IF YOU LOOK FOR ME,
I AM NOT HERE

IF YOU LOOK FOR ME, I AM NOT HERE

Sarayu Srivatsa

Bluemoose

First published in 2016 by
Bluemoose Books Ltd
25 Sackville Street
Hebden Bridge
West Yorkshire
HX7 7DJ

www.bluemoosebooks.com

British Library Cataloguing-in-Publication data
A catalogue record for this book is available from the British Library

Hardback ISBN 978-1-910422-13-7

Paperback ISBN 978-1-910422-14-4

Printed and bound in the UK by Short Run Press

for Rosa Maia

If you look for me, I am not here.
My writings will tell you where I am.
... they point out my life like
Lines drawn in the map of my palms.

From *Babur*
Dom Moraes

It was the hottest summer since the English left the country. The silkcotton trees burst their pods before their time and tiny parachutes of silk sailed in the wind, scattering colonies of seeds all over the red soil. The burning sun lay on the crops, roasting them crisp, sucking all the moisture out of them. The wind howled in pain and, when it could suffer the heat no more, it abducted straying rain clouds and steered them towards Machilipatnam.

The tar road outside Machilipatnam Railway Station had melted in the heat; inside, cobwebs of dust had settled everywhere. The platform was bright with noise and activity: vendors tinkled trays of cold drinks; a radio warbled a popular tune; children waved at passing trains; a woman vomited; unwashed young men with bloodshot eyes watched pigeons defecate in the trusses, and Swami, the crippled boy, crouched beneath the statue of an Englishman, George Gibbs (1814–1862). Although a hundred years old now, the bronze figure gleamed in the morning light. Swami sat up and spat out at the statue: Motherfucker. Fucking bastard.

On a bench nearby were Patti and Amma, waiting. Their train to Madras was two hours late. The smell of refried snacks, sweaty feet, vomit, and ammonia clung to the air. Amma was irritable and nauseous, but it was not entirely because of the offensive smells or the indefinite wait: she was pregnant.

Patti was uneasy. Her silk saree was the colour of worry: a nagging dull brown. Chandan dotted her forehead and an ashline underlined the dried blob. She smelled of sandalwood, incense and deep disquiet. She rummaged in her handbag and

1

fished out a framed photograph of Lord Shiva, touched it to each eye, *touch-touch*, and mumbled a prayer.

Just then a group of hijras entered the platform, clapping their hands to announce their presence. Besides the noise they made, the way they were dressed drew people's eyes to them: gaudy nylex sarees, kohl round their eyes, flowers in their hair, night-old stubble clouding their chins bluegreen. Sweetie-Cutie, the youngest of them, approached Patti and Amma. She was no more than twenty-one. Her bloodred saree had silver sequins on it. She had coiled her hair at the top of her head, and to one side was fixed a red rose. Her face was heartshaped, with a broad forehead and angular cheekbones. Her thin, flat lips smiled redly at Amma, who covered her face with her hands like a child.

'Don't hide your face,' Sweetie-Cutie said to her, 'you are fortunate to be so beautiful.'

Amma was beautiful. Her skin was the colour of cashew, her eyes the purple of aubergine, and her glossy black hair tumbled to her knees. She smelled sweetly of jasmine. Two diamond studs shone on the sides of her nose like clots of pure mercury.

Sweetie-Cutie caressed Amma's cheek. 'Give me a smile, my love. That's all I ask from you.' Then she turned to Patti. 'Spare some money, ma and I'll bless you with a grandson.'

Patti joined her hands together, dismissing Sweetie-Cutie with stubborn silence and staring adamantly at the rails. Luckily for her, the train to Madras arrived just then and people scrambled to board it, followed by coolies carrying tiers of luggage on their heads. Patti grabbed Amma's hand and rushed toward their compartment. They found their berths and tucked their bags underneath. As the train drew out of the station Sweetie-Cutie waved to Amma and blew her a kiss. Amma smiled and waved back.

Sweetie-Cutie clasped her hands at her fake bosom and shouted: 'I am so fortunate.' But her body knew otherwise.

The train sped out of the city. It passed fields of stunted trees and one station after the next, where people waited with trunks and cloth bags. At the end of one platform, an old man sat holding a rope tied around a goat's neck: a big fat goat, its horns painted yellow and bright red ribbons tied to them, readied for ritual sacrifice. Redeyed.

The train pulled into Madras Station early next morning. Patti and Amma got off and boarded a bus to Chiroor. It was late evening when they arrived at the village. In the light of the moon Patti found Ratnamma sitting on a rope cot outside her hut. Spread out on a mat on the ground around her feet were several jars containing herbs, seeds and chunks of bark. Next to her feet was a human skull, the eye sockets large and gleaming in the moonlight. Not far away, an old potter turned his wheel and the smell of clay rose into the night air: moist, muddy. Next to him on the ground was a row of clay idols of the Snake Goddess, their faces black, with algae-green eyes and red tongues.

Ratnamma motioned to Amma, asked her to sit next to her. Amma did as she was told. Ratnamma clasped her hands to her chest and gravely looked deep into Amma's eyes. 'Look at you. So tender, like a baby cucumber.' Ratnamma tweaked Amma's cheek. 'All men want their women to be green, untouched and innocent. You must be careful of men. All men: father, brothers, husband and even sons. They will clip your wings so you can't fly anymore. Remember, it is a burden to be a woman, a disgrace, because we are always captive in one way or another. Large rocks are tied to our back and we sink deep into dark waters.' Ratnamma pointed to a spotted insect and then crushed it with her foot. Red ants appeared out of nowhere and swarmed around the dead insect. 'See those ants,' the old woman said to Amma. 'Men are like them. Be careful. Men will wait until you are helpless, and then take over your body and mind.' Amma

3

watched the ants disentangle the insect's legs and pull it towards a hole. She would remember this in the years to come.

Patti made a rumbling sound deep in her throat. 'We have to get the last bus back,' she said impatiently.

Ratnamma yelled out to the old potter. He covered the clay with a wet sack and rubbed his hands together, releasing tendrils of clay that fell to the ground. He walked over with an idol; Ratnamma took the Snake Goddess from him and thrust it into Amma's hands. 'Pray to her every day,' she said. 'She will bless you with a healthy child.' She pressed packets of black seeds of the magic peepal tree into Amma's hand. 'One a day,' she said, raising her finger. 'Eat the seed before or after the midday meal. But remember, it is before the meal for a boy and after for a girl.'

Patti paid the old woman and walked Amma back to the road, carrying the clay idol and a month's supply of magic seeds. They didn't have to wait long for the bus. It was crowded, but Patti and Amma found seats at the back and soon they were off into the sultry night. Amma was tired and hungry. The motion of the bus rocked her to sleep. At dawn the bus made a stop at a wayside hotel for breakfast; Patti and Amma had coffee and fried vadas and chutney. The bus wouldn't start and they had to wait for nearly an hour. Patti was edgy and Amma was wholly worn-out. It was midday when they reached Madras Station, just in time to get the return train to Machilipatnam. Minutes before the train pulled out, the attendant from the refreshment room at the station came with two South Indian Thali meals and handed them to Patti and Amma.

'Mallika, now don't forget to eat the seed before you start,' Patti said, joining her hands together in prayer. 'Oh Lord Shiva, bless me with a grandson. I have already named him Siva after you.'

'I want a daughter,' Amma retorted.

'You must have a son.' Patti slapped Amma's arm. With the birth of a son, Patti explained to her, three generations of the family would cross over from heaven into eternal bliss. Without the birth of a son in the family they would be reborn again and again as snakes or rats, or even mosquitoes, into this cruel world.

Amma took a seed out of the packet and held it between her fingers, then tossed the seed into her mouth. She ate the rice and potato curry; she finished the pachadi and the sweet. Then, after she'd eaten, when Patti was not looking, she swallowed two more seeds.

That was the precise moment when Siva's fate looked at him cockeyed.

***

They travelled all day and night and most of the next day. It was evening when Patti and Amma returned to Machilipatnam and to their home, Victoria Villa. The tall trees around the house cast ghostlike shadows; the branches trembled and set free sparrows that flew across the moon. Large moths rose into the air in a white cloud that settled on the front veranda like a soft duvet. The house trembled and creaked in the wind; the windows wheezed and let the breeze in. Amma took a deep breath and opened the front door.

Amma was tired and she retreated to her room. Patti got busy in the kitchen. She was making vattal kozybambu for dinner. She fried sundried berries and popped them into spicy tamarind curry simmering on the stove. She shredded cucumber and mixed it with fresh yogurt and tempered it with mustard seeds, curry leaves and dried red chillies. She boiled the rice and fried the papadams. Then she went to the dining room and spread a cloth over the old table; she sang a song as she set steel plates on it. In the centre she placed a glass containing assorted spoons, and around it the bin of papadams, a bowl of sour curds, lime pickle, and steel tumblers of water. She would bring in the rice and tamarind curry, piping hot, when they sat down to eat.

Up in her room Amma changed into an old cotton saree and then lay down on the bed. From the bedside table she picked up Georgette Heyer's *Convenient Marriage* and, so that she wouldn't fall asleep, she started to read aloud from the page where she had stopped, when Sir Robert Lethbridge kissed Horatia Winwood and told her rather flippantly that he intended to steal her virtue. Amma closed her eyes and thought about Lethbridge. A smile tickled her lips and they fell apart, waiting, wanting. White moonlight hit the glass window and two squares of light shone on the floor: a pair of ghostly eyes, witness to everything. The window was shut but the breeze blew through the gaps, made an eerie sound. The room was alive: breathing and waiting. Amma had fallen asleep.

Appa returned late. He stood by the bed looking down at two mosquitoes perched on the edge of the pillow. He brought his hand a few inches over them and whacked them hard. Amma woke up with the sound. The corners of her mouth curved upwards, and her aubergine eyes smiled. Appa sat beside her and pulled away the palav of her saree. He stroked the hollow of her neck, her breasts and her bare waist and then he gently undressed her. He picked up a bottle of scented oil and with utter tenderness rubbed it all over her body. He held her carefully lest she slip out of his fingers. Then he kissed her lips, crushed cherrypads, once, twice, and thrice. Amma giggled. When he kissed her neck, she giggled. He sucked her nipples; he thrust his tongue into her bellyhole; he licked her feet, the insides of her thighs. She giggled. Then he turned her on her stomach, stroked her back, cashewtoned, spicesmelling, spicetasting, all the way down to her buttocks, such harvestheaps, Then he ran his thumb down her spine and licked the trail. Amma laughed.

Her laughter penetrated his heart and he turned her over again and took her passionately. Amma could smell the damp breath of his pentup longing. Her heart throbbed wildly, recklessly, and then missed a beat. And oh, by God, good

6

heavens, by Jove... Amma gasped. She let out a huge, roaring laugh and exclaimed in mock dismay, 'Good God!'

To which Appa whispered ecstatically: 'Oh, Rukmini, Rukmini...'

Amma raised her head and stared at him with accusatory eyes. 'Why are you calling out to your mother?'

Appa looked at her in dismay. A buzzing sound saved him from answering. He rolled over and slapped Amma's cheek. He held her face in his hands and kissed the spot where the mosquito had bitten her. Turning his head and looking into her eyes, he began to speak, softly. 'Mallika, did you know, it is the female mosquito that bites? She pierces the skin of people and animals to suck blood. She can't see clearly, but the temperature of the body produces an infrared picture for her and she is attracted to carbon dioxide. The male is a vegetarian, poor fellow; he lives on fruit and flower nectar but the female requires a blood meal to develop her babies. She is called Anopheles.'

Amma sat up and gently touched her palm to her stomach: skin-touching-skin, warmth against warmth.

'What is it, my sweet Anopheles?' Appa asked teasingly.

'I can feel our daughter moving.'

Appa smiled. 'It could be a son.'

'It's a girl,' Amma retorted, her voice shaking. 'It has to be a girl.'

Siva trembled deep inside her womb. It was by instinct that he did so, for he didn't know about Amma's fixation then. By the time he got to know it was much too late: he had arrived in the world embroiled in others' fates and handcuffed to his own destiny. There was no escape from all that was to come after this, and all that had happened before he really began.

Before she was married, Amma had lived with her father in a mango-coloured house on Gibbs Road, not far from the market. B.K. Vishnu was the owner of the Victoria Dyes factory. He was also a musician; he played the violin. When he was 35 he married Vatsala, a singer, fifteen years younger than him.

Amma never got to know her mother: she died the night Amma was born.

Appa's name is P.S. Raman Iyer. He holds a Masters in Biological Sciences from the University of Sussex. He had been part of a research team in London known as the Mosquito Behaviour Unit. After working in London for some years Appa returned to India, where he was appointed the deputy director of the Malaria Research Centre in Madras. Here, he made good progress in the genetic mapping of the Aedes, Culex and Anopheles mosquito genera, using molecular approaches for reducing or eliminating vector-borne diseases. In support of his research, the Indian government repaired and revived the old George Gibbs Institute, which had been inoperative for many years. It appointed Appa as its director and relocated him to Machilipatnam, giving him Victoria Villa as his new home. It had belonged to the Englishman, George Gibbs; the house and some of the contents were over a hundred years old.

When Appa arrived in Machilipatnam, he pulled up to the house at 23 Gibbs Road in a battered Ambassador. Seated beside him was his widowed mother, Patti – Mrs Rukmini Iyer, smelling of Amrutanjan Balm. She had accompanied her son with a stainless steel tiffin-carrier, a small khaki-covered suitcase, an old English holdall, a lantern, a jar of balm, and a mosquito net that had been darned in a number of places. These six items, according to her, comprised her life: food, clothes, sleep, light, no-pain and no-bite.

However, as soon as Patti settled in the old house she began complaining about the rundown place. There were holes in the roof and missing windowpanes. The thin reed screens covering the windows let the sun in, the wind blow in. Appa was too excited about his new job to be bothered. Malaria epidemics had plagued the town and Appa worked late into the night at the George Gibbs Institute.

Meanwhile, Patti occupied herself looking for a girl who would be a good housekeeper and wife for her son. She hired the local astrologer, Perumal Krishnan, to guide and assist in her search. It was not long before Perumal arranged Amma's marriage to Appa. She was all of nineteen, and a stranger to Appa, as he was to her. Both were unaware of all the feelings knotted deep within them, breathing, wanting, waiting to unravel, even though theirs was a marriage of convenience. Love was meant only for the deviant affairs of the heart, not for the utilitarian alliance of bodies and mind. This is how it was in those times.

Amma had come to Appa's house with a single trunk, a photo frame with her mother's picture in it, her mother's coral beads around her neck, her mother's old Singer sewing machine and a ragged doll. The doll's body was made of cloth and its head of papier-mâché, golden locks tumbling from it; it had sea-blue eyes and long lashes that went updown when rocked. Amma loved her doll; it had comforted her through all those lonely years and let her hope, wish and dream. Before the year was over, Amma was expecting. She nurtured one deep, achefull dream: she longed for a daughter she could be a mother to, a mother she never had. She had already chosen a name for her, a name for stars: Tara.

As for Siva, he did not exist for her.

***

Appa woke up to the heady aroma of coffee. Amma was already in the kitchen roasting coffee beans. When they were done she held a warm bean against her tummy, warmth touching warmth. She took a fistful of coffee beans and ground them in a hand grinder. She put spoonfuls of the powder into the filter and poured hot water over it. Patti stepped through the doorway carrying a vessel of fresh milk and stumbled over a loose floorboard and spilt some of the milk on the floor.

Appa came up behind her. 'The house is a terrible ruin. I must call the carpenter. Mallika, when are you going to put up the curtains?'

'Yes-yes,' Amma said looking for a rag. 'I will fix the curtains today.' Then as she bent down to clean the mess on the floor Siva bumped his head against her wombwall and his sister flipped to her side. Ouch. *Ouch.*

When Appa left for work Amma got down to serious work. She fixed two layers of curtains on each of the windows, the shorter inner one fixed by a spring that went drrriiiiiing when stretched. She hung khus mats in the veranda and on the floor she laid a pai woven with thin, silky, reeds. Then she moved the bamboo screen from the veranda to a corner of the kitchen to make Patti a small private corner for prayer. When she was done, Patti arranged her gods on the low table: a plaster of Paris idol of Rama, a clay idol of Ganesha, the clay Snake Goddess, thumb-sized idols in silver and brass of various other gods and goddesses, and a photograph of Gandhiji in a metal frame. Beside them she set the lamps, a bowl for flowers, a jar of holy ash, a packet of incense and a brass pot, the size of a fist, filled with rice grains. With Amma beside her, Patti stuck joss sticks into the rice pot, lit the lamps and chanted aloud to all the important gods to bless her with a grandson.

Just then there was a rattling at the gate. Patti and Amma rushed to the front veranda. Sweetie-Cutie stood outside in a bright yellow saree. She had flowers in her hair. 'May the good lord bless the house and your family and may you be blessed with a grandson,' Sweetie-Cutie shouted in a hoarse, carrying voice.

Patti signalled her to come through the gates. Sweetie-Cutie sauntered to the veranda and stood at the steps smiling redly at Amma. Patti undid the knot in the end of her saree and retrieved a hundred-rupee note and thrust it into Sweetie-Cutie's hand.

She tucked the note into her blouse. 'What about the rice, ma? Everyone gives me a sack of rice.'

'They do, do they?' Patti retorted. 'Then go to them and collect your rice.'

'You should know better than to disappoint a hijra, ma,' Sweetie-Cutie said, an edge to her voice. 'We were cursed when we were born. And our curse is more deadly than a snakebite.' Sweetie-Cutie stepped up to Amma. She waved her hand over Amma's head. 'May you give birth to a daughter,' she smiled, then turned around and walked away.

At once Patti retreated into the kitchen to pray away the hijra's curse. Amma began to clean the house, moving from room to room with a duster. She gazed up at the old portrait hanging on the wall. She climbed up on a stool to wipe the cobwebs. Staring down at her was an image of a pale, bearded young man in a pair of high-waisted trousers, a shirt with decorative trim tucked into them. At his waist was a belt buckle with a symbol on it: three Ts joined at the bottom, and between them the letters E I C. The man stood against a backdrop of velvety curtains, a sword in one hand and a cap in the other. Amma read aloud the words stencilled below the picture: George Gibbs. The East India Trading Co. 1839. 'Well, if it isn't my lord Gibbs!' Amma looked up into his blue eyes. 'How kind it is in you to be thinking of me. I am fine.' Then she ran the cloth carefully over the surface of the picture.

'Mallika, go get a bunch of ripe bananas,' Patti yelled out from the kitchen.

At the back of the house Amma reached out to the bunch of rastali bananas drooping from the plantain tree and pinched the fruits one by one. Then, on a whim, she turned around and climbed the steps to the attic. She had never been up there. Her bare feet were black with dust as she stumbled through the debris on the floor. A bat darted across the room and she screamed. Siva started kicking in fright. His twin kicked him back. Amma stood still for a moment staring into the distance. She tiptoed to the far end of the attic, stepping over bundles of old newspapers and files, past a heap of mattresses, two broken umbrellas and wooden cases, to a tin trunk partially covered with an old bedsheet. Inside the trunk she found a bale of cloth wrapped in muslin with a paper tag attached to the end of it. *Kalamkari on silk – Tree of Life.*

Amma tore open the muslin: handpainted on the cinnamon-brown silk inside were peacocks, parrots, interlacing leaves and plump pink lotus flowers. She touched the soft, musty fabric to her cheek.

The light from the attic window revealed a thick ledger which had clearly been undisturbed for a very long time. Amma lifted it and blew away the dust. Particles glinted in the sunlight and a thread of dustlight traversed the room. Amma opened the cover carefully. On the first page, yellowed and stained, in indigo ink were the words:

George Gibbs
Victoria Villa
23 Gibbs Road
Machilipatnam

Amma turned the page:

Victoria Dyes April 1853.

Allejaes. Red and white. Striped and checks. Medium quality. 16 yards long, 45 inches wide.

Callowaypoos. Patterned. Medium quality. 14 yards long, 45 inches wide.

Chintz. Block-printed.
Dungarees. Plain white. Coarse.
Gingham. Dyed. Medium quality.
Sallampores. Dyed. Medium quality.

Very quickly Amma flipped through the pages of inventories of cloth, chemicals, natural dyes, and detailed records of costs, written in short rushes. Here and there, interspersed, were jottings of a more personal sort, of things that happened each day. These accounts were mostly several pages long, scribbled hastily, some even shabbily; some others were not more than a condensed sentence:

Made chicken curry last night.
January 1853 – Elizabeth Arrives.
April 1854 – John arrives.

Amma turned over clusters of pages. Closer to the end of the ledger, after a folded and marked page, were carefully worded notes, fragments really, a diary perhaps, not of the events of each day but a short summary of entire seasons. These notes were written neatly, widely spaced in slanting handwriting, unusually large. The 'Y's had long tails made with a flourish of a steel nib, and like musical notes the 'Y's rained through the pages. Amma caressed the words with a forefinger, finding pleasure in touching what George Gibbs had written so many years ago.

Carrying the bale of silk and the ledger, Amma stepped out of the dark attic. Then, on an impulse, she sat on the sunlit landing and opened the ledger.

September 1840 – December 1850.

A giant wall of water rose and the wind roared, swirled round the ship's hull and thumped it on the sea. I stood on the deck, swaying, my heavy robes encrusted with droplets of seawater. Salt seared my nostrils and eyes; the wild wind deafened me.

It was still summer in London when the English East India Trading Company ship put to sea. It had carried more than 500 people, guns, supplies and cargo. The water on the ship was unfit to drink and the staple ration of salt pork and rice was inedible. Some of the seamen, ravaged by typhoid and malaria, made stifled sounds of suffering. The healthy ones drank toddy until they were drunk and nauseous, uttering pitiable moans. Only 400 people were left by the time the ship reached the Cape of Good Hope. Carrion birds hovered in the sky.

Towards dawn, many moons later, gongs and drums were beaten, a trumpet brayed, an announcement blared. The ship had docked at Machilipatnam, on the east coast of India. The air was moist and warm, and heavy with the stench of fish.

I dusted my coat with a handkerchief, swept my hair back with both hands, and looked up at the still dark sky. The stars in it were not English: they glittered anyhow.

***

Birds shrieked and shrilled all day long and the sound of wingbeats filled the air; overhead a white skein of eagles unravelled the sky. The labourers were alarmed by the bird cries, but they continued digging the earth for the foundations of the house. At the back of the site they found a grave, with human bones embedded in the dust. A skull smiled up at them from the dirt. A ripple of shock spread through them and they fell back, collected their tools and left the site.

The contractor asked me to find another location for the house. His men were terrified of ghosts and evil spirits, he said. I regarded him coolly and then burst into laughter, upon which the contractor gravely told me that ghosts had memories and they looked for someone to latch on to. If I lived here on this land, then the dead person's memories would seep into me and haunt me all my days. The contractor was serious. His men didn't report for work the next day so I decided to send Matthew Thekkel, my cook, butler and general factotum, hotfoot to the tribal workers who, according to Matthew, had long ago devised a way to deal with spirits.

The tribal workers came at once: a bunch of forty, attired in nothing more than loincloths, with blue-black markings on their arms. They built a low brick wall on the North side of the site and left lime and terracotta handprints on it. They knelt around it and joined their hands in prayer. They beseeched the ghost to go away. They made shrill sounds which to my mind seemed like a collective fit of hysterics.

However, Matthew assured me that the ghost had been banished and the house was finished without any further hitch.

It was three storied with an attic; the roof, which was cut at the top in notches, arches and pinnacles, fell in graceful sweeps like a voluminous skirt. The two verandas, one in the front and the other alongside the kitchen, resembled two arms of the house folded across its chest. I named it then and there, and without too much thought – Victoria Villa.

Some distance from the villa, where the swamps gave way to fields I built a factory to manufacture natural dyes and named it Victoria Dyes. It was not very different from the villa except for the tall clock tower. But one stormy night an eagle flew straight into the face of the clock and broke one of its hands. Over the years the clock remained one-handed, timeless.

The tribal labourers had more work to do. They laid big stones on the mud path connecting the villa and the factory. With loud cries of haiya-haiya they filled the gaps between the stones with smaller pebbles, over which they drizzled gravel from large jute sacks. Haiya-haiya. Dusty clouds cluttered the air overhead. With jute cloth tied to their hands and feet, they poured hot liquid tar on the gravel; other workers rolled a heavy drum over puddles of sweaty tar. Haiya-haiya. And up ahead the path had been big-stoned, small-pebbled, gravelled, tarred and flattened. Here, a worker had put up the wooden road sign: Gibbs Road; and further on, the top of the new Gibbs Road curled like an uncoiled ribbon and rambled all the way to the beach.

There I stood, lost in reverie, looking far out to sea.

Amma could hear Patti move about in the kitchen below. She would have to return to her soon. But George Gibbs' notes thrilled her: she lived in the house he had built, and her father owned his factory. How extraordinary was this! Teased by curiosity, she read on:

The factory was hot as an oven. The outer walls had blistered in the heat. The stone floor inside was splattered with dye, red, yellow, indigo, black and brown; the room had a musty, tart smell. I stood by a large vat, the thick brown ledger in my hands, watching Chotoo, a dwarf, stirring the dye. Sunlight refracted through the glass roof tiles above and made him squint.

'I daresay it could do with a touch of more red, Chotoo,' I said. 'Bright red but deep, and one that changes colour in the sun.' I turned the pages of the ledger to the dog-eared leaf with my notes in indigo ink.

Red – bark of Manjista.
Yellow – skins of pomegranate.
Dark blue – indigo plant.
Brown-chocolate – Kasikalti.
Black – Kaseem mineral.
Purple-brown – Surupattal, catechu.

'Add more Su-ru-pat-tal,' I said looking up from the ledger.

Chotoo lifted up the bucket of purple-brown dye; standing on his toes he poured it into the tall vat and stirred the liquid with a stick. For a dwarf he had big hands.

'By God, fellow, that's it,' I said when the colour was just right. 'That's it!'

I walked to the adjoining hall. All along its indigo-stained walls were bales of dyed silk, muslin and chintz; endless yards of silk hung from the roof. They had been previously washed in water, bleached by soaking them in buffalo dung solution and sundried for several days. Two workers dipped cloth in a trough of milk and the juice of myrobalan fruit. I asked them to add more milk. It would prevent the colours from running and tauten the fabric. I turned to two artists outlining the shapes of a peacock and a lotus on cinnamon-brown silk held tight by wooden frames. They dipped tufts of goat hair held in split bamboo sticks into a basin of iron filings and molasses, then painted fine lines on the cloth. This is a local craft, called Kalamkari. I tapped the centre of the cloth with my forefinger, 'Make that lotus fuller and add more leaves here, and yes, a parrot.'

At a distance the temple bells rang and sonorous chants rose into the sky. Like a counterpoint, the loudspeaker from the mosque blared out: la ilaha ila allah. On cue, even as I stood there watching them, the Hindu workers shut their eyes and folded their hands, the Muslim workers spread their mats on the floor, and together they remembered their separate Gods.

Amma was now terribly excited. The bale of silk that she had found was most probably the same cloth that George Gibbs' workers were painting. She tapped the cloth roll on the floor beside her and mimicked in a deep voice: Make that lotus fuller and add more leaves here, and yes, a parrot. Then she went back to the ledger, turning several pages at once and started to read the account dated February 1851:

I followed Chotoo through the woods, a lantern in my hand. A whine of music and the dolorous wail of voices rippled the air. We walked on in the direction of the sounds. Beyond the trees closer to the sea, hidden by an outcrop of rocks, were some thatched huts. A great deal of noise came from them: the thuds and squeals of musical instruments accompanied by shrill ululations. We walked into a central court flooded by light from what seemed like a hundred lanterns. There, a gawky person dressed and made up as a woman danced. She had stubble on her face. On one side of her sat the musicians – all of them men dressed in colourful sarees and glittering ornaments. And on the other side were a host of villagers who sniggered and clapped.

'That is Sita, the eunuch queen,' Chotoo said. 'Tonight she will chose her man and pump him to such levels of ecstasy no woman can ever provide.'

Sita writhed her hips and heaved her large counterfeit breasts. Now and then her enraptured audience shouted words of endearment as they flung coins at her. She smiled sweetly at them. Then she looked up and her eyes rested on me and she gave a cry of delight; holding up her saree with her hands, she hurried toward me. The crowd cheered, the drums began to beat. I stood still for a moment, mesmerised, then I turned around and ran into the dark. The eunuchs called out after me. The drums beat louder, harder. I ran out of the woods and down the road. I didn't stop at my house because my feet had got used to the speed with which I had escaped; I ran on and on. I was panting by the time I reached the factory. The workers had left. I rushed into the main hall and stopped to catch my breath. In the light of the moon I saw the cinnamon-brown silk cloth painted with lotuses and peacocks hanging on a string to dry. I stood back and stared at it, then on a whim I swirled the cloth around my body; like the eunuch queen I had just seen, I pirouetted, round and round. And round...

All at once I stopped and, flushing a little, I discarded the silk on a pile of cloth. Then I strode down Gibbs Road. When I entered my home I could smell smoke, cinnamon and cardamom. Butter too, melted. I made my way to the kitchen and found Matthew frying something on the woodfired stove. The kitchen was dark, lit only by the faint light of a lamp in a corner and the red glow of the fire.

'Oh, good heavens! What's that awful smell?' I asked as I walked through the door.

'Chakka sar, they all be ripe.'

I looked at the bowl next to the stove containing what seemed to me odd oversized beans.

'They being chakka seeds, sar,' Matthew said. 'I have roasted them.'

I peeled a seed and popped it in my mouth. It was not bad at all. I took another.

'Don't eat too many of them,' Matthew said. 'It is being a hot food. If you eat too many, stomach gets loose.'

'Oh, good heavens! I must have no more of that! What's for dinner?'

'I am make roast pork for you? You be liking that.'

'Good lord no, not again. You made pork last night and two days ago. Come to think of it, I have to say I fancy a curry. Chicken curry.'

'No problem sar. I make chickan curry now.' Matthew brought down a bottle from the shelf.

'What's this?'

'Curry powder. I make it.'

'Of what?'

'Turmeric, whole coriander, dry ginger, dried red chillies, pepper, cumin, cardamom and clove. All being ground together.'

'Splendid. Tell you what: let's make the curry together,' I said, laughing heartily at Matthew's visible discomfiture. 'Now tell me, what do I do first?'

'You be chopping onions and making paste of ginger and garlic, then cutting chickan into squares.'

'I'll cut the chicken and chop the onions.' I pushed up the sleeves of my shirt.

'Very good sar,' Matthew said in a doubtful voice.

When the chicken and onions were chopped and the garlic and ginger pounded, I had tears streaming from my eyes. 'Now what?'

'Now sar, we be heating oil in pan. Frying onions brown. Adding ginger and garlic and curry powder and little bit vinegar. Then cooking till oil be separating out. Adding a pinch of salt then and water, and cooking and cooking until the chickan pieces are becoming cooked.'

I ate the chicken curry with rice dyed yellow by turmeric.

'By Jove, this is really good!' I said to Matthew. 'I must say I like chicken curry. Certainly, I do.'

Patti's voice came from below. 'Mallika, are you getting the bananas or what?'

'They are not ripe!'

***

It was getting overcrowded in Amma's womb: Siva's twin had taken up all the room. She had grown bigger than him. He couldn't kick his legs or move his arms. His sister's body pushed him against the wall of the womb, and his head was squashed against her chest. Now and then she put her finger on the top of Siva's forehead, then slowly ran it over the ridge of his nose, down its tip, over the lips, the chin and all the way down the neck to the hollow under it. Then she curled her finger into the dip, sheltered and safe.

Siva sucked his fingers all the time; he was restless and waiting to be born. Amma was restless too. That evening as always Amma stood at the dining room window pulling at the spring curtain and it went driiing-driiing-driiing. The sound announced the close of the day. But today, as Amma pulled at the spring, her day was not over. It was time for the Valakappu ceremony. It was time to pray for the sex of her unborn child.

Amma went to her room to get ready. She donned a blouse and saree made out of the cinnamon-brown silk she had found in the attic. She fixed a string of jasmines in her hair, and smeared her eyes with kohl. From the cupboard shelf she took down the baby frock she had stitched with the leftover cinnamon silk, and clutching it to her breasts she cooed: my Tara, my sweet Tara. Then Patti called out to her and Amma hastily put the frock away and rushed to the veranda.

A group of women sat in a circle singing, clapping their hands and swaying to the rhythm. Amma sat amidst them. Patti, because she was a widow, sat at a distance supervising the event. The young women slipped pairs of red and green glass bangles on Amma's wrists. Then they smeared turmeric paste on her arms and face. Beside her feet they arranged the quill of a porcupine, Udambara leaves and an ear of paddy. Another young woman put sweets and savouries into the palav of Amma's saree and tied it around her waist. They were meant to be food for the baby.

Meanwhile Munniamma, the maidservant, had put a vessel of rice on the floor. The women walked around it, sprinkling flowers and chanting. They clapped their hands loudly so that the baby would not be born deaf. Then the women started to pray to Rika, the deity of the full moon. They beseeched the Goddess to make Amma's pregnancy fruitful and bless her with a son who would be as beautiful as the full moon, and whose intellect would be as sharp as the porcupine's quill. After the prayers were over, Munniamma brought coffee, savouries and sweets.

Amma didn't eat anything: she was meant to fast until the stars came out in the sky. Patti didn't eat either. Her brow was creased with worry. 'Where is that Perumal?' she said, when the women had left and she and Amma were finally alone. 'He should have been here fifteen minutes ago!' Just then there was a rattling of the gate. Patti looked up to see Swami, the crippled boy. 'Munniamma, give the poor boy something to eat.'

Munniamma returned from the kitchen with food parcelled in a sheet of newspaper and hastened to the gate. She held out the parcel; Swami grabbed it from her hands and shouted, 'You fucking whore!' Munniamma reached out and tweaked his nose. She was not a bit annoyed. Everyone knew about Swami's bouts of intermittent insanity when he let out coarse words, which he didn't mean and didn't seem to remember he had spoken.

Swami was no more than ten years old, and a homeless orphan. In the daytime he went house to house begging for food. In the evening he was at the market selling limes, chillies and green coriander. When he had made enough money he closed his little stall and bought a bottle of Coca Cola, a treat for his endeavours. He lived one day at a time, one Coca Cola at a time, before he made his way to the railway station where he slept away the hours before the next day began.

'Go get your horoscope, Mallika, and Raman's too,' Patti said. 'They are in the box in the prayer room. Perumal should be here soon.'

'I am hungry,' Amma said.

'Drink water, ma. You can't eat for another hour at least.'

Amma went into the kitchen. Munniamma had cleaned the dishes and put them away, all except one plate by the stove covered with a napkin. Amma lifted the napkin slightly to reveal bondi ladoos, coconut burfi and different kinds of vadais. Amma looked around her, and then she picked a laddoo and stuffed it into her mouth. 'That's for you, Tara,' she said aloud, rubbing her hand on her stomach. Amma quickly tossed a coconut burfi into her already full mouth and pressing it down with her fingers she dashed into the prayer room. She opened the tin box on the shelf and from it retrieved two paper scrolls and brought them to Patti.

Perumal Krishnan walked through the gates dressed in a starched white veshti, barechested, his Brahmin thread looped over his shoulder. He climbed the steps to the veranda. He was tall and extremely lean. He had brought with him several notebooks and charts. He set them down on the pai and sat down in front of Patti and Amma. Patti gave him the horoscopes.

Perumal adjusted the sacred Brahmin thread over his shoulder. He fanned his armpits with a fan made of dried leaves. The astringent odour of Lifebuoy soap and perspiration laced the air. Patti's nose twitched and she covered it with the end of her saree. She sniffed the air to ensure the brief breeze had blown away, before dropping the saree from her nose.

Perumal now surveyed the scrolls of paper matching house for house, planet for planet and star for star. He looked through the frayed notebook in which he had made interpretations of the positions of the moon. He made notations of planets and stars on a page and put down lunar calculations in the margin. Then with a shudder of his chest he blew the air out of his stomach and burped. 'A girl,' he pronounced.

Patti said, 'Look-look, see properly. It has to be a boy. I didn't go all the way to Chiroor for nothing.' Tears had pooled in her eyes.

Perumal stared at Patti's open mouth. 'A... a beautiful boy,' he said with a wavering smile.

Patti's mouth closed and then ever so slowly it widened into a smile. She clasped her hands together, stretched them in front of her and pressed them out until her finger bones cracked. Twin dimples appeared at the back of her elbows.

'Definitely a boy,' Perumal repeated firmly. But his eyebrows remained knitted together, as though they had a mind of their own and they didn't entirely agree. Perumal smoothed out his eyebrows, collected his books and hurriedly left. Patti had not missed the doubt etched on his face.

With renewed determination, Patti took Amma straight to the Shiva temple at the end of Gibbs Road. She offered two coconuts, a basket of flowers, an entire bunch of ripe rastali bananas and fifty-one rupees to Lord Shiva. The pujari rotated the plate with the burning camphor with one hand and rang the bell with the other. Looking intently into Lord Shiva's eyes, Patti folded her hands and prayed. When the pujari stood in front of her with the plate of burning camphor, Patti covered the flame with her hands and touched her eyes and face. She drank the holy water that the pujari dropped into her palm with a silver spoon. She looked up at Lord Shiva and added, 'Now don't forget to make sure it is a boy. I have named him Siva after you, after all.'

***

Late in her ninth month, Amma often got breathless and she could hardly sleep at night. She had grown terribly big and, to a lesser extent, so had Siva and his sister. Siva had shed all the downy hair on his body and his skin was smooth. He had moved further down in the womb and it was getting intolerably cramped. He hung upside down from a cord and his sister swayed backforth like a trapeze artist. And when Amma sat in a particular way their heads collided: ouch-*ouch*. But Siva didn't seem to mind this at all; he kicked his legs excitedly. His twin was asleep most of the time, her finger curled into his, until he too fell into sleep.

That afternoon Amma sat under the cool shade of the neem tree reading the old brown ledger; she read it almost to the end. Tears tumbled down her cheeks and she wiped them with the end of her saree. Suddenly, she felt her womb heave and squeeze, and she involuntarily said aloud: 'Nooo, by Jove!' The heaving and squeezing happened again and Amma felt a firm grip like a clamp around her womb. Hugging her belly, she bent double and retched all over the trunk of the tree. The violent heaving and squeezing began once more. Each time, her heart skipped a beat. She felt as though her life had turned into water and it was oozing out of her. Amma bellowed – By God! Good heavens!

Patti rushed to her. 'Your water has burst,' she said and at once sent Munniamma for the midwife. Holding Amma by the arms, Patti led her beyond the hallway to the dark storeroom for the birthing so that light and wind wouldn't startle the newborn. The walls of the storeroom were lined with gunny bags containing red rice from the local fields; they gave off a homely starchy smell, meant to be good for babies. The midwife came with Munniamma and both helped Amma squat on the floor, then they held her shoulders, gently laying her down. 'Munniamma, go get the bottle of balm from my room,' Patti said, 'and rub it on Mallika's back. It will relieve some of the pain.'

The hours passed. Amma felt each minute in its entirety, and the separate grain of each second. Inside her, Siva was kicking feverishly while his sister seemed to have momentarily passed out. Appa, who had been summoned from work, paced up and down in the hallway. He clutched his nose, unaccustomed to the smells of birthing: Spittle. Birthblood. Sweat. Balm. Then Amma screamed. It pierced the night like lightning.

Siva's sister struggled in the slimy water, bobbing up and down, and then gulping water. More water. More water. She sank to the watery bottom of the womb-bed, landscaped by deep shadows and silence, and the twisted root of the birth cord, already old, curled around her neck, and then she choked, once, twice. Her heartbeat rose and fell like a leaf detached from its tree. Her finger she had curled into Siva's let go bit by bit.

Amma gave a big push and Siva's sister arrived into the world, headlong, the umbilical cord still coiled around her neck. The midwife cut the cord and held up the baby. Patti stared stupidly at her granddaughter as she kicked her legs in the air. Amma held out her arms for her daughter. The midwife slapped the baby hard on the buttocks. The child didn't cry as they are meant to; instead she rounded her mouth and sang out their wombsong – oo-oo-oo – and her eyes glittered with newborn tears.

Outside, the wind howled: ooooowr-oooowar-oowat-oowata-oowata-r, as though it was thirsty. Amma would not forget this peculiar lament of the parched wind. A flash of lightning brightened the dark room for a still moment, and then shadows appeared, on the ceiling, walls and floor. Amma wouldn't forget the shadows either. It started to rain hard – large hyphenated lines tossed from the sky. The midwife looked up at the windowpane etched with lines of water, raindrops drumming at it. She looked alarmed. It was only April: too early for rain. It was a sign, this summer rain. It meant that something untoward was to happen.

The midwife pressed the baby to Amma's breast. Amma touched the baby's hair, stiff with birthblood. She touched her lips to the baby's cheek, kissed her with neverending love. It was a moment Amma would never forget. Then she breathed the name into the baby's ear: Tara.

Appa stood at the door, his shirt sweatdrenched, worried, wondering. Just then Munniamma stepped up to him with the newborn baby and raised her into his arms. Appa looked down at his daughter, wonder in his eyes. He laughed with joy. The baby twisted, cried, turned blue, and then was still. He continued to laugh, tears in his eyes.

Munniamma wrenched the child out of Appa's arms, walked back and laid the child next to Amma. Her voice shaking, she said, 'She died, ma. She died in her father's arms.'

Amma writhed and moaned. The midwife turned to her, and pressed Amma's stomach with her hands to force the placenta out of her womb. It had occupied all the space, pushing Siva's sister into the coils of the cord of birth and death.

His heart pounded loudly. The sound was amplified in the hollow he now inhabited alone. Then, even as he stayed moored to the very root of his beginnings, his body was caterpillared down the narrow passage and out. His mouth quivered open and he opened his eyes to the light of an oil lamp.

The midwife raised her bloodied hands. 'It's a boy.'

And thus I was born in a room that smelled of raw rice and balm.

1

It was early morning, but the sky was unusually dark and the moon was still out. An eagle perched on the roof of Victoria Villa looked up, watching, waiting. Dawn broke and cracks of light emerged from the dark clouds. The eagle spread its wings, felt the wind in its feathers and flew with flawless grace into the morning sky.

Light filtered through the leaves and faltered over my face as Patti stood under the neem tree, gently rocking me in her arms. I felt the pangs of hunger: a gnawing, dull ache, as though a mouse was nibbling at the inside of my belly, scratching-itching. I wailed, not so much because of hunger but because something was missing: the scent and the warmth I had got used to. Amma had abandoned me since the day I was born; I was now three months old.

Holding me close to her chest Patti walked into the kitchen. She was short, stumpy, but not fat. She was solid with hard work and childbearing, although Appa was the only one of her children who had survived. Three daughters had died in different positions in her womb. Her umbilical cord was a tragedyloop, Patti told everyone. It had coiled itself around a babyarm, babyleg and a babyneck and coaxed the life out of them. Patti was always dressed in nine yards of cotton the colour of an aged deerskin, and this she wrapped around her body and twisted between her legs. Somewhat like frilled trousers, her saree reached her ankles, and her bare feet moved quickly-deftly through each day. She wore no blouse because she was a widow and for the same reason, as per custom, her head was tonsured.

She pulled the saree tightly over her bosom and her head. She smelled of the scent and the heat of balm.

In the kitchen, Patti pulped a piece of ripe rastali banana and fed it to me with a silver spoon. I rolled the pulp in my mouth. Patti gave me another spoon and then another, so sweet and starchy. But by afternoon I had set up a howl. Patti dribbled tablespoons of gripe water into my mouth. The aniseed rivulet cooled my stomach and soothed the cramp in it. The next evening Patti crushed a piece of homegrown papaya and asked Appa to feed me. I ate it greedily, raising my open mouth for more, Patti would tell me.

Appa would come home with different kinds of papaya, she told me: the long ones, the round ones and particularly the small ones, which came from the western coast, called disco papaya. They were honeysweet. I loved papaya, Patti said. In fact it was the first word I learnt to speak. Each time Patti brought my evening feed, I would kick my legs in the air. *Pa-pa, pa-pa, yaaaa.* Patti told Appa I was asking for him. Appa smiled, showing all his teeth.

Appa was lean, tall and dark skinned, and wore gold-rimmed glasses. Hair sprouted out of his ears. His teeth were crooked and when he concentrated on something he ground them hard. In the evening after Appa returned from work, if he was not fussing over me, he was in his study at the back of the house, grinding his teeth.

In the study were a mock-Elizabethan chair, a rattan bench that had given way in the centre, a wormeaten table, its crevices filled with the dirt of years, and an old English safe. The safe contained little money, but in it were bundles of papers and reports Appa had recently prepared on the behaviour of a certain species of female mosquitoes. Above the safe was a painting of a young woman dressed in a cinnamon-brown silk gown painted with parrots, peacocks and pink lotus flowers. Her hair, under the threadnet bonnet, was cut short and her deepset eyes were blue like the sea. She was slightly swollen at her waist. At the bottom of the painting was a plaque: Elizabeth Gibbs.

Attached to the study and connected by a door was a garden full of flowering shrubs enclosed by steelnet and partly covered with dark canvas to keep the interior dim, warm and moist. In large glass trays of slimy water, larvae grew into adult mosquitoes. Families of the Aedes, Culex, Culiseta and Anopheles buzzed, copulated and multiplied. This was Appa's favourite place. The drone and whine of a thousand mosquitoes thrilled his ears and his absolute power over them energised his mind. He ground his teeth vigorously. It was in his study that Appa introduced me to the world of insects: flies, moths, butterflies, ants and mosquitoes.

'Did you know Siva,' he told me, 'the mosquito goes through four stages of life: egg, larva, pupa, and an adult. The larva lives in the water and comes to the surface to breathe. It sheds its skin four times, growing larger each time. The larva changes into a pupa. After two days the pupa splits its skin and an adult mosquito emerges. It rests on the surface of the water, waiting for the wings to harden. Then it flies in the air.'

Appa paused and looked at me. 'Now tell me what does the pupa do?'

And I said, kicking my feet in the air, pa-pa-ya-pa-ya.

***

Amma's father, Vishnu-thatha, was tall. He had a sharp face with deep penetrating eyes. His hair was long, tied into a ponytail. His smile was almost angelic, as though he wished something good for everyone, though tragedy had struck him early and left him lonely for all his life.

That evening when he came to see us I was lying on the pai on the veranda floor. Patti sat next to me, fanning me with a dried leaf fan. Not far from us she had lit a bowl of Queens Mosquito Repellent Powder; its bitter fumes bewildered the mosquitoes and they buzzed away. Patti lifted me onto grandfather's lap when he sat down beside her. He stroked my cheek that had railwaytrack marks from the pai. He took a silver rattle from his shirt pocket and shook it over my face.

Ting-ting-ting.

'He's got Mallika's eyes,' he said, tickling me under my chin. Vishnu-thatha thrust the rattle into my hand and closed my fingers around it.

Ting-ting-ting.

Grandfather's voice wavered as he enquired after his daughter. Patti averted her eyes as she told him that Amma was still in the storeroom. Vishnu-thatha became stiff and pained; a gush of shame spread over his face. He lifted me into Patti's arms and insisted on seeing his daughter. Patti led him across the hall to the storeroom. Vishnu-thatha knocked on the door and called out several times. The door opened a crack and there Amma stood, her hair dishevelled and her face stained with tears. Ammasmell. Wombsmell. I waved my hand.

Ting-ting-ting.

Vishnu-thatha held Amma by both her shoulders and gently shook her. She looked at him vaguely, then turned away and went back to her corner. Vishnu-thatha turned to Patti. 'Her daughter died, ma. It is because of grief that Mallika refuses to see her son.' His voice was broken.

Patti looked at me, sadness in her eyes. I felt someone's fingers curl into mine.

Ting-ting-ting.

***

Soon everybody got used to Amma's goings-on. She came out of the storeroom early each morning, washed, changed into fresh clothes that Munniamma had left on the kitchen table, ate leftovers, then returned to the storeroom. All day long she sat in a corner staring at the shadow on the floor, as one in a trance, as though the shadow was calling out to her. The dry wind blew through the gap in the window: ooooowr-oooowar-

30

oowat-oowata-oowata-r... When Munniamma went to her, Amma pointed to the shadow and said, 'Why did she have to go?'

'Because she had no After,' Munniamma said, wrapping an arm around Amma's shoulder.

'I want to have no After,' Amma said.

And whenever Munniamma took me to her, Amma shut her eyes and would not look at me. Each time Appa stood before her, cajoling her, she shut the door in his face. Hurt and bewildered, Appa let her be. He had me. Only a week ago Appa had had the cloth cradle moved from Patti's room to his. When I woke up at night and cried, Appa pulled the rope fixed to the cradle and sang as he gently rocked me:

> *I'm a little mosquito, l have little wings,*
> *I fly around and smell all things.*
> *When I see a little boy who smells simply great,*
> *I buzz out to all of my mosquito mates.*

***

It was early September, and the sun had switched on its heat. Frogs leapt into mirage puddles, dogs ran zigzagged in the streets, tails between their legs, tongues hanging out of their mouths. Then the heat cast its eyes on people. It squeezed them dry until their eyes wore a permanent squint and their brows a lasting frown. They whined and hissed like the hot wind.

My skin was prickly and sore. I heard wombsounds: whispering and hissing, and the slosh of the sea that had contained me. I moved my tongue and echoed the sounds: ssh-ssh, hizz-hizz. I pressed my tongue to the upper palate to try and make the slosh of the sea, but it came out as a cluck. This alarmed Patti.

Appa was in the rear garden examining a dish full of larvae, singing *Hang down your head Tom Dooley* as he did so. It was his favourite song. I had memorised the tune: Lala-la-la-la-lala. Patti stepped out of the study door holding me in her arms.

The pungent smell of balm preceded her. 'Look at this place swarming with mosquitoes,' Appa said without even looking up. 'There are around 300 million cases of malaria in our country and about three million people die every year. Only fifteen years since our independence, and look at the state of our mosquito-ridden country.'

'This country has only you to fight mosquitoes or what?' Patti slapped my arm, brushed away the squashed mosquito. 'And what about your son? He has heatsores and all day long he hisses and wheezes and makes clucking sounds with his tongue.'

Appa smiled. 'He must be imitating some of the sounds he hears.'

'Only snakes hiss and sish and hens make those clucking sounds and there are no snakes or hens here for him to imitate.

'Hen,' Appa repeated. 'Now where did I see the hen?' Momentarily distracted from his task, Appa rushed out of the rear garden door and up the stairs to the attic. Straddling me on her hip Patti followed behind him. Appa walked past bundles of old newspapers, files, a heap of mattresses, broken umbrellas and wooden cases to a trunk. He pulled away the bedsheet and opened the trunk. Stacked in it were several cloth bundles. He looked into one; it contained half a dozen baby frocks, silk, dyed in vegetable colours. He looked into the next one; it contained a number of boy's clothes brought all the way from England. Under them were a few shoes and feeding bottles, a plate, and a cup. From amongst them he pulled out a wooden toy – a hen, one claw broken and one eye-bead lost. Appa turned to Patti and me and thrust the toy into my hands. 'There must have been children in this house a long time ago. This toy must have belonged to them.'

Patti looked at the toy hen suspiciously. 'I wonder if the mother of those poor children cared for them,' she said. 'Old houses store memories and the past repeats itself.'

Appa laughed. 'Of all the silly superstitions!'

'Superstitions are not silly, okay. Something must have gone wrong with the people who lived here and it is affecting us.'

'Only George and his wife Elizabeth lived here. He was a fine man, and one responsible for malaria research in this part of the country. Do you know the Queen's Mosquito Repellent was started by him?'

'Oh forget the queen and her mosquitoes! Why don't you do something about Mallika, eh?' Patti snapped. 'By ignoring the problem it is not going to sprout wings and fly away like your mosquitoes. If you're not going to do anything about it I will, and right now. I am not afraid of her. You are a coward, Raman. You are frightened of your wife.'

Appa's endurance broke. Grinding his teeth he rushed down the stairs and into the house. Patti followed him to the storeroom. After several knocks on the door Amma opened it. Her face was swollen and her saree was dirty. Appa held her gently by her shoulders. She swept Appa's hands away, retreated into the room and threw all those things that would break: bottles, glasses, and the old mirror. She threw old newspapers and magazines, and Appa's old files and then the thick brown ledger flew up in the air and landed at Patti's feet, open. Its faded, yellow-grey pages rustled and turned in the breeze from the open window. Part of the red spine had torn from the ledger and lay curled on the floor: a thumb ripped away.

'Why are you angry with me?' Appa looked at her beseechingly. 'What did I do?'

Amma rushed at him and beat his chest with her fists, her eyes wide with rage. 'You killed Tara.'

Appa held Amma's arms and gently but firmly pulled her out of the storeroom and bolted the door. He called out to Munniamma to get the padlock. Amma ran out of the hall, up the stairs, all the way to the spare room on the second floor.

Patti stood still, looking at the broken glass and debris all around. She looked down at the old ledger at her feet; some of its pages had shifted out of the binding. A gust of wind blew from the window and the pages crackled like dried leaves as they turned, more pages, more pages, and a swatch of silk flew out and rolled on the floor: cinnamon-brown, painted with a peacock, parrot, leaves and a lotus.

Patti stared at the square of silk on the floor. Holding me to her chest, she bent to grab an edge of the fabric. Her eyes widened. 'Now why didn't I think of this?'

***

The spare room on the second floor was crowded. Suitcases and trunks were stacked in one corner; two steel almirahs stood against a wall; steel and brass utensils lay in a heap. On a bed, under a small window in the adjoining wall, was Amma. She held me in her arms and caressed the cinnamon-brown silk of my new frock. Amma kissed me on both my cheeks and pressed me to her breasts. My mouth opened wide and I made smacking sounds with my lips. Amma unbuttoned her blouse and thrust her nipple into my mouth. Appa and Patti stood watching outside the bedroom door. Patti struck her tongue on her palate and produced a defiant cluck.

That night, Appa brought Amma down to their room on the first floor. He held her close as she lay beside him. They seemed happy just like they did in their wedding photo in the hall, in which Appa looked fondly at Amma and she looked shyly down at her toes. Appa lifted his head to check on me; he pulled at the rope that rocked the cradle. He sang:

Eenie, Meenie, Miney, Mo.

Catch a mosquito by her nose.

If she buzzes don't let her go.

Eenie, Meenie, Miney, Mo,

He turned back to Amma and said, his voice deep, 'Do you know, Mallika, mosquito is a Spanish word. It means little fly. It belongs to the insect family cu-li-ci-dae which is derived from the Latin word culex meaning midge.'

Amma giggled.

Eenie, Meenie, Miney, Mo.

After that day, whenever Appa was travelling Amma laid me to sleep next to her each night. She bundled me in a soft quilt at the slightest hint of breeze. She tucked peppercorns under my pillow to keep bad dreams away. She kept the rattle next to the pillow and whenever I woke up in the middle of the night she went *Ting-ting-ting* with it. She not only left the night light on but hung wind chimes on the window which tinkled through the night, a lilting music to my dreams.

An echo went off in my head:
EenieMeenieMineyMo.
Who was that?

2

And thus my life began due to an inconsequential Spanish fly. Had it not been for that probing parasite Appa would have never come to Victoria Villa; he would have never been married to Amma. I would never have been born. But by the mysteries of destiny I had tumbled forth onto the storeroom floor in Georgie Gibbs' old house, amidst sacks of rice. Whispers soaked into the old walls told me that my sister had died the day I was born. Her name was Tara.

But Amma called me Tara. And Appa called me Siva. Patti called me both Tara and Siva. I was both a boy and a girl to her. Only I didn't know whether I was a boy pretending to be a girl or the other way around. I was four years old.

I was allergic to dust, the heat gave me a cold, milk brought out a rash and green vegetables made me itch. I contracted quite a surprising number of slight ailments. Dr Kuruvilla's visits to the house became a regular routine. I still wet my bed and still sucked my thumb. The doctor had said this was due to congenital fear. Patti was perturbed. 'What is it about this child, so delicate?' Patti asked Appa one morning as he left for work. I was down with a cold. 'And sensitive to heat? Have you ever heard of anything like this? Sensitive to heat? Ha! In Machilipatnam? With the sun blazing 365 days of the year?'

'Stop pampering him, ma,' Appa said. 'Don't bathe him in warm water. It is habit-forming. Bathe him in cold water. Let him cry, it's good for his chest. Mallika shouldn't cover him with that silk quilt when he sleeps and she shouldn't leave the lights on. He should get used to the dark and the cool breeze. How long will Mallika dress him in these silly frocks eh? Surely she knows he is a boy.'

'She is only pretending.' Patti rounded her eyes and shook a finger at Appa. 'But don't you say anything to her.'

'What will happen when she finds out?'

'You don't worry about that.' Patti was worried nonetheless. When Vishnu-thatha came to the house a few days later Patti confided in him. We were out on the veranda.

'Siva and Tara were born together,' Vishnu-thatha said. 'I am sure Mallika knows the child who survived is Siva. But to battle her grief she needs to make believe he is Tara.' A frown of concern came upon his face. 'I am more worried about Siva. Like his mother, he must miss Tara. Twins often develop a strong attachment in the womb. He will feel the loss of her.' Then Vishnu-thatha held my face in his hands and looked deep into my eyes. 'Terrible things happened, Siva,' he said, 'and your mother got very sad. She thought of someone who will make her happy, and this person became the real thing. But a day will come when she will not want to fool herself anymore. When this will happen I can't say. But this much I know, she will one day.'

The 'one-day' had yet not come and Amma's illusion blossomed and bloomed.

I was Tara, and Tara, her world.

Amma was always telling me stories about my birth. I was singing when I was born, she told me. And when she looked into my eyes she could see the whole world. There was a stormy wind the night I was born, she told me, and it howled: ooooowr-oooowar-oowat-oowata-oowata-r, as though it was thirsty. I was a little shadow in her tummy, she said, and then I grew my skin, flesh and bones.

She pulled away her saree and tapped her belly button, 'You came out of here.'

I put my mouth to my birthhole and blew hard; it made a farting sound. I tried to peep into the birthhole but I couldn't see inside it. 'Was there only me?'

Amma's face went blank and her eyes filled up with tears. I did what Amma did to me when I was hurt. I put my hand on my mouth and fisted it, and then raising it to Amma's mouth I pasted a smile on her face.

She said, 'Only you, Tara.'

Something throbbed inside me in a strange sort of way, like a twin. Tara?

***

One afternoon, when Patti was resting, Amma dressed me in long silk skirt, the colour of wet paddy, and a red blouse. She kohl-lined my eyes; on my forehead she smeared a vermillion pottu. She fixed a string of jasmine to my long hair, which she had refused to cut. We were going to the temple.

We walked down Gibbs Road. Low houses lined the street behind lines of drowsy palms; the houses were set back and far apart, all crowned with terracotta-tiled hats, scorched brown by the sun. From each of the houses music could be heard: Carnatic, Hindi, Telugu, English, and even Appa's favourite *Hang down your head Tom Dooley* song – Lala-la-la-la-lala; film music, godsongs, jingles for toothpaste and balm, from different radio stations. Between houses there were the vacant plots that resembled a yawn or a toothless grin depending on their size. In front of them sat new hawkers who smelled of distant migration.

As we approached the market a confusion of smells filled the air: coffee, curry powder, pickle, sour rice batter, tender shallots roasting in ghee, ripe bananas, jackfruit, and the scents of jasmine, kadamba and roses. It was a mixedup smell that lingered from the beginning of the market street to its end, and beyond, where the sea took over.

Old greengrocers had laid out their vegetables on the ground: the snaking gourds, the rolling pumpkins and pimply yams – their colour dull as dried earth. Beside them, younger merchants had arranged in baskets purple aubergines, red tomatoes, green peppers, all rubbed with oil to make them shine. Fruit sellers had put out their bananas, apples, pears and grapes, all of them arranged in cardboard boxes, tier upon tier. Old women with nineyard silk coiled between their legs, and younger women in bright nylex sarees, ambled through the market aisles, halfmoons of sweat at the armpits. They bought flowers for their hair and for the Gods, then headed down the road to the Shiva temple.

Amma held my arm and pulled me along. She pointed to a mango coloured house across the way. It was Vishnu-thatha's, she told me. The shutters of the window nextdoor were painted a bright green. Behind the window, stood a young girl and an old woman. I recognised them. The old woman was Rose Coelho, Patti's friend. She came to the house now and then to collect old clothes, old books, everything that was old, and money. Patti always had something to give her. It was for the poor, she told me. And the young girl was Rose-aunty's granddaughter, Rebecca.

Rose-aunty combed Rebecca's hair, plucked the loose hair from the comb, balled it up and tossed it from the window. Screwing up my eyes, I followed the hairball as it floated in the air, whirled, downdown, caught on a branch of a tree, blew off and stuck to a lamppost, and then rolled down the pavement like tumbleweed. A signal had been given.

We passed Ranga Roses, a roadside stall that sold roses in papercones, and Yusuf's Pet Shop beside it. A cow sat in front of it. Unlike the animals, fish and birds in Yusuf-uncle's shop, the cow was not for sale: it was a homeless holy cow. We stopped at *Mohan's Fruit & Juice* stall next door. I watched Mohan feed sweet limes into the mincing machine. He pushed them down with a rounded stick, collected the frothy juice in a steel jug, then scraped handfuls of pith, which he flung into the bucket crying *six* if all went in, *four* if half went in and *no-ball* if all

39

dropped out. He was mad about cricket and he played his game substituting the pith for the ball and the bucket for the cricket stumps. Flies swarmed around the *sixes* and *fours*, and the holy cow looked up from its bundle of grass and licked the *no-balls*.

'Here, kanna.' Amma held out a glass of sweetlime juice. I gulped it down, so lemony and sweet. I heard a slurp in my head.

A crippled boy limped closer to Amma. He smiled at her and displayed the knob of his leg.

Mohan smacked his hands. 'Go away, Swami. Stop pestering my customers.'

'Give Swami a glass too,' Amma said and paid for our drinks.

'You stupid cow,' Swami shouted, 'I don't want juice. Give me money for Coca Cola. Stupid cow. Stupid cow.' Amma clutched my arm and dragged me on.

The temple was similar to a house with a tiled roof, except its outer walls were painted yellowochre with a band of red at the bottom. We walked around the temple to the backyard. A pujari sat in front of the ritual fire on the rear veranda. Amma sat down before him and pulled me down in her lap. Amma took a lollypop out of her bag, unwrapped it and stuck it in my mouth. Lala-la-la-la-lala. The pundit spooned ghee into the fire. The mole on the tip of his nose grew red as the flames hissed and shot upwards. The man in a white vesthi next to him wiped the sweat off his face with a towel. I was restless; I tried to free myself but Amma held me tight. Sweet syrup trickled down the corners of my mouth, mixed with sweat. Lala-la-la-la-lala.

The pundit continued to feed the fire with ghee: onespoon twospoons threespoons of pure homemade ghee. My candycoated tongue stuck out, licklicked, then disappeared. I screamed when the man in the white veshti pierced my ear and twisted a gold wire into the hole. A scream sounded in my ears. The man quickly pierced my other ear and I started to howl. Amma hugged me. She balled her saree in her hand, blew warm air on it and pressed it to my ears, one at a time. She whispered,

'Now the hurt will go away.' She held me to her breasts and rocked me gently. 'Look Tara, there are stars in your ears.'

I touched my ears. I put my finger on the top of Amma's forehead, then slowly ran it over the ridge of her nose, down its tip, over the lips, the chin and all the way down the neck to the hollow under it. Then I curled my finger into the dip, sheltered and safe. I felt someone else's finger curl into mine. Tara?

We were by the lake behind our house. White lilies grew in it and butterflies flitted over each bloom. Green-brown toads croaked in unison. The trees around were tall. A few cicadas mistook day for night and screeched in chorus. Amma sat down on a grassy mound under the old chakka tree. I sat down beside her. The ground was still damp from the night's drizzle, and drops of water fell down from the leaves above. I tried to catch them in my palm.

'What is rain made of, Amma?'

'Water.'

'And the lake?'

'Rain water.'

'And the river?'

'Running water.'

'What is the sea?'

'Tides in water. And the ocean is the biggest water with the sea in it,' Amma said. She leaned back against the tree trunk and shut her eyes.

Not far from me a lone caterpillar sat curled like an O. Its body was the colour of fresh moss made translucent by the sun. Then teased by the wind it began to unwind its body and heaving updown it moved away on endless legs. I heard a whisper in my ear. 'Tara, is that you?' I felt her fingers lock into mine. I felt her heartbeat, a bit fainter than mine. All of a sudden I felt numbness spread through my body. I felt her leave me bit-by-bit: one arm, the other, one leg, then the other; eyes, ears, nose, heart and lungs, and then she tumbled out of me. She walked to the water's edge, then a splash and she disappeared. I ran to the water; I saw Tara's face in it. I saw her struggling in the slimy water, bobbing up and down, gulping water. More water. More water. Then she sank to the bottom of the lake, and I could see her no more. The last thing I saw was the water exhaling in bubbles. It was definitely possible, I knew then, to pick a moment, then be ready to slip away: feet first, then legs, waist, arms, heart, and lastly the head. It would be over.

But it was not 'over' time yet. I let out a cry. Amma rushed to me and held me in her arms. She looked at the edge of the water and she froze. The slimy water swelled and something leached into it similar to an inkdrop. The inkwater spread like a shadow and then disappeared below. Amma stared at the hollow in the water the dark shadow had occupied. The wind howled: ooooowr-ooooowar-oowat-oowata-oowata-r. Amma gasped and looked away. 'Don't go near the water,' she said. 'It will swallow you.'

I buried my head in her bosom, in its deep warmth. Tara returned to me bit-by-bit-by-bit. I was whole once more. 'Don't ever go near the water again,' I whispered. 'It will swallow you.'

That night in my dream I flew with Tara hand in hand to the place we had come from. Here the hills were light and soft like the breeze, the land was yielding like the sky, the sky was hard like glass reflecting the light of a single bright star; the trees grew tall and dropped fruits and flowers on a silky twine, and the river was made of clouds and on a tentative sunnyrainy day it spilled over and stretched in an arc across the earth's sky.

3

Those early years were full of happy times. Amma was with me, Tara in me. We were a threesome core family tied together by an invisible wombcord. Patti, Appa, Vishnu-thatha and Munniamma were present too, but they were outside our inside world. And there was Rose-aunty and Rebecca, somewhat outside our outside world. As my inside world grew, the outside world expanded with it. It was the time for games, stories and lessons, and the lessons learnt from them. Catch-n-cook, hide-n-seek, Simon says, L-O-N-D-O-N Lo-n-don... Amma played these games with me. And sometimes when Rose aunty came with Rebecca to meet Patti, Rebecca and I played Statue. Every time Rebecca pointed a finger at me and said *statue*, I had to be very still. But deep inside me Tara giggled and I lost the game. Lesson: play to win the game. Con-cen-trate.

Patti told me stories about the Gods and demons. Lesson: good always wins over evil. Amma taught me ABCD and 1234, bluegreenyellowred and nose-eyes-ears-head-fingers-toes. I was clever, she said, hugging me. Lesson: it pays to be clever.

Amma taught me a rhyme:

What are little boys made of?
Frogs and snails and puppy-dogs' tails;
That's what little boys are made of.
What are little girls made of?
Sugar and spice and all that's nice.
That's what little girls are made of.

Lesson: girls are nicer than boys.

The best lessons I learnt from Appa. He would often be with me in his study going through a picture book of insects. I liked being with Appa. It was *EenieMeenieMineyMo,* Tara whispered. She liked learning to learn. *Yay.*

'Tell me, Siva what is this?' Appa asked pointing to a page in the insect book.

'Ant.'

'Good.' Appa turned some pages. 'And this one?'

'Butta-fly.'

'Very good. Now tell me what this is?'

'Catta-pilla.'

'You can't see its legs but it has six in the front and many in the middle. Its head has six eyes on one side. And what is this?'

'Silk-orm.'

'That's correct. What is this?'

I shook my head.

Appa said, 'This is a praying mantis. It is the only insect fast enough to catch flies and mosquitoes.'

'Pider, pider,' I said pointing to the adjoining page.

'Spider, not pider. Spiders are our friends because they eat those horrible mosquitoes that carry disease.'

Appa turned some more pages. 'What is this?'

'Muk-si-to.'

'Mosquito.'

'Muk-si-to.'

'Say Mos-ki-toe.'

'Muk-si-toe.

'Mos-mos.

'Mus-mus.'

'Ki-ki.'

'Ki-ki.'

'Toe-toe.'

'Toe-toe.'

'Right. Mos-mos-ki-ki-toe'

'Mus-mus-ki-ki-toe.'

'Mos-qui-toe.'

'Muk-si-toe.'

'Tell me which one?'

I stuttered. Appa laughed and pinched my ear fondly. 'Silly, you don't even know what this is? Look at its wings. It has black and white scales on them. It is an A-no-phee-lees. Repeat after me – A-no-phee-lees.

I jumped up and down. Aa. No. Phil. Liss. Aa. No. Phil. Liss. And Tara joined in: *Aa. No. Phil. Liss. Aa. No. Phil. Liss. Aa. No. Phil. Liss.*

'That's right,' Appa said. 'The anopheles is a female mosquito. She is very bad.'

'You are telling Tara stories about mosquitoes again.' Amma walked through the door with tumblers of coffee and ovaltine. 'Mosquitoes are not all that bad,' she said setting the tumblers on the table. 'They never bite me.'

'Because mosquitoes prefer some people over others,' Appa attempted a calculated smile. 'Some people's sweat simply smells better.'

Amma pursed her lips and jerked her head back. 'As if.'

'It's true. Our body odour is made up of carbon dioxide, octenol and other compounds in different proportions. Did you know a mosquito has 72 types of odour receptor on its antennae, and at least 27 are tuned to detect the nonanal chemicals in our sweat.'

'Non Anal?'

'Nonanal is an alkyl aldehyde. It has an orange-rose smell and is used in flavours and perfume.'

'Are you saying I don't smell nice?' Amma narrowed her eyes.

Appa's eyebrows arched; a conspiratorial smile quivered on his lips. 'That's why mosquitoes don't bite you, Mallika. There are no fruity-flowery chemicals in your sweat that attract them.'

'But surely the mosquitoes can see me.' Amma tilted her head back, adjusted a curl of hair behind her ear. Her long dark hair was still wet after her evening bath. She smelled of

45

the astringent and lemony bacteriological soap that Appa had got a large supply of from his institute. The soap was a part of his experiment with mosquito repellence. The soaps were no good; they didn't froth. A good reason the mosquitoes didn't like them much.

'Mosquitoes don't see very well,' Appa said with a mysterious smile. 'They have two compound eyes with multiple lenses and blind spots separate the lenses. Therefore, they can't see you until they are near and even then they can't make out the difference between a person and a drum.'

Amma looked accusingly at Appa. 'Are you now saying I look like a drum?'

Appa bunched his shoulders and grinned. He held a truce hand out to Amma. But Amma was not ready for a compromise. With a wave of her angry hand she walked away.

'Aa. No. Phil. Liss. Aa. No. Phil. Liss.' I cried. *Aa. No. Phil. Liss. Aa. No. Phil. Liss,* Tara echoed.

Appa gathered us in his arms.

***

The most important lesson I learnt was on the day we went to see Jungle Book. I was by the pond in front of the house that afternoon. There were many fish in it: Goldfish, Carps, Guppy, Molly, Swordtails and a lone Angelfish – all of them with yawning mouths and bags under their eyes, due to lack of sleep. The Angelfish, turned on its side, floated by: dull and colourless. 'Angelfish too sick,' I said.

Amma said from the stone bench nearby: 'I think it's dead.' Then she went back to Georgette Heyer's *False Colours.*

I heard the sound of a car. Appa had come home. With my arms in the air I called out to him. 'Appa, why Angelfish die?' I asked when he stood beside me.

'Because of stress.'

'Stess is what?'

'Stress, not stess. It is a disease. Like malaria. But stress is not caused by bacteria or germs. It's caused by too much worry.'

'Why Angelfish too much worry?'

'Maybe it didn't have a friend and it was alone.'

'So I can get stess also?'

Appa laughed. 'You are too young, kanna.'

Angelfish was too young too. So I could surely get stess. But I decided not to have too much worry about it. In any case I was not alone. I had Tara.

Appa walked over to Amma and sat down on the bench next to her.

'How come so early?' Amma picked up a leaf from the ground and placed it on the open page of the book.

'I thought I'd spend some time with you.'

'As if. Don't lie.'

The light was fast fading. The buzz and whines of mosquitoes filled the air. Appa pointed to a swarm of mosquitoes around Amma's feet. 'You shouldn't sit outside. It's the time for the mosquitoes to come out. They will bite you.'

Amma looked at him triumphantly. 'You said the mosquitoes wouldn't bite me. Anyway, I am not scared of mosquito bites.'

'Mosquito bites are not bad. It's their saliva that is harmful.' Appa turned around to face Amma. 'Now listen to me carefully,' he said with the sudden excitement of someone revealing a secret. 'A special protein in the mosquito's saliva makes it an anticoagulant and...'

'Anti-co-what?'

'Anti-co-agu-lant. It's a chemical that thins their blood so that the mosquito's proboscis does not become clogged with blood clots. Its saliva also carries the malaria germs. So when an infected mosquito bites us the germs from its saliva gets into our blood and kills our blood cells. If malaria is not treated on time, especially P. Falciparum, then it can lead to many problems: high fever, vomiting, sweating and shakes. In some cases even death.'

Amma bent over and wiped her feet with the end of her saree.

Appa looked at his wristwatch. 'It's only five thirty. Let's go see a film. Let's see Jungle Book. Patti will love it and so will our child.' Appa never called me Siva when Amma was around. It was Patti's BEWARE with two round eyes and one finger up. 'It's playing at Eros Cinema,' Appa said. 'We can have dinner out.'

'But I've made puliodhare and cucumber pachadi,' Amma said. 'It's your favourite.'

'I'll take it with me for lunch tomorrow,' Appa said. 'Promise.'

Patti, although reluctant, walked with us to the cinema house. I sat between Appa and Patti in the hall. Amma sat on the other side of Appa. The hall was big and there were not many people in it. 'Must be a bad film,' Patti grunted.

'It's a children's film, ma,' Appa said, 'and it's the evening show after all. The afternoon show, I am sure, must have been houseful.'

'In our time, Patti said, 'there were mainly religious films. So many people went to see these films, morning or evening. Night even. People would simply love to see their hero singing to Lord Krishna, Lord Vishnu, and to hear the Gods singing back. What heavenly music. A-ha-ha.'

Then the lights went out and I clasped Appa's hand. Some minutes later when I saw Ba-geera the Black Panther on the big screen, I felt stess in the back of my neck and loud beating in Tara's heart. 'Appa we go home,' I said. 'I get stess.'

'Don't be scared,' Appa whispered, 'it's only a movie.'

I heard Tara wail in my ear. 'Don't be scared,' I whispered, 'it's only a movie.'

'What? Did you say something?' Appa asked.

I covered my face with my hands and watched the screen though the gaps between my fingers. In my comic books the animals didn't move and they spoke through bubbles that rose over their heads. But in the movie Ba-geera actually spoke. I saw the little boy Mowgli and slowly dropped my hands, but when

Kaa the python appeared I shut my eyes tight. But I could hear him sing *Trust in me* in a mesmerising voice.

Tara laughed out loud when the elephants marched – a shrill, undulating laugh that I inherited, and which in later times would become my own. I liked the big bear Baloo and his song, *Bare necessities*. And the vultures. I liked the way they spoke.

When the movie was over and the lights came on Appa asked me, 'So did you like the film?'

I slapped my thighs with both my hands and then clapped them over my head, sprang up and spun around like Baloo the bear. 'Yes-Yes-Yes,' I said.

Amma had tears in her eyes.

When we were out on the road I asked Appa: 'Whatweagonnado?

'What?' Appa asked.

'Whatchawannado?'

'Speak clearly, kanna,' Appa said.

Amma laughed. She said, 'Letsdosomething.'

'Okwatchawannado?'

*Okwatchawannado?Okwatchawannado?Ok...*I slapped my head to keep Tara quiet.

We walked down the lane to Good Morning Café, which also served Good Evening dinner. Nayak-uncle, the owner, showed us to a table by the window. Rose-aunty, Rebecca and her father were seated at the table in the corner. Rebecca waved to me. She got up from her chair and then her father said something to her and she sat down again. Tommy Gonzalves stepped between the two tables. He turned to Appa and with a nod he uttered, 'Confucius,' and walked toward the other end. Just then the waiter came to us for our order. Patti ordered a Mysore masala dosa. Appa ordered two plates of idlis for Amma and him, and thayir vadai for me. I liked thayir vadai. It did not take long for the waiter to come with our order. There were two vadais on my plate. One for Tara, the other for me. Tara liked thayir vadai too. I heard her slurp in my head.

After Patti had eaten all of the dosa, she said, 'Mallika makes better dosas. And the chutney was too watery. They are stingy with the coconut. We should have stayed at home and had that nice puliodhare Mallika made.'

Appa laughed. 'But you've finished everything on your plate, ma.'

'Then what! Gandhiji said: To a man with an empty stomach food is God. We must not waste food.'

Amma held Appa's hand and said, 'Thank you.'

Outside the restaurant, across the road, a mob of men in saffron clothes was gathered around Yusuf's Pet Shop. Arms raised to the sky, they screamed: Only Hindus. No Muslims. Only Hindus. Muslims go to Pakistan. Appa gathered us close and walked quickly down the road.

'Who are they?' Patti asked when we were further away from the mob.

'They belong to the Hindu National Party,' Appa said.

'Why are they shouting?'

'To keep the Muslims in their place.'

'Why?'

Appa told her: A riot had broken out one time. It had started with a quarrel between Yusuf Ali, the Muslim owner of Yusuf Pet Shop, and Ranga, the Hindu owner of Ranga Roses. Ranga considered the holy cow that sat outside his shop to be lucky for him. People on the way to the temple stopped at Ranga's shop for flowers for the Gods and also bought grass to feed the holy cow. But Yusuf, next door, considered the cow to be his worst nightmare. It produced piles of dung that were covered with flies. The flies drifted into his shop and parked themselves on his birds and animals. They lingered on his glass of tea and the fried pakoras he liked to eat with it.

On that fateful day just as Yusuf stepped out of his shop to go to the Mosque for his prayers, Ranga's holy cow let fall a stream of piss. It spattered all over Yusuf's freshly washed salwar. Yusuf cursed and beat the cow fiercely with his fist. The next morning a pig was found tethered to a pillar in front of the Mosque. Suddenly what started as a squabble between Ranga and Yusuf swelled into a bigger and a more dangerous tumult between Muslims and the Hindus in the market.

At the break of dawn on the third day of the quarrel, in front of the Shiva temple, muscular Muslim men turned their spit above a fire and cooked the slaughtered holy cow, sparks flying into the holy Hindu air around. Four cow hooves lay on the ground, a visible testament to their deed. That night a group of Hindu men set fire to many Muslim shops and houses in the market. Timber, paper, plastic, cloth and treasured memories of togetherness went up in flames.

The Hindu National Party was founded about this time. Its Hindu members constantly quarrelled with their Muslim neighbours. Theirs was not just a quarrel over Gods, or home or land; or between a man and another man, or about animals, but also a war over fundamental rights – about who had the right, and who had the right to decide this.

'Bloody fellows,' Appa said when we were halfway home. 'Instead of getting rid of Muslims they should help in eradicating the bloody mosquitoes from this place.' We passed the old wooden sign that had painted on it: GIBBS ROAD. The wood had rotted, the paint had flaked and the post tilted to one side. Appa turned to Amma. 'Do you know the mosquito *Anopheles Gibbinsi* is named after Gerald Gibbins, a researcher on mosquitoes and black flies. He was investigating a yellow fever outbreak in Africa. He was speared to death, because the locals believed that the blood samples he was taking were intended for witchcraft. He was only forty-two, and he had so much more to do.'

Amma clutched Appa's hand. 'Promise me you will never go to Africa,' she said.

Patti and I had walked ahead. I turned back to look at Appa and Amma. Appa had his arm around her shoulder. He whispered something in her ear and she giggled.

Patti asked, 'Siva, did you like Bagheera, Ka, Baloo or Shere khan?'

'Baloo,' I replied and did the bear dance once more.

'And don't forget what the bear said,' Patti added, patting my head playfully. 'Life is made of small-small things. Don't look for things you can't get, you can't find. Forget them and the small things,' she spread out her arms, 'will become big-big-bigger, as big as life.'

EenieMeenieMineyMo, Tara whispered in my ear.

The moon above was large and round and the shadow on it looked like Ba-geera. I felt nicely de-stessed. It was a good day, and so was the lesson I learned from Baloo, the bear.

Amma and Tara were the barest necessities of my life: breath and heartbeat. I couldn't live without them.

Then there was Georgie Gibbs of course; he stared down at me from the wall in the hallway every time I passed by. And sometimes when no one was looking I talked to him. But he was a different matter. He was not family; he did not belong to our inner or outer world. He belonged altogether to another world.

4

I was introduced to God early in my life. I can't say He did me much good. To know me, just me, would have been difficult even for Him, as it would prove to be for me. There was no escaping my fate, no, not even with His help. I seriously doubted if He would help, or if He could. In any case, who was God? Some questions don't have answers; science has still to find them, Appa had told me, that's why people believe in God. God was important. I knew this. I also knew that God had a lot of answers. But I couldn't understand why He didn't have answers for everything.

Most of what happened to me, with me, was not in my control but I had found a way of filling in the gaps, finding hidden clues, swimming the tide to become who I was meant to be. The gaps and clues were tiny at most times but it was the enormous tide that eventually swept me off my feet. But first about those gaps and clues:

I now knew a lot of words, some of them with their spelling:

G-i-r-l = girl. B-o-y = boy. Many 'girl' = girls. More than one boy = boys. Like a girl = girl-ish. Like a boy = boy-ish. I had worked out in my mind the difference between Girl and Boy.

Girls: Patti, Amma, Munniamma, Tara, Rebecca and Rose-aunty. Girls were sweet and cried easily. They cooked, cleaned and did not go out to work.

Boys: Appa, Vishnu-thatha. Boys were strong, they had hair on their face; they were very busy and they went out to work.

But were there boys/girls who were half-and-half? Boys who were strong and cried easily? Girls who were sweet and had hair on their face? I didn't know. These were un-answerable questions, at least for me. As for God, God only knew.

Appa was fully a boy, and thank God for this. He was strong; he had hair on his face, and he left early to work and returned late in the night. Girls surrounded me all day long, old, older, oldest: Amma, Munniamma, Patti. Now and then Tara whispered in my ear: ssh-hiss. Except for Georgie Gibbs, if he could be counted as a man. Then there was the chakka-man who parked his cart under the chakka tree. But he couldn't be counted; he was outside. Until the morning Mani arrived at the gates with a tattered suitcase. He was a cook and Appa had hired him.

That morning Rose-aunty had left Rebecca in my house and gone to Sunshine Home, the school for the handicapped and poor that she looked after. Rebecca and I were in the kitchen watching Patti churn curds with a stick to make fresh butter. Patti saw Mani from the window and went out to meet him. Rebecca and I ran after her.

Mani leaned on one hip against the gate, scrutinizing the property. One arm was flung carelessly behind his head. As we approached, he stroked the side of his head, and pushed his hair up. His face was smooth and his teeth were so even and white that they put a Colgate smile to disgrace. He was girl-ish. 'My name is Mani,' he said in a squeaky voice. 'I was a cook in the Indian army. I know English cooking very well. And an Englishman I worked for said my chicken curry was the best.'

Patti grunted. 'There is no army here. Just three of us, and this little one here,' she said pointing to me. 'English cooking? Chicken curry? Look at me. Do I look like some pale English woman to you? We are vegetarians. No eggs. No meat.'

'I know South-Indian cooking too, ma,' Mani said beaming. 'And North-Indian. Bengali, Gujarati dishes also.'

'Okay-okay.' Patti let him in and led him into the outhouse at the back of the kitchen.

54

As Rebecca and I followed them important questions came to my mind. Important, because only God had the answers to them.

- Mani was a boy but he cooked. He was girl-like; he waddled.
- Munniamma was a girl but she went out to work. She was strong; she had muscles.

Amma had told me about Exceptions. In English one thing could become many things by adding 's'. Like banana and banana-s, apple and apple-s. But cherry became cherr-ies and mango became mango-es. And the more difficult one, knife became kni(f)-ves. These, Amma said, were exceptions to the rule. They were special. So I concluded that Mani and Munniamma were exceptions. They were a bit of both – a girl and a boy. Like me. I was an exception too. I was two people at once: one a half of the other. Being an exception was special. I liked Mani. Exceptionally.

In the outhouse Mani put his suitcase down and opened it. He took some of his things out and laid them on the floor.

'You can unpack later,' Patti said. 'First cook the rice.'

'Cook rice? Now?'

'Yes. I want to feed the crows.'

'Crows?'

'Crows are the spirits of our ancestors and feeding them brings good fortune and peace to the family. Don't you know this?'

'Okay, ma. I will come in a minute.'

Rebecca and I returned to kitchen with Patti. Amma was grating coconut and Munniamma washed the utensils. Just then Rose-aunty arrived to fetch Rebecca. Some minutes after they left Mani stepped into the kitchen in a lungi; his chest was bare. Patti stared at the blue-black tattoo of a heart on his arm.

'What happened to your shirt eh?'

'It's so hot, ma.'

'I don't care. I can't have your sweat and hair falling into my food. Go, put on a shirt.'

Amma ground the grated coconut with green chillies, ginger and cumin seeds and added the paste to the stewed pumpkin. She now added the buttermilk left over from the curds that Patti had churned. Mani returned to the kitchen in his blue shirt and got busy boiling the rice. When it was cooked he heaped some on a plate and held it out to Patti.

Patti stepped out into the garden with the plate of rice. She rolled the rice into balls, then standing on her toes she placed them in a row on the garden wall. I had seen her perform this ritual every morning and sometimes she even made a tiny rice ball for me and thrust it into my mouth. Ka-ka-ka. She called out to the crows. Before long, she had a response. I looked up and saw a large black crow with a cut near its left eye staring down at her. 'Oh. It's you,' she smiled, 'so many years and now you show your face eh? Your son is doing well. Raman has become the director of the Georgie Gibb Mosquito Institute here. You would have been proud, had you been alive. And yes, you have a grandson, Siva.' She didn't tell the crow about Tara. 'Now don't worry about me. Your son is looking after me well. When he is not running after those mosquitoes, that is.' She hurried back into the kitchen and returned a few moments later with another ball of rice. She held it up to the waiting crow. 'Here, eat this one, I have mixed it with fresh homemade butter that I churned this morning only.'

But the crow flew out and up over the palm trees. Ka ka, ka, Patti shouted to it as she walked further into the trees, her arm outstretched with the ball of rice. There, hidden by lantana bushes, she saw a tomb made of broken laterite. The stone had crumbled and grass grew out of its pores. The inscription on the weathered headstone was worn.

Ge rge Gi bs.
Ap il 13, 1862.

Patti dropped the riceball and covered her mouth with her hands and screamed. Munniamma and Amma came running past the palm trees.

Amma pressed her hand to her mouth, and her eyes grew wide. 'It's George Gibbs' grave.' She glanced at the date. 'By Jove! It's a hundred years old.'

'What Jove, Jove!' Patti retorted. 'You silly woman! Don't you even know that the dead person's memories will seep into each of us and make us live his life and think his thoughts?'

'Don't you worry ma,' Munniamma said. 'I know someone who can drive spirits away.'

Patti folded her hands, looked up, and prayed to the Goddess of unhappy spirits: Oh Periyachi Aaman, keep the English spirit away from us.

***

A half hour later Munniamma returned with an old man wrapped in too much cloth. Patti and Amma were waiting for her in the garden. Patti asked, 'Munniamma, who is this human cocoon?'

'He is the fakir who sits near the Mosque.' Munniamma rubbed her hands together. 'He will drive away the evil spirit.'

'Ye di Munniamma, could you only get a halfstarved man to do the work?' Patti asked. 'And can't you see he is a Muslim?'

'With ghosts, religion doesn't matter ma,' Munniamma whispered. 'And it is an English ghost after all. I can tell you this much, ma: the spirit will be gone just like that.' She clicked her fingers in the air. 'He says he will do it for fifty rupees.'

'Fifty rupees!' Patti hissed. 'What does he think money grows on? My bald head?'

'He has to send the ghost away all the way to England, no?'

'I don't care if he sends the ghost to England or Kanyakumari,' Patti retorted. 'I am not paying more than twenty-five.'

The fakir raised three fingers, shook them in front of Patti's face. 'Thirty rupees. You have to pay first.'

Patti opened the knot she had tied with the end of her saree and retrieved several notes. 'Here's twenty. Five I will give later.'

The fakir spread a black cloth on the ground. I stood behind Amma and peered at him as he arranged coins on the cloth, stones and bits of wood in a circle. From his bag he took out a small roll of cloth no bigger than his palm. He wound a piece of twine around it and placed it in the middle of the circle and thrashed it with a broom made of leaves. Then he sat on the ground and shut his eyes and swayed back and forth. His body shook and he wailed as if in terrible pain. Spit spewed out of his mouth.

Patti asked, 'Ye di Munniamma, why is this man howling like a mad dog?'

Munniamma raised a finger to her lips. 'Sshh, it is the English ghost tormenting him.'

The wind became steadily fierce. The fakir stood up and with his arms flailing above his head he circled round and round. He rushed to the pond and just when it seemed to me that he was about to jump into it, a branch of a palm tree snapped and fell into the water. The fakir crashed down in a heap on the ground. He foamed at the mouth and his body shook. Amma watched, her hands covering her mouth. I stood close to her. Tara had set up a wail in my ears.

'Achicho, he's having fits or what?' Patti screamed. 'Mallika, go get my old slippers and leave them next to him and, yes, get an iron key and shove it into his mouth. Go! What are you waiting for eh?' Munniamma cupped her hands, filled them with water from the pond and sprinkled it on the fakir's face. She held him by his shoulders and shook him. 'Why are you shaking him like that?' Patti said. 'Can't you see he's already shaking?'

The fakir opened his eyes, wiped his face with the back of his hand, sat up and pointed to the branch fallen in the pond. 'That was the ghost,' he said.

'That branch?' Patti asked.

'Yes. The spirit entered me, and then flew to the tree, slid down its branch and dropped into the pond.' The fakir held out his hand. 'Give me the rest of the money, ma. The ghost is gone.'

Patti looked at the branch fallen in the water. Although my grandmother believed in the supernatural, logic was stamped in her Tamil brain and it often intercepted her blind faith. There was no way she was going to believe the fakir. 'The ghost has not gone anywhere. It is still in the pond. Floating. It is an English spirit after all and it can certainly swim. Go now.' Patti waved her hand at the fakir.

Disgruntled he walked away. Mani had come out into the yard by now, having heard the ruckus. 'You should get a dog, ma,' he said. 'Dogs can see spirits. And they bark loud and scare the spirits away. Yusuf has a pet store in the market. I can get a dog from him, but he is expensive.'

'Why pay for a dog when so many of them run about in the streets eh? Go look for one and bring it here. Feed it for a few days. Then it will remain faithful and guard the house and keep the ghost away.'

Half an hour later, Mani returned holding a rope tied to the neck of a mangy white dog. It smelled of an old gunnysack. Patti inspected the dog, walking around it. She slapped her forehead. 'Aiyooo Rama. Why is it so thin and white? Those English people left behind their dogs or what? Chi-chi, God only knows what illness it has. Feed it outside the gate, Mani. So it will stay there, under that chakka tree, near the chakka-man.'

'What to call it?' Mani asked.

Patti thought for a bit. 'A nice name. A name of a king perhaps. Or a hero.' Her eyes lit up. 'Yes, yes, I know what to call it. Churchill.'

I shaped my mouth and said something like 'Cha-chi.' *Cha-chi-cha-chi*, Tara went on and on in my head.

***

Not entirely convinced by the fakir's tomfoolery or the dog's extraordinary powers, Patti sent for Perumal Krishnan to offer prayers to Periyachi Aaman to ward off the evil eye of the spirit and, unbeknown to Amma, to read my horoscope that he had cast the day after I was born.

A horoscope is like a stamp from nature's own manufacturing company, which lists important features as:

Manufacturing Date
Batch Number
Composition
Indication
Expiry Date

Just like on a pack of medicine.

As soon as Perumal arrived Patti sent a reluctant Amma to the medical store to get her a jar of Amrutanjan Balm. Perumal sat on the pai in front of Patti. She told Perumal about the grave she had found and handed him my horoscope. 'A good fate can beat an evil spirit any day. Read carefully,' Patti said, 'and see if my grandson is going to be a great man one day. Perhaps a great leader like our Gandhiji.'

Perumal giggled.

'What are you giggling for eh? Tell me, would Gandhiji's mother have ever imagined her son would be a great man one day? These things happen. Yes, they happen if fate allows it.'

Perumal studied my horoscope; his nose twitched now and again. 'He will have a soft body and face, wide forehead, deep eyes, bright countenance and a prominent nose. He is of the type – *Satyameva Jayate*. He will not hesitate to sacrifice his own life for upholding the truth. He will also be of the adamant type. Once he takes a decision it will not be easy for others to change his mind. While he will be very intelligent and have a good grasp of complex things, he will be very soft in his heart.

Patti clasped her hands in front of her chest. 'See, I told you.'

'Your grandson is born under the Mrigasira constellation of stars,' Perumal added. 'Its ruling deity is Parvati. Those born under these stars are on a quest; they are always seeking. He will be a wise one, and know many secrets. He will have excellent memory and the powers of premonition, and he will be prone to clairvoyance.' Then Perumal looked up at Patti conspiratorially. 'However, we must be careful, ma. The Mrigasira person frequently follows a mirage and this gives rise to duplicity, fickleness and mental exhaustion in him and those around him. Let us be warned, Mrigasira is known to bring temporary contentment, deep disillusionment and sorrow.' Perumal now looked into his charts and notes to check the position of planets, the celestial houses they occupied and their transition between houses. 'Scorpio is the ascendant,' he declared. 'The Sun is in Pisces and Saturn is in Gemini. Saturn will cause a lot of damage when it transits from the house of Gemini.' He looked up at Patti, wearyeyed. 'This is far worse than the evil eyes of spirits, ma.'

Patti covered her open mouth with her hand. 'What am I going to do?'

'To ward off the evils of Saturn you must pray to Shaneeshwar, the Lord of Saturn, the son of the Sun God and the Goddess of Shadow. Everything will be all right, ma,' Perumal said. 'You must have trust in the superior powers.' Perumal joined his hands, closed his eyes, drew in a deep breath and prayed, Aum praang preeng proung Shanaye namah...

Patti closed her eyes and prayed to Shaneeshwar to look after me, damned by the itinerant Saturn. Cha-chi howled all night. Tara sang to me in my sleep – Kaa's hypnotic *Trust in me* song.

5

The Lord of Saturn cast his benevolent eyes on me, at least temporarily. He blessed me with a fair share of intelligence. I was bright and Amma was overjoyed. She taught me s-c-i-e-n-c-e. The same science that knew lesser answers than God. I learnt that my head was made of bones, and thoughts were inside it, and yesterday's thoughts became memories. Thoughts were the fruits of my mind, Amma told me. I wondered if thoughts were made of flesh, like papaya flesh. Skin like banana skin. Or bones like mango seed. Or juice like orange juice. I asked Amma and she said: God only knows.

So I asked Patti. She hugged me and said, 'My intelligent seeker. Don't forget, God resides in every thought.'

There, the clue. God was invisible. He was touchless, odourless, tasteless. He was pure air. So thoughts were made of air. I imagined my thoughts blowing inside my head, round and round, and now and then coming out of my ears, my nostrils, and when I yawned God came straight out of my mouth.

Amma also taught me maths. She taught me to minus and plus, and told me everything could be minussed and plussed. 'What is A+B?' I asked her.

'That is called algebra,' she said laughing. 'Algebra is alphabets plus maths together,' she explained. 'It has ABCD and XYZ. You can plus or minus them, divide or multiply and the letters can be given any value like 1,2,3,4...'

'Tara is so clever,' Amma told Appa that evening. 'She was asking me what A+B was.'

Appa fondly pinched my cheek. 'Our child is going to be a scientist one day.'

Of that, I wasn't certain, but I had learnt early that living was all about plus-ing and minus-ing and like in Al-Zeb-Ra everything had a value, more or less.

***

Vishnu-thatha told me about the colours besides bluegreenyellowred – which made me nostalgic – the colours that on a rainysunny day spread on the sky's face and made it smile. I made my days wear colours. Instead of Sunday-Monday-Tuesday-Wednesday-Thursday-Friday-Saturday I had Violetday, Indigoday, Blueday, Greenday, Yellowday, Orangeday and Redday. Seven days for seven colours. It was easy to remember them. I liked Violetday the most because Amma dressed me in a Sunday frock and took me to Vishnu-thatha's house and left me there all day. He taught me to draw: standing lines, sleeping lines and lines that went round and round. I drew the sun, mountains, a river, birds and trees. I also drew Georgie's ghost: one standing line, a wisp of smoke, disappearing into nothing. And *Eenie, Meenie, Miney, Mo*: one line holding two lines spread in a V, like two arms outstretched: Yay. Tara liked *Eenie, Meenie, Miney, Mo* the best.

One Violetday Rebecca and I were out on the veranda in Vishnu-thatha's house. I was colouring the sketch I had drawn, a sort of map. It had Gibbs Road winding to the blue-blue sea, Vishnu-thatha's mango-coloured house, Rebecca's house with green shutters, the temple with red stripes, and my house with red rooftiles...

Rebecca pointed to the wispy grey thing in front of my house. 'What is this?'

'That is the ghost.'

'There are no ghosts, stupid.'

'We have a ghost in my house. He is from L-o-n-d-o-n. His name is Georgie.'

Rebecca broke into a rhyme:

Georgie Porgie Puddinand Pie,

Kissed the girls and made them cry,
When the boys came out toplay
Georgie Porgie ranaway.

'He didn't run away. He's here.'

'What's he doing here?'

'He died here so he left behind his ghost.'

She pointed to the sketch. 'And who's that, next to the ghost?'

'Amma. And this one is Appa, and here is Patti. This is Mani and this one is Munniamma. This is Cha-chi under the chakka tree. And this one is the tamarind tree at the back...'

'And who's under the tree?'

'This is me, and this is you.'

Rebecca leant toward me and kissed me on my cheek.

We went with Vishnu-thatha to the lake in the woods that day. When I clapped, the birds in the tall trees were startled and ruffled the leaves as they took flight. We went to Pinto's ice-cream parlour with four flavours: vanilla, orange, chocolate and pistachio. I sat with Rebecca on the railing outside and we licked our ice-cream cones in rhythm: 1-2-3-4 Lick. 5-6-7-8 Lick.

'Let's see who can lick faster,' Rebecca said.

12345678... I licked away all the ice-cream. 'I won,' I said. 'You lost.'

Rebecca dashed her cone to the ground. She looked at it grumpily. 'Look what you made me do.'

Next to Pinto's was the old barbershop with frosted glass windows. We peeped through it, watched men with soap on their cheeks, ready for a shave. We pressed our ice-cream mouths to the glass and then watched the spit bubbles pop-pop-pop. And beside the barber's was the greengrocer with yesterday's vegetables in small cane baskets in the front, going at a discount. While Vishnu-thatha talked to the grocer, Rebecca dropped the old vegetables into the fresh vegetable bin. I heard a giggle in my head that wouldn't stop until I tapped my head hard.

'Why are you slapping your head?' Rebecca asked.

'Because it's giggling.'

'Heads don't giggle, stupid, only mouths do.'

'I have a mouth in my head.'

'Don't be smart. Okay. And why do you always wear a frock? And why do you wear earrings? You are a boy.'

'I am an exception.' I said.

'Why exception?'

'Because I am special.'

'And why does your mother call you Tara?'

'Because it is my other name.'

'How can you have two names?'

'You have two names. Rebecca, and Rose-aunty calls you Becky.'

'Becky is my pet name.'

'So Tara is my pet name.'

'Pet names are only used for people with long names,' she said. 'Becky is short for Rebecca. Your name is already short.'

'Patti said other names are used for those who are loved. And Tara means star. I am Amma's star.'

'But Tara is a girl's name. How can you have a girl's name?'

'Because I am an exception.'

And then there was the fruit vendor I liked so much whose shop smelled like a jellyorchard in the sun.

***

The next Sunday Vishnu-thatha took Rebecca and me to Victoria Dyes factory. He had bought it from the government after the country had got its i-n-d-e-p-e-d-e-n-c-e, he told me. George Gibbs built it, he said, the same Englishman who had built my house and the road that curled all the way to the sea. I liked Victoria Dyes factory; it was old and big like my house and had many rooms and a tall clock tower, though one of the clock's hands was broken. It was a cripple clock. It had no time.

Vishnu-thatha took us into the main hall, where workers were dyeing cloth in large troughs. The stone floor was splattered with dye; the room had a musty tart smell. It was oven-hot inside. The paint on the walls had blistered in the heat. One of the workers came up to Vishnu-thatha and showed him a piece of dyed cloth. 'Red, make it more red,' Vishnu-thatha said. 'Add more Surupattal.' Then he took us to another room stacked with bales of cloth where we played the Before-After game.

Vishnu-thatha said, 'Let's get to the Before of Honey. Where does it come from?'

Rebecca flapped her arms and made a buzz-buzz-buzz sound.

Vishnu-thatha held up his leather slipper next and waved it about. Rebecca walked on all fours. Moomoomoo.

Vishnu-thatha shoved his hand into his trouser pocket and held up piece of paper. 'Your turn, Siva.'

I looked at the sheet of paper. It was a square leaf. I tapped my head with my finger so that my thoughts would think. Maybe there was a paper tree that grew paper leaves. *Siss-siss-siss*, Tara whispered. I stood on my toes and raised my hand up in the air and swung it about. Siss-siss-siss.

'That very good, Siva. Paper comes from trees.' Vishnu-thatha unclasped his wristwatch and held it up. 'Now tell me what is the before of this.'

Rebecca didn't know. Neither did I.

'Time,' Vishnu-thatha said.

'But that's not a thing,' Rebecca said, 'like the cow or the bee.'

'Correct,' Vishnu-thatha smiled. 'Time is not a thing. It is an idea. Great thinkers made it up. They got three big cardboard boxes, packed Time into them, called them Before, Now and After. If Time had not been made up,' Vishnu-thatha explained, 'if it had not been separated in three boxes, everything would happen all at once. What happened long before, or was to

66

happen after, would be happening right now. It would be like having only one big cardboard box called NOW.'

I shut my eyes and imagined time: ticktock, ticktock, moving from the After box to the Now box with each tick, and then with a tock to the Before box, and remaining there ticktock-ticktocking like a million heartbeats, getting fuller and fuller, heavier and heavier.

Vishnu-thatha said, 'And one more thing, the Before box is the heaviest. It contains memories. And the After box contains imagination, dreams. It is the lightest. So light, it can fly.'

And then we played an imagination game:

'Close your eyes tight,' Vishnu-thatha said. He tapped his finger on my brow. 'This is your mind's eye. Concentrate hard and you will be able to see what you can't see, and get whatever it is you want, just by imagining it.'

'Anything?' I asked.

'Yes. When you are particularly sad, imagine something that makes you happy and you will forget your sadness, even if for a short time. Remember, you can always find a solution if you use a little imagination.'

Fixed to one wall of the hall was an old frayed map. Vishnu-thatha imagined that his finger was an aeroplane. He flew it to distant places, told us about them: their hills and rivers, climate and wind, the big sea that held them. Then he made me imagine that my finger was an aeroplane; it carried me far far away, landed me in unknown places. I let my finger soar over the magenta coloured mountains and the blue ocean, I let it circle over the red USSR, the orange China, canary yellow America, candy pink Australia, purple Africa and back to brown India. I landed my finger with a thud on a torn and threadbare spot on the map. *Ma-chi-li-pat-nam.*

***

A heap of chiffon lay piled in one corner of the room. Rebecca buried her face in the sheer silk. I wriggled into its folds, warm and secure. 'I knew my caterpillar was here,' Vishnu-thatha said, pulling me out of the cloth. He plucked out a silk thread stuck to my hair. 'Did you know, it is the silkworm's spit with which it makes its cocoon,' he said. 'And when the worm is sleeping inside it, it dreams of the day it will become a beautiful butterfly and fly far away to Paradise.'

He told us a story:

Once upon a time there was a young caterpillar. He lived alone on a bush. One day he met a beautiful butterfly. Her wings were orange, purple and a deep blue. They became friends. The butterfly told the caterpillar that it was time for him to build his cocoon, and then he would become a butterfly like her and fly away to Paradise. The caterpillar looked down at his soft green body and shook his head. He was used to the bush, the caterpillar told the butterfly, this was his world and he was happy with it.

The butterfly told him then that he had to be what he was meant to be. He had to do what he was meant to do. If he didn't build his cocoon soon then he would be alone and he would surely die. She couldn't wait for him any longer; she was going away to Paradise. She pointed her wing beyond the lake, beyond the mountains. It was a heavenly place, she told him, full of beautiful flowers, with nectar as sweet as syrup. She flew away.

Soon the caterpillar felt weak and listless. He thought of what the butterfly had told him. So he started to build a cocoon with his spit. It took him a long time. He crept into it and went to sleep. It was dark inside and he was afraid and alone. He could feel his wings grow on either side of his body. He couldn't wait anymore; he missed his friend. So he pushed through the cocoon door and flew into the air. But he had come out too soon; his wings had not soaked in the colours of the dark; they were white.

Butterflies flew around him flapping their colourful wings. They laughed at him. The white butterfly flew far far away to

Paradise where he met his friend. She was happy to see him. He was so beautiful, she told him. His wings were like the skin of the moon.

Rebecca spread her arms out and fluttered them. 'I am the beautiful butterfly.'

'And I am the caterpillar,' I said, 'in my silk cocoon.'

Vishnu-thatha said, 'When the caterpillars are fast asleep silkfarmers pluck the cocoons and put them in hot water. They boil them for a long time with lots of salt. Then they make silk out of the cocoons.'

'What happens to the caterpillars? They die?' I asked.

'They don't really die,' Vishnu-thatha said. 'The sky's million mouths pop open, and they suck them into Paradise where they become tiny fairies with lights in their eyes. But sometimes in the night when they are sad and homesick they drop down from the skymouths to look for their cocoons. But they are all gone; they have been made into silk. So if we tie silk threads on branches of trees, they will know we care for them.'

Vishnu-thatha opened a cupboard and took from it a reel of white silk thread, and then he led us to the back garden. He broke the thread into bits and gave them to Rebecca and me. We reached up to a low branch of the Parijat tree and tied bits of thread on it. The day went suddenly slack and the first rain of the season broke loose from the clouds. But it didn't last very long. Soon the slanting lines ///// became dots .... We stood together, Rebecca and I: a butterfly and a caterpillar, moistened by the brief rain.

***

That evening Vishnu-thatha and I walked through the fields at the back of his house. I ran past the palm trees, across parcelled crops, and parted the wet paddy leaves thisway-thatway before I swishawayed to the beach beyond.

We sat on the sand and watched the sea. I could hear Tara hum in my ears. 'Why does Amma call me Tara? Am I Tara?

'Tara is dead, kanna. You are Siva. Whenever you have doubts about yourself, shut your eyes tight and look inside your head, in every nook and corner of it, inside your inner thoughts and try and find who you are. Deep inside your mind, where your feelings are stored, you will see yourself. Not Tara. But you.

'Thatha, where do people go after they die?'

'People who are unhappy become ghosts. They wander about in the place they have lived. But the happy people become spirits and they go all the way to Paradise. They come back now and then to watch over us.'

'Where did Tara go?'

'She didn't live long enough to become unhappy. She is a spirit. She is in Paradise. If you close your eyes and think of her you will hear her in your ears.'

'Where is Para-dies?'

'It's a lovely island in the sky, far far away.'

I looked up at the dusky sky. The setting sun had streaked it in crimson and pink. I raised my arms to the island in the sky. 'When I die, I will go to Para-dies and meet all the butterflies and fairies with lights in their eyes. And Tara.'

6

Although I couldn't count beyond 50 I knew Patti was 10+10+10+10+10+4 years old and I was nearly 6. Patti was oldest and I was the youngest. Everybody had to obey the oldest. I had to obey everyone – Patti, Appa, Amma, Vishnu-thatha, Munniamma Mani, Tara, and Rebecca too, although she was not family. Though come to think of it, Georgie was the oldest, and if inanimate things were to be counted, Victoria Villa was older than my grandmother. Like old people, it groaned and moaned with the changes in its seasons. It possessed a voice of its own – a creaking, whining one. Often I pictured the house as a living thing and I swear I could see the cracks on its skull, blisters on its hands and feet, an old smell issuing from its aged flesh, almost like bad breath, and its skin completely dried out.

I should have feared the worst, therefore, when Appa started messing around with the storeroom on the first floor. It had been untouched all these years. Piles of old things lay on the corridor outside and Mani and Amma were sorting them out, putting them away in cardboard boxes: Before, Before and more dusty Before. Old dust smoked the air. Tara sneezed; I wiped my nose.

Amma found an old threadnet bonnet. She perched it on her head, and posed with her hand upon her waist. 'See, I look like Elizabeth Gibbs.'

'You look ludicrous.' Appa laughed.

To which Amma promptly replied, 'Say no more I pray. Am fine.'

I found an old leather belt with a brass buckle. I wrapped it around my waist. 'Appa, I can keep this?'

Just then Patti called out to Mani. I could hear her come up the stairs, muttering. 'Here you are, Mani,' she said from the top of the stairs. 'I have been calling out to you. Have you got ears or buttons? Who's going to cook lunch eh? Go down to the kitchen right now. And Mallika you go help him. And feed that dog. He has been barking and whining all morning.' Patti smacked her hands hard and Amma and Mani scuttled down the stairs. Now Patti's eyes swept across the corridor and rested on the mess on the floor. She strode up to the Appa, her hands on her hips. 'What are you doing Raman? One day you are at home and you make this awful mess.'

'Look, this room must have been a bathroom. The floor and walls have stone tiles, and look,' Appa pointed inside the room, 'there is an old chamber pot, a washstand and a tin tub.' He looked up at Patti's stern face and said firmly, 'I am building a bathroom here. Siva is starting school soon. It will be more convenient.'

A silence fell between Patti and Appa signalling a quarrel. Patti would soon be terribly angry. I knew the language of her eyebrows: menacingly arched, the hair on them taut and upright. And Appa would have his way in the end. He had that look in his eyes. I didn't want to be in the midst of their impending squabble. The belt clutched in my hand, I sprinted down the stairs and out of the front door to the garden. I sat down on the stone bench and looked closely at the belt. The buckle had a symbol on it: three Ts joined at the bottom, and between them the letters E I C. Then I heard Patti's raised voice, and Victoria Villa sighed in the wind, its breath sour.

However, despite the groaning and moaning, creaking and whining, and Patti's precariously arched eyebrows, by the end of the month the bathroom was ready. Appa had it fitted with a blue washbasin and a mirror above it. The commode was blue too. When Appa pulled the flush the water in the commode was sucked away. Then the tank gurglegurgled and filled up the commode with water once more.

Patti was wonderstruck. 'Gleaming like a pearl with a wide-open mouth and saliva in its throat,' she said. However, next morning as Patti was in the prayer room, which was right below the toilet, she heard the flush and the gurgle of a giant gargle. She rushed up the stairs and knocked on the bathroom door. 'Raman, come out, this very minute. Whatever you are doing in there, come out now!' She punched Appa on his chest as he emerged out of the bathroom, a towel around his waist, and shaving cream on his face. 'Aiyoo da, that dirty seat is right over the prayer room. You are shitting on top of Gods' heads.'

Appa laughed; bits of shaving cream fell off his face. 'Don't worry. Plumbing is a modern science, ma. Not at all like the hole in the floor in the outhouse.' He tried to explain to Patti about modern plumbing and how her Gods were safe from its exigencies. But the discourse on fluid mechanics and the behaviour of water collapsed.

Patti slapped her chest, burst into a wail. 'Aiyoo Shiva-Shiva... No one will use this toilet as long as I am alive,' she wailed. 'Upon my dead body will anyone use this dirty seat. Otherwise I will pack all my Gods and leave this wretched house where Gods can't even reside in peace without worrying what is happening over their heads.'

'Don't get hysterical, ma,' Appa said. 'If there's any leak I'll lock up this bathroom. Okay?'

'Not even a drop of water, mind you.' Then with a grunt Patti walked away. From that day on, as she prayed, her eyes were fixed to the ceiling instead of on her Gods. Almost a month later she asked Appa, 'Where does all the muck go?'

***

My school, Convent of Jesus and Mary, was in a lane off Gibbs Road, and not too far from Rebecca's house. She was two years senior to me and she walked me home after classes. My school uniform was a white shirt and blue shorts. Amma didn't like it. What was more, Appa had had my earrings removed, and this upset Amma even more. Cracks had appeared in her illusion and, like a mirror, it threatened to break into a million little pieces. All this was very bad for her, and for me, even more. What was worse, I had my own room now, next to Appa's. It was a small room with a large window and a balcony overlooking the road. It contained a small bed, a desk and an old wooden cupboard, a full-length mirror on its shutter.

In a drawer inside the cupboard I found stones, smooth and perfectly rounded like marbles. I wondered who had put them there. Georgie? I arranged the stones on the desk on which I had set the old toy hen with one eye missing. On the wall above the desk Appa had fixed Georgie's picture from the hallway; I had asked him to. I liked sharing the room with Georgie; I didn't feel alone. He must feel lonely too; his eyes were sad.

It was my first night in my new room. Amma stood at the door. 'Come Tara, it's time to sleep,' she said.

'Tara is dead,' I said. 'She is in Para-dies. And if you close your eyes she will whisper in your ear.'

A big crack in the mirror. Amma walked away. That night as I lay in my room I heard a loud crash, similar to the tinkling crash when a mirror hits the floor, and then Amma's scream. 'You killed Tara. You killed my Tara.'

The next morning Amma moved her things to the spare room on the second floor. She didn't come out of her room all day. She stared out of the window all the time, Munniamma said. The tamarind tree outside shivered in the heat, and Amma, feeling its mild turbulence, trembled out of habit. Far far away, in the haze of the sunlight, she saw a dazzling sheet of white water, as though the land had been blanketed with the salted slimy sea. She remembered the salty sea in her womb, and how it had gushed out of her, flooded her, flooded her daughter. The old familiar sadness rose like water inside her, and in the distant white salty sea Amma saw a little shadow struggling in the water, then it stared at her with big watery eyes. The thirsty wind howled: ooooowr-oooowar-oowat-oowata-oowata-r-w*ate-r*, before it was swept away. Munniamma had gone up to the spare room a number of times. Amma said to her, 'Look look, far away in the sunlit water. Can you see the little shadow?'

'She's just standing in front of the window and staring out,' Muniamma told Patti.

'She'll be fine tomorrow,' Patti said. 'Let her be.'

But Amma wasn't fine. As days passed she became more remote and absent. She grew cheerless and confused and stayed away from me. After her chores were over for the day she pedalled on the sewing machine for hours on end: swish-swish-swish. She didn't stitch anything. Only swish-swish-swished.

My bare necessities became bare. I despaired, and so would Baloo the Bear despair. I should have known then, it was the beginning of 'over' time.

O-V-E-R.

7

There was less of Amma when she was around and more of her when she was not. I found myself dreaming of her and waking up with her name on my lips. But she was not there for me. She was just not *there*. Each day I chose an aspect of her: her aubergine eyes and how they crinkled when she smiled, or her aquiline nose with the dazzling mercury clots on them, and the way her nostrils flared when she was annoyed, and her smile, as red as crushed cherries, until she was *there*, there right in front of me. Then I felt warmth surging through me, turning to fondness, and ultimately, inexorably, to love. Unrequited though it was. I turned to the next best thing: Patti. I was with her most of the time. She was there for me.

Patti had planted more plantain trees at the back of the house where the soil was red and bleeding. They had grown tall and one of them had given fruit: plump fingers of mustard yellow rastali bananas. New anthills had cropped up under the tamarind tree: the home of lonely ghosts, full of old loneliness. Its ghostly arms reached up, swayed and sang in the breeze. Bats hung on its branches, upsidedown, watching everything around downsideup. When I sat under the tree its leaves lisped to me in eerie fashion and when I touched the leaves to my cheek they felt soft like ghostly skin.

Don't sit under the tamarind tree, the ghosts will climb into your dreams and nightmare you, Patti often told me. I was not afraid of ghosts. Georgie must live on the topmost branch of the tree. From there he would see the sea and far far away toward London. He was farsighted. Further down from the tamarind tree, on a low brick wall someone had left white and red impressions of their palms. Who had done this? I heard footsteps behind me.

'Here you are.' Patti stood before me holding a plate of semolina ladoos. She set a laddoo at the base of the low wall.

'What is this, Patti?'

'It is a shrine. Here's one for you,' she said pressing a laddoo into my hand. Then she walked to the huddle of plantain trees, reached out to a cluster of bananas and pinched one of them with her thumb. 'They are almost ripe,' she said and walked away.

I broke the laddoo and dropped bits of the sweet around the anthill and watched ants scurrying around them. I crouched on the ground. 'Come, come,' I called out to ants, 'come and eat sweet laddoo.' I held my breath lest I blew the ants away. As the ants moved with their sweet burden, I plucked a hair from my head then with my cheek against the ground, I nudged each ant gently on its way with the strand of hair, 'Go, go,' I whispered as I guided them to the anthill.

Go go, Tara said.

Not far away from the anthill I noticed a caterpillar. The garden was full of them. They wandered out because of the heat, Vishnu-thatha had told me. This one was on its back and it wiggled its life away leg by leg by leg. Ants marched towards the dying creature in mock Brahmin ritual.

'Shoo,' I shouted at the ants.

Shoo. Shoo.

I breathed hard and blew them off the scene of extinction. A lone cricket chirped: cri-ket, cri-ket, crik-et... and then I heard Patti call out to me. I picked up the dead caterpillar and ran to the kitchen. Patti was sorting mangoes from a basket, picking out the ripe ones. She heaped a plate with food and then sat down on the floor. I sat down beside her and put the dead caterpillar on the floor. 'Why does everything have to die?' I asked.

'Time ripens the creatures, Time rots them.' Patti thrust her head back in an operatic manner. 'From the Mahabharata, 1.1.188.' She was good with numbers. She was always quoting from religious books. She had once told me that when we died our souls rose and followed the way of the spirits, through nights, dark fortnights, along the northern course of the sun, and eventually came back to the earth, clinging to the raindrops to be born again. It was from Chandogya Upanishad 5.3.1. – 5.3.10. She was really good with numbers.

Patti rolled the rice, sambhar and vegetables into a small ball and pressed it into my mouth. 'I'll tell you a story about death,' she said. 'When the gods built the world, there was no death. So creatures and people went on and on being born. Soon the earth was full. So many people in it with so many problems and wants that the gods could not attend to them all. So what to do? The gods thought and thought and then introduced Time. So the young ones grew old, the old ones grew older, and the older ones grew still older. The tired ones wanted to rest. Those with pain in their bones cried out. The gods became worried. So they came up with the plan of death. They made categories, and then decided who should live and for how long. They made the germs live the longest, flowers the shortest and the trees, birds, beasts and people in proportion to their need on earth.'

Patti stuffed another ball of rice into my mouth. 'So, Siva, that is how death came on earth,' she said. 'And always remember what the Bagavad Gita 8.24 says – *what is gained depends on the path followed.*'

'What that means?'

'What comes after depends on what happens before. So if you live this life properly you will live forever in Heaven.' She put the plate away and picked up a ripe mango.

'Why did God make Tara die? She was not old.'

'How I wish Tara had lived. Everything would have been all right. But I knew Tara would die the moment she was born. She was so weak and yellow like this mango. I know who will die soon and who will die later. The gods drop the children from heaven with special smells and return dates stamped on their foreheads.' Patti sniffed the mango. 'See, like this mango. The children who have to die, smell over-ripe.' Her eyes filled with tears.

I blew air into my palms and pressed them to Patti's eyes. 'Now your hurt will go away.'

***

The sky was darker than usual that evening. Rebecca and I were out on the veranda. Patti stepped out of the door with a silver tray. Arranged on it were a lamp, a tumbler of water, a bottle of raw rice and sesame seeds, and flowers. 'Come, it's time to feed our ancestors,' Patti said. 'It is Amavasya today.'

'What's Ama. Vas. Ya?' Rebecca asked.

'It's the night when there is no moon in the sky,' Patti explained. 'It is the time for new beginnings, the time to embrace the promise of new light.'

We went out into the garden. Patti looked up into the moonless sky, clutched a fistful of jasmine and dropped the flowers on the ground. She took a pinch of rice and sesame seeds from the bottle and sprinkled it on the soil.

'Why do you do that, Patti?'

'Sesame seeds are magic seeds, they can change rice to any food of the dead person's liking.'

'Can they change rice into ice-cream?' I asked.

'Oh yes.'

'Rice can't become ice-cream,' Rebecca said.

'And chicken curry?' I asked. 'Mani said the Englishman he had worked for loved the chicken curries that he made for him.'

'Don't listen to Mani's stories,' Patti said. 'He's a fibber.'

'But can the seeds change rice into chicken curry?'

'Oh yes. But kanna, not one of our ancestors was English. They were all vegetarian only.' She poured water from the

79

tumbler into her hand and sprinkled it about. 'After feeding them you have to give them water.'

I took a pinch of the rice and seed and sprinkled them about: ice-cream for Tara. Chicken curry for Georgie. Then I took the tumbler from Patti and poured some water out, then drank what was left in it. I felt happy in my belly. It now contained the same water Tara and Georgie had drunk.

To all of these curious things was added, a few days later, a friendly chameleon that showed me the way to the attic. It emerged out of a hole in the neem tree: brightgreen at first, then sunbleached, then stonebrown. It hopped off the tree, scrambled down the low stonewall to the stairs at the back of the house, then leapt up on a step. It cocked its head and looked up at me, swishing its tail in a friendly fashion, and then with a change of colour it disappeared into a crack in the wall.

I climbed the stairs to the top. Up on the terrace I tried the door and it opened into a small landing. I climbed the steep flight of steps 1-2-3-4-5-6... 11, and stood in the doorway. The corner of the attic leaned as though it was looking out. There was a hole in the attic-roof where the tiles had fallen off and birds flew in and out through the hole. I went on my knees and hands and crept around the floor trying not to make any sound. The attic was home to many insects.

Moths flew like mini aeroplanes navigating the dark space; frogs watched them through binocular eyes, and spiders with thin, long ballerina legs spun in a creepycrawly dance. Lizards fluttered their tongues and made tut-tut sounds. Dragonflies teased the air; confused cockroaches ran helterskelter like people did in the rain; rats squealed from crevices and big fat mosquitoes buzzed around me, sucked at the blood and left crimson hillocks on my skin. Crickets sang their evening song in the day. A butterfly flitfluttered and flew away.

I picked up dead cockroaches, spiders, a frog, a dragonfly, a rat, a lizard, and a small bird: all dead. I put them in a box I found on the floor then took it down into the garden and set it under the neem tree. Then I fetched water in a bottle and sprinkled water over them. Some days ago I had asked Vishnu-thatha why he was watering a dead plant. He told me that the plant would live if I watered it. Then on a whim I rushed to the grave at the back and poured the remaining water on Georgie's grave. Where was Tara's grave?

I was often in the attic. It was filled with old things: furniture, rugs, magazines and books. Appa told me they belonged to George Gibbs. I liked being in the attic; I liked being surrounded by Georgie's things; I liked being with Georgie. I talked to him, and sometimes Georgie answered with signals. Like on the day when an old coin fell from above. I looked up: a rat scurried across the wooden beam and a pigeon was perched on the rafter. Neither the rat nor the bird could have dropped the coin. It had to be Georgie. I was sure about this.

I made it a point to come up to the attic almost every day. It was from here that I called out to Tara, *Taaraa*, far away in Para-dies. Sometimes I would take a plate of goodies to the attic for Tara and leave it there so she could eat later. I talked to her about the Hide-and-Seek game the clouds and the sun played. I told her about the moon and the stars, which were torchlights in the sky and how the soiled sky had a shower in the rain and when it was clean a rainbow popped out of its mouth like a multicoloured smile.

On some days I was in the attic with the comic books Appa had got me. I read aloud to Tara the tales of the Li'l Bad Wolf, Bugs Bunny, Donald Duck and Uncle Scrooge, Mickey Mouse and Goofy and tried to talk like them.

When a cobweb stuck to the hair on my arm, I heard Tara whisper in my ear.

Whazz this?

Cob-web. The spider makezz it.

It livezz in the web, eh?

Yeah. It asso traps other insectz in it.

Why?
It likez to eat 'em.
Why?
Thass how it iz on eartz.
Thass awful!
How it iz in Para-dies?
Eenie,MeenieMineyMo

Then I lay under the hole in the roof and watched the blue sky. I saw a plane flying past. I saw its huge belly. I saw birdbellies flying. It was so different seeing the big sky in the open and seeing it through the hole in the roof. The sky became so small that it belonged only to Tara and me: our bright blue sky with planes and birds that flew on their bellies.

Whenever I needed to be with Tara, I hid in the attic. It was Tara's and my wombworld, our own Para-dies on earth, with a tiny tiny sky.

8

After weeks of sizzling April heat and the air thick with dust, suddenly daylight dimmed and the wind held its breath for a moment, only for a moment, and then with sidelong gusts and a deafening roar it lacerated the descending rain. In the prayer room Patti lit the lamps one by one. She lit the incense sticks next, and then from a small silver jar she took a pinch of holy ash and smeared my forehead with it. I had on the new clothes Appa had got me the previous day: a pair of mudbrown shorts and a white t-shirt with red and blue aeroplanes on it. 'It's your star birthday today Siva,' Patti said, 'and you are six years old.'

'What is star birthday?'

'The Calendar was made by the English to control people all over the world,' Patti said. 'English birthdays are according to the calendar. But Hindus are born under stars. We have a special group of stars for each of us. Yours, Siva, is called Mrigasira. And when these stars come in the sky, it is your birthday.' She added, her eyes moist. 'It was also your sister's birthday.'

It was not a day I liked; it was not a day that Amma liked. She needed to be with Tara. Even though dead Tara was most alive that day. And I needed to be with Amma.

Amma's back was turned so she didn't see me at the door to her room. She seemed to have just returned from the market. She took paper packages from a shopping bag and set them out on her bed. She opened one of them and plucked out a frock and laid it on the bed. From a box she lifted out a cake, pink and white with red roses on it. She set it next to the frock. From another box she took out six candles and planted them in a circle on the cake and lit them. Then she blew the candles out. She cut the cake into wedges, then shut her eyes and began to sing: Happy birthday to you... happy birthday dearest Tara...

I stood by the door, ten thousand ants eating at my heart. Making as little noise as possible, I crept up to the bed, picked up a piece of cake and bit into it. A dollop of icing stuck to my nose. I sneezed. Amma opened her eyes; they grew large and round. She slapped me hard on my face. My eyes full of tears, I ran out of the room and into Munniamma, who was standing by the door. 'Why does Amma hate me?'

'She doesn't hate you kanna,' Munniamma said, wiping my face with the end of her saree. 'She loved too much too soon. She doesn't have any love left.'

***

Up in the attic I collected my pencil, butterfly notebook and the envelopes I had hidden behind a trunk. I had found the notebook some days ago in the attic. On its pages were scribbled in scrawny handwriting:

D-O-G
C-A-T
C-O-W
F-A-H-T-E-R
G-O-R-G-E
S-E-A

But on one of its pages was a dead butterfly, secured with glue. Its wings were orange, purple and green. Then there were pages coloured blue and blue and more blue. Ghosts were messengers, Vishnu-thatha had told me, like postmen really. They lived in the in-between world and conveyed the thoughts of those living to those who were in Para-dies. So I wrote often to Tara and put the letter in an envelope addressed to:

Georgie the GHOST.

And under it:

T-E-L-I-G-A-R-M

Because Patti said it was the shortestfastest letter. I wrote 'Happy birthday TARA' on a sheet of notepaper and put it in an envelope and addressed it. Then I set it on the heap of old letters on the trunk, which I knew Tara had read and returned through Georgie the GHOST.

That done I leapt up and ran to the window and stuck my head out of it. I could see the grey folds of the sky. I looked to my left at the chakka tree outside the gate. The chakka leaves are fleshy and a darker shade of green. When clean they shine like the rexene sofa in our living room, but these chakka leaves were covered with dust and the greywhite droppings of pigeons and the black waste of bats. I peeped further out of the window so I could see the peepal tree with thin skinlike leaves. The chakka leaves made a *swish-swish* sound in the breeze. The peepal went *sis-sis*, similar to the sound Munniamma made when she was furious. Some of her teeth were missing.

Kuttan the chakka man was under the chakka tree as usual. He parked his cart there every day next to Cha-chi. The tree did not belong to him but long ago he'd claimed it as his own. The shade of the tree was his. The tree's fruits were his. Even Cha-chi had become his. Every day Kuttan wheeled a cartful of bulging jackfruits, a large, dissected one placed on top, its entrails exposed. As he dug into the fruit with his fingers and prised the nuggetlike seeds from its sticky tentacles, it made noises. To accompany this, he made obscene noises with his tongue. Only a week ago, when I was playing with Cha-chi outside the gates, the chakka-man had made squishy noises with his mouth. His eyes turned lewd, his smile leering, as he shifted his lungi and pointed between his legs where, it seemed to me, a branch had grown. His hand moved over it. S-l-o-w-l-y. Fasterfaster. I didn't quite understand but instinct warned me what he was doing was wrong. Tara trembled deep inside me. We were afraid of him.

85

I leaned out of the window looking the other way. Electrical cables divided the sky: untidy sleeping lines. On Gibbs Road a bus, a horizontal red band, rattled past and following it, like a yellow bug on a mission, a taxi. It started to rain: hyphenated lines, vertical-vertical, and as the wind moved through it, slanting-slanting. Horns honked as people ran thisway-thatway in the rain. Another bus hid the people across the street. I peered at the advertisement on the bus: Godrej Hair Dye, with the picture of a woman with lustrous, jetblack hair. Lobo-teacher at school also had bootpolish shine in her hair. When freshly dyed her hairline was lower, like the new watermarks on old buildings. The Godrej Hair Dye bus passed. I saw a man on a cycle grab the back bar of the bus and steer through the crowd, steel bands on his ankles holding up his trousers. He was getting his ride free; he seemed happy. And then the bus went over a pothole and the man lost control of his cycle and fell. Tara laughed in my head.

Just then I heard Munniamma call out to me from the garden; I scrambled down the stairs. She came to me in her floral nylex saree. Her long black hair was combed back and tied into a knot covered with a shiny black nylon net. Two golden pins with fake rubies held wisps of hair behind her ears. She waved her hands over my head and then, making fists of her hands, pressed her knuckles to her own head and cracked them.

'Why did you do that?'

'So that I take away any blemish in you into myself. Come kanna, Patti said we must go to the temple.'

'Why?'

'Because God wants to see you. He wants to talk to you. He wants to say Happy Birthday.' She grabbed my arm and led me into the house, up the stairs into my room. She combed my hair, gathering it into a tight ponytail and then rubbed talcum powder all over my face. She made a kissing sound with her lips. She held my chin between her thumb and forefinger. She touched her finger to her dark kohled eye and smeared the soot on my chin. 'Now this will keep the evil eyes away.' She patted my back. 'Let's go.'

Cha-chi set up a loud bark followed by a friendly whine as we walked out of the gate. Kuttan whistled.

'What are you whistling at me for eh?' Munniamma leaned toward him and poked her finger into his ribs.

'I am whistling at him,' he said, pointing at me. 'So pretty.'

Munniamma hissed through her teeth. 'I'll pull your tongue out and you'll never whistle again.' Then grabbing my hand she pulled me down the road built of big stones, small pebbles and gravel. Munniamma and I trundled on, the Gibbs Road under our feet, old tar melting in the heat.

I stopped at Sweet Heaven Cake Shop. 'Let's buy a cake?'

'We can't,' Munniamma shook her head.

'But it's my birthday.'

'You know we can't celebrate your birthday, kanna.'

'But Amma celebrated Tara's birthday.'

'She was only playing Pretend.'

We walked on. Closer to the temple, Munniamma stopped at Ranga Roses. 'Leave your sandals here kanna,' she said as she slipped her own inside the stall. 'Ranga will look after them.'

I took my sandals off and dropped them on top of Munniamma's. She bought a cone of roses from Ranga. A tall woman approached us, smacking her large hands together. She stood before me and with a delicate movement of her hand she caressed my face. She circled her hands over my head and then, making fists, she touched her knuckles to her own head and cracked them. 'Sweetie-Cutie blesses you with happiness and wealth,' she said. Pouting, she added, 'Although your grandmother refused to give me rice when you were to be born. I won't forget that.' Clapping her hands she walked down the road.

I stared after her. 'Is she a man?'

'Yes,' Munniamma nodded.

'Then why is he wearing a saree?'

'Because she is a hijra.'

'Confucius.' Tommy Gonzalves had walked up to us. He was the owner of Tommy's Garage, and an ardent follower of the Confucian way of life. Everyone called him Mr Quotes. He frequently quoted others' quotes but mostly his own, most of them derived from others' quotes. One of his favourite Confucius quotes was: I hear and I forget. I see and I remember. I do and I understand. Appa's old Ambassador was regularly in Tommy's Garage for repairs and Tommy-uncle would say: The Ambassador is a manly car with a womanly temperament. It is a hijra automobile!

Now Tommy-uncle asked, 'So Siva, where are you off to?'

'God wants to talk to me.'

Tommy-uncle laughed heartily. 'Remember son, when you talk to God, people will say you're a God-loving man. But when you tell them God talks to you, they will say you're insane.' And with that he walked away, laughing.

The temple's main hall was noisy: young and old people praying with raised voices so that the Gods could hear them. Piety had a mixedup smell: jasmine-rose-milk-ghee-sandalwood-jaggery-incense-camphor-sweat. God must like the smell a lot but it made me nauseous. Munniamma pulled me through the crowd and the God-awful smell to the front. There she shut her eyes and chanted aloud over the din. Some moments later she opened one eye and followed my gaze up to the pigeons on the wooden rooftruss. It wasn't the pigeons I was looking at. I had drifted off into Taraland; I was listening to the song in my head, the song without words: our wombsong – Tara's and mine.

Munniamma slapped me on my back. 'Close your eyes and pray to God or he won't talk to you.'

I looked up at the picture of Lord Shiva framed in glass. Two bulbs were reflected in his eyes, affording them a divine glow: yellow, shiny. In the picture of Jesus Christ in my school, He had a heart, all red and glowing, and shaped like the Ace of Hearts in Appa's deck of cards. I focussed my eyes to the spot where Shiva's heart should be; it wasn't there.

At school we prayed to Jesus Christ: Avur Father who art in Hay-ven halloo-d be Thy name... At home Patti made me pray to lots of Gods: Shiva-Rama-Vishnu-Krishna-Ganesha-Murugan etc. and all their respective wives and their families. Jesus was strong; he did the work of all our Gods; he did not have a wife or children to help him. Our Gods were choosy about their work: Ganesha for good luck, Lakshmi for money, Saraswati for intelligence, Shiva for peace, Vishnu for goodness and so on. What was more, Patti made me pray in Sanskrit; the words were long and difficult to mouth and I didn't understand what they meant. Jesus understood English, which was very fine, and my prayers to him were precise and short, all ending with *Amen*. My schoolteacher had told me that Jesus was everywhere so I looked up at Lord Shiva and prayed to Our Lord Jesus. 'Please send Tara home for one day, please. It is her star birthday today. *Amen*.'

Prayer done, I turned around and darted through the crowd and out of the door. Munniamma caught up with me at Ranga's shop. We collected our footwear and in silence walked up Gibbs Road. I stopped in front of Rebecca's house and called out to her. Munniamma gave me a light pat on my head and holding my arm she dragged me homeward.

Kuttan was fast asleep under the tree; Cha-chi barked, then wagged his tail. I ran past our house down the mudpath and Munniamma, sissing through her teeth, rushed after me. We walked through the woods to the lake. There we sat under the old chakka tree. The leaves swayed in the wind, made chakchak sounds. Milky sap oozed from its trunk and jackfruits, like big, bloated balls, grew from the wrong places: not from the branch ends but some place in between. Munniamma looked up at the tree trunk, at the markings chiselled all over it: half-circles, like pockmarks on skin. Some of the markings looked to me like GG. Below the pockmarks there were more markings: Yusuf Loves

Meena. Gita Loves Mukesh, Cindy my darling, my sweetheart, and so on. I read each one out loud, one syllable at a time.

Munniamma made a grimace. She scooped out damp soil with both her hands. She patted the soil into a mud cake. 'Appy baday to yoo, kanna,' she said.

I picked up dried twigs and stuck them in a circle into the mud mound. 'Happy birthday Tara.'

9

The small occurrences of daily routine kept me distracted from worrying about the bigger ones. An entire year passed this way: eating, praying, studying, playing, more eating, some sleeping and, looming over them all like a dark cloud, Patti's forewarning, the Before-After bit: *what is gained depends on the path followed.* Path followed? Did I have a choice? My 'gains' had been pre-calculated and they didn't amount to much. My life had a shape to it and had I stared at it hard enough I would have known its form and the route it would take. But I got to see it only in silhouette.

A different kind of darkness had come over Amma. It was as though there was a weight on top of her, something that pressed her down. Although she helped with the cooking she did not dust the house or tend to the garden. It was not that she was lazy; she didn't see the dust anymore, and the plants, she told Patti, were meant to grow. The plants grew, the weeds too. Dust covered them, and everything else.

As for Appa, he was too busy at the institute to be bothered about home, though it must be said that he tried several times to talk some sense into Amma. But something had changed about her. Appa knew a great deal about the behaviour of female mosquitoes but he didn't know much about women. He did not understand what had happened to Amma. So he let her be.

However, Patti never stopped trying to ease matters between Amma and Appa. 'And how long will this go on? This arrangement of separate rooms, eh?' Patti confronted Appa one morning as he was leaving for work.

'She can come down when she wants to, ma,' Appa said wearily and stepped out onto the veranda.

Patti followed him with a duster in her hand. 'After all these years you don't understand women even,' she grunted. 'Mallika won't come down until you ask her. Women need to be asked, not told or ignored.'

'Let her be,' Appa replied.

'And what about me?' Patti screamed at him. 'Do you have no responsibility towards me? If only your father had been alive. Seeing me in this wretched state he would have promptly died. Have you any idea how much work there is in this house, eh? Mani and Munniamma can't do everything. Everywhere there is dust and more dust.' Patti slapped the duster in the air to stress her words. 'And the bulb in the outhouse is fused. Do you even know this? And look at the garden, so overgrown.'

'Let me be.' Appa walked away.

Outside the gate Cha-chi barked, adding a footnote to their exchange.

Patti dashed into the house and reprimanded Amma in the kitchen. 'If you carry on like this, Mallika, the bottle will soon replace you, and then Raman will find another woman. Men are unstable and no man can live alone. First whiskey and then woman. That's what will happen. Mark my words.'

But Amma didn't mark her words. Appa started leaving early for work and coming home late. He would have already eaten in the canteen at the institute. Once home, he shut himself in his study, drank rum and played Solitaire. He was tired of Amma's ways. I knew this. This is how I knew: Appa forgot his pocketbook and I looked through it. Most of the pages were filled with notes about mosquitoes and experiments in the institute, of all things that had to be done each day. Here and there were jottings of a more personal sort, written in small antlike handwriting, as though Appa didn't want them to be read. Some of these notes were long and others not more than a sentence.

- *Why does she blame me? What did I do?*

- *Why can't she accept that Tara died? Babies die all the time.*

- *She looks so unwell, so unhappy. What can I do?*

- *Is something wrong with this house? Should I go back to London?*

- *Must call the electrician.*

- *The pursuit of mosquitoes is for me the only exhilarating thing left of life to pursue. Mosquitoes are at least mostly predictable and responsive, and they never are unyielding. Women are something else really. I can't understand them.*

- *Must get new shoes for Siva.*

- *I remember the day she came to Victoria Villa. She was all of seventeen, shy and innocent. And how much she giggled and laughed those days. She was happy. What happened to her? And now whenever she crosses my path she looks at me with the heavy hurt of betrayal. If she speaks to me at all it is only about mundane matters: of reminders about money or repairs. The tone she adopts invariably humiliates me. It is as though she has said: now why do I have to ask you? Or why did you have to do this to me? Her unyielding eyes defeat me. I have had enough of their silent accusation. They have destroyed my quiet.*

- *Must get a vacuum cleaner. Must hire a gardener.*

- *I can't take this anymore. Let her be. Let me be.*

Some months later when Appa returned from a trip to London he brought back a vacuum cleaner. He showed Patti the way to use it to keep the house clean. Patti looked suspiciously at the gleaming red thing with a long elephant's trunk. She left the machine in the prayer room for safekeeping. On occasion she would use it, the button in normal position, to vacuum the prayer room so her Gods remained tidy. And she learned to use it in the reverse position, to blow the husk of new rice. As she blew and blew the husk away, she kept at her refrain about Amma whenever Appa was within earshot.

Then one afternoon, when Patti was taking a nap, Rebecca and I used the vacuum cleaner in normal position to blow away the husk from rice that Patti had spread out on a mat on the kitchen veranda. The grains were sucked in with a ssss, and I quickly, quietly put the machine away. Some days later when Patti used the vacuum cleaner it rattled and roared and choked from within. Then it coughed and stopped. Patti wound an old red silk saree around the broken machine and set it in the prayer room on a low table as though it was a different sort of God, all sacred red with a long black corrugated snout.

She didn't stop her daily refrain. 'And what if I die?' I overheard Patti ask Appa one evening. 'Who will look after the house?' She paused, then drove home the punch: 'Look at your hair, it has already started graying. Soon you will go bald even. You are getting old, Raman, very, very old. Who will look after you then?'

What if Patti dies? This thought worried me. It worried Tara too.

***

I was out in the garden overgrown with creepers and flowering bushes. I circled my arms around a bunch of wild daisies that I hadn't noticed before. I gathered the blooms around my face, rubbed my nose into their petals. I watched the tiny black ants chase the sweetsmell on the stickystems of flowers. With a dried leaf I soaked up the morning dewdrops on the spiderwebs on the grass.

Appa walked out of the door. Patti came up behind him. 'Why do you have to go to work today eh? It's Sunday.'

Appa stepped into the garden without a word. He wore that Fullstop look in his eyes. He had many punctuation looks, which he used instead of words. He had the Bracket-look when he was sad. His face shrank and seemed contained. Now he waved to me with a Semi-Colon-look (this one is a To-Be-Continued look), walked to his car and drove out of the gates just as

Munniamma walked through with the shopping. He gave her his Ellipsis-look, which mostly meant Go On... Get On With It... without actually saying it.

Patti spread the pai on the veranda floor. She sat down on it and held her head with both her hands.

'What's the problem ma?' Munniamma climbed up to the veranda. 'Headache?'

'A big headache.' Patti hit her head. 'And it's all Mallika's fault. Women should know how to manage their men and keep them.' Patti's eyes became moist. 'I must have committed some grave sin in my last birth to deserve this.'

'Don't blame yourself, ma. Gods have a hand in these matters. Everything happens for a reason.'

'The only reason the Gods created women is so that they would look after their men and give them children.'

Munniamma moved closer to Patti. 'Sometimes ma, we have to help our Gods in their work. Tell me, what do you do with the jackfruit seeds?'

'That Mani roasts them and eats them all.'

'You must roast the seeds, powder them and mix them with sesame seeds and jaggery and then make small laddoos from the mixture and give them to Raman-aiyah every night.' Munniamma beamed and slapped her thigh. 'Then watch. Aiyah may be one mile away from his wife but in the middle of everything, he will run to her. So much thirst, ma, so much heat, he will not be able to control. He will just run, run, run. Nothing can stop that ache between a man's legs. Not even his bad temper.'

Patti at once called out to Mani. He strutted out of the door in a new red shirt. Patti looked censoriously at him. 'Ye da Mani, is this the only shirt you could find to wear? If you walk on the street people will mistake you for a postbox and shove letters into your mouth. Go, cut that jackfruit you got yesterday. I want each and every seed, mind you.'

Mani chuckled. 'When I eat those seeds they make me so thirsty that I have to drink gallons of water. My stomach gets so full that I want to sleep all day. And if I stand all day long all the water rushes to my feet and they swell up. I can hardly walk.'

'What do you know about water in the feet?' Patti grunted. 'Anyone would think you are pregnant.' Mani chewed at his fingernail, and then spat it out. Patti screamed, 'I'll chop your fingers off if you bite your nails. Now don't stand there like a buffoon. Go cut that jackfruit and after you have taken out all the seeds, go get yourself a haircut. Look at your hair growing all over your head like a paddy field. And get that barber to clip the hair growing out of your ears. Chi-chi-chi.'

After Mani had trotted off to the market Patti hurriedly roasted the seeds. She ground them to powder, mixed it with sesame seeds and melted jaggery. She made small laddoos and put them in a steel box and hid it in the kitchen cupboard, which she locked. That evening I saw Patti leave two laddoos in a bowl in Appa's study.

'Don't eat that, Siva,' she said. 'It's for your father. I have put some medicine in them. If you eat them you will get a stomachache.'

Patti had told the truth after all. Appa woke up with a terrible ache. With a Bracket-look he moaned and groaned and paced the living room, his hands pressing down on his belly. He didn't go to work. Instead he kept running to the toilet. Then late in the morning he sent for Dr Kuruvilla. The doctor checked Appa's temperature, his throat and tongue. Then he listened to his lungs with the stethoscope. He tapped his belly with his forefinger. 'Wholly gas,' he said. 'What did you eat last night?'

'The usual,' Appa said.

'He ate laddoos,' I said.

'What laddoos?' the doctor asked.

When Patti told him what they were made of the doctor threw back his head and laughed, and then he looked at Patti and gave her a big wink. 'So much heat in them they can send a man running in every direction.' Turning to Appa he said, 'They have melted the insides of your stomach.'

I would have laughed, but honestly, what with the way things were at home, and between Appa and Amma, between Amma and me, nothing was a laughing matter anymore. I had been tricked by my own destiny. If anyone, anything, were to be held guilty it was fate, a blessed piece of paper with squares, notations scribbled in them: my horror-scope – the damned inventory of life stamped on my brow. And as fate would have it, one evening a week later Amma was by the stove, boiling tamarind water with turmeric and sambhar powder. Her faded cotton saree had turmeric stains all down the front. Her hair was uncombed, and her face sweaty. Otherwise, the day had turned out to be rather nice. Nothing exceptional, only ordinary, but even that was somewhat special given the circumstances. Except my left eyelid had been twitching all morning.

'That's good luck,' Patti said. 'Left eye for the boy, right for a girl. Today is your lucky day.'

It was evening and nothing terribly fortunate had happened yet. Mani hummed a song as he grated coconut. Patti shouted at him from the door. 'Hurry up with that. Raman-aiyah said he would come early today. He's bringing a scientist with him.' She turned to Amma, 'You go up, ma, and change your saree. Comb your hair nicely and put flowers in. Be nice, okay, be very very nice.'

A half hour later Appa stood in the doorway with a woman standing beside him. I had not seen anyone like her: she was tall and fair-skinned, with big, bright eyes. Her face was made up like a film star and her hair was cut short in a chic bob. She wore fitting black trousers and a sleeveless blue chiffon blouse that seemed to me like she had wrapped the sky around her. And the sky smelled of perfume.

They entered the living room, and Appa called out to Mani asking him to bring two glasses, a jug of water and lime. He took a bottle of Old Monk from a paper bag and set it on the table. Minutes later Mani stepped into the living room with a steel jug of water, glass tumblers and a lime cut in quarters. He stood rooted to the spot as he stared at the woman for some moments and then walked back to the door where Patti stood. I hid behind her. Patti sidled up to Mani. Between her teeth she hissed, 'What are you standing here with your mouth wide open like that? Before you know, a pair of mosquitoes will go in and lay their eggs inside your stomach. Then you will die of malaria of your stomach. Go!'

Appa looked up at Patti. 'This is Rukmini Swaminathan,' he said.

Patti looked surprised. 'She is Tamilian?'

'That's right. Rukmini is originally from Madras. She was with me at the institute in London. She's now the chief researcher in a very big pesticide company there.' He turned to Rukmini, 'My mother, Rukmini Iyer. And my son, Siva.'

'Hello Siva.' Rukmini rose, looking queenly and radiant. 'Good evening, Mrs Iyer. My namesake.' She smiled.

'Evenin-evenin.' Patti wondered what the woman had meant by 'Name Sake'. Name, she understood, but what did she mean by Sake? And whose sake? Hers or hers?

Appa poured the dark contents of the bottle into the glasses, topped them with water and dropped the quarters of lime in them. He held out a glass to Rukmini. 'So what are you working on now?'

Rukmini took a sip from her glass. 'We are studying the single frog.'

'Frog?' Appa repeated. 'Single?'

'That's correct. The highest rates of hermaphroditism are to be found in frogs when larger volumes of DDT are used for mosquito control. Some frogs have complete ovaries as well as complete testes. Pesticides have altered hormones of wild animals but frogs show the effects of ecological change more quickly or more noticeably than other species.'

'So it's the concern for frogs that has brought you to India. I mistakenly thought you had come to see me.'

'You were in London recently, weren't you? But you didn't even try and see me.'

Appa scowled. 'I didn't think you would want to see me.' Then he smiled. 'It's good to see you, Rukmini. I was both surprised and pleased to hear from you.' He put on his Parenthesis-look, one where his face would widen and swell with delight. His face had become unaccustomed to such joyous swelling.

Rukmini leant forward and held Appa's hand. He curled his fingers around it. Their eyes met and held for seconds. The air in the room was still and silent. The seabreeze could be heard in the distance. Then Rukmini pulled her hand away. She looked in her bag, scooped out a packet of cigarettes and a lighter. 'Tell me about your work here,' she said as she pulled out a cigarette from the packet and lit it. She took a long puff and sat back in the chair.

'We have discovered a virulent and invasive strain of the Chikungunya virus spread mainly by the Aedes alpictus mosquitoes,' Appa said. 'These mosquitoes can be identified by the white stripes on their black bodies and legs. They are aggressive daytime biters, active during the early morning and late afternoon, unlike the Anopheles mosquito, which is active at dusk. Typical symptoms of Chikungunya could include fever, headache, crippling joint pain, rash, minor bleeding in the eye and skin, and nausea. What is alarming is that this virus could spread from mosquito to mosquito and not just through a human host. This would result in outbreaks that last longer and affect more people. The strain is in its primitive stage but in ten or more years it could lead to severe epidemics across Asia.

'Growing cities and the increasing size and density of human populations will only hasten the spread of the virus,' Rukmini replied. 'Not long before this will become an emerging worldwide health threat.' She took a long drag on her cigarette and exhaled a wisp of smoke that went up, up and disappeared.

Patti turned on her heel and grabbing my arm she walked back to the kitchen. There she seized Amma by the arm. 'Look what is happening in front of our eyes, eh?' she said. 'This shameless woman is blowing smoke all over your husband's face. And look at your dirty saree, and your hair all out of place. Have you not even washed your face eh? Have you no idea how to be a proper wife?' Patti hissed through her teeth. 'You have to be cunning. Conniving like a cat. And you have to learn to control your husband without him even knowing it. Men are not as tough as they appear. They are easy to impress and confuse. I told you didn't I? First whisky and then woman. He's doing both at the same time.'

Loud squeals of laughter came from the living room. Patti flushed and the veins in her neck stood out. 'Just listen to her laugh,' she said. 'Chichichi, this Rukmini has no shame. Just imagine, she is a Tamilian like us and her hair is cut short like a man's, and do you even know what she is wearing? Tight-tight pants and a transparent blouse without sleeves even.'

Amma looked at Patti with a queer smile. 'So this is your son's Rukmini,' she muttered, 'your namesake.'

'And what do you mean by that? Patti retorted.

Amma stopped the sob that rose in her throat and then turned around and ran up the stairs. After the meal Appa left with Rukmini, to drop her at Queen's Hotel. Patti and I stood by the front door. I felt as if my chest was crushed and I couldn't breathe.

'Is Rukmini-aunty going to be my new Amma?'

Patti turned around and smacked me hard on my head.

***

I liked to dream. Not the dreams that come with eyes shuttight but those that happen with eyesopen. There was a way to do this. I would lie back in bed and stare at the dented fan blade as it went round and round. And then the dream would drop down into my eyes. My best journeys were in such dreams, spinning on the brink of sleep. They were soft and light: dreamy. It was bright in these dreams and not dark, unlike the sleepfull dreams; I could travel anywhere, with the moon in my eyes and my finger on a map. I never got lost, or felt loss either. I was always with Tara in my eyesopen dreams. We flew over distant rivers and seas, and on grassy fields ate corncobs in the sun. Sometimes we burrowed back into the womb, to the splosh of the sea within.

This time I flew with Tara all the way to London. We were in skysmelling Rukmini-aunty's house and all the rooms in it smelled of flowers. The wind was cold and the sky was a different shade of blue, deep and bright just like in the pictures Appa had shown me. Rukmini-aunty took us to the Queen's big house, Hide Park, Pika-dilly and all the other places Appa had told me about. The roads there were so good and the cars moved in straight lines. And yes, we went to the London Bridge that we learnt about in school: London Bridge is falling down, falling down, falling down, my fair lady...

Then Rukmini-aunty took us to a restaurant for Chinese near Tra-fa-ga-square. I never had Chinese food before. Tara didn't eat, she didn't have to, and I didn't eat much because I don't eat meat. So Rukmini-aunty got me ice-cream afterwards.

Tara whispered: *Who she?*

Our new Amma.

Tara screamed. I shut my eyes and ended the dream.

10

Something changed about Victoria Villa after Rukmini-aunty's visit. Like Amma, the old house heaved, drew a hood over its head and its insides became dark and gloomy. A window rattled tic-tic-tic and somewhere water dropped d-r-i-p, d-r-i-p, drip. A gust of wind swept through the window and the pages of a book on the sill went flap-flap-flap. A door slammed shut above. These were subtle indications. The ominous house was waiting for the right timing, and I should have known it did not intend to let me be.

Timing is everything, Appa would say. Sometimes, saying or doing even the right thing at the wrong time does not turn out well. You need to be in the right place at the right time. This is not coincidence, it is providence. And then you must do something about it at the right time, and this is neither coincidence nor providence. A good sense of timing, that's what it is. It wasn't providence surely, but I couldn't decide whether it was a coincidence or a good sense of timing that my sister died the day I was born, and on the day Amma was born, her mother died.

It was my grandmother's death anniversary, and Amma's birthday. The morning had warnings written all over it. Moreover, Rebecca had quarrelled with me the previous day. I didn't even know what the quarrel was about except that she wanted to have her own way. I didn't want her to have her own way. So we had squabbled and Rebecca had her own way and I was not in the best of moods.

Amma didn't come out of her room that morning. Patti sent Munniamma to fetch her. Amma stood in front of the old cupboard, staring at her reflection in the mirror fixed into the shutter. She rubbed her hand over her gaunt stomach. 'I have become fat,' she told Munniamma who stood by the door. Amma gathered her thick hair in a knot at the nape of her neck. 'My hair has thinned,' she said. Then she bent closer to the mirror and inspected her bony chin, the three strands of hair sprouting out of it. 'Oh no. I am growing a beard.' She started laughing; her voice was shrill but her eyes were full of tears.

In the kitchen, Patti was making aviyal. Vishnu-thatha was coming for lunch. I liked aviyal, it had lots of vegetables in a curry of coconut and yogurt. Tara liked it too. Patti cut an obese brinjal on a blade shaped like a hook. The blade cut through the brinjal's tight flesh, slicing it; not a drop of sap dripped from it. Then she cut each slice into strips. She had already cut many vegetables into strips of the same length: potatoes, beans, drumsticks, raw banana, yam and carrots. I had arranged the strips like a railway track on a steel tray: potatobeandrum-stickbananayamcarrot and Tara was waiting to add the brinjal strips to them.

Amma stepped into the kitchen and the old house heaved and creaked. Outside, Cha-chi set up a howl and then abruptly stopped. Mani ran through the door some minutes later, bewildered. 'It was howling one minute ma, and the next minute it fell to the ground and died. Cha-chi died.'

Patti's hand flew to her mouth. 'Achicho, that's a very bad omen. Something bad is going to happen.' She muttered a prayer as she sliced the brinjal faster, the slices thinner, and when a shadow fell over her she looked up. Vishnu-thatha stood at the kitchen door. I ran to him.

'Don't be late for lunch,' Patti said.

'We'll be back in an hour,' Vishnu-thatha replied. 'Come Mallika, let's go.'

'I want to go,' I said, looking up at Amma.

Her eyes had taken on a new sort of emptiness. Her mouth was empty of words, or almost. She had stopped talking to Appa

103

after Rukmini-aunty's visit. If he asked her something she said yes or no with her head or eyes, but she didn't talk to him. And she didn't talk much to me. Appa and I were in the same boat, one that tilted and tossed in dangerous waters. What was more, I didn't know how to swim.

'Take him with you,' Patti said to Vishnu-thatha. 'And Siva, take your water bottle. It's a hot day.'

Vishnu-thatha drove us in his old car to the market. He bought flowers from Ranga's Roses and a cage of lovebirds from Yusuf's shop next door. He drove all the way to the end of the woods; I climbed the steep hill, clutching my water bottle. Amma didn't say a word. Neither did Vishnu-thatha: he was deep in thought. Although the day was hot, the air was fresh and light high up on the hill. The valley spread out below us, the paddy fields woven into it like tapestry. Boulders speckled the hillside, and wild grass that had been roasted brown by the sun. A garland of white clouds hung from the sky. The breeze smelled of flowers. It was a good day.

Under a Parijat tree, next to small piles of pebbles, Vishnu-thatha laid the flowers with a prayer and a song. 'This was your mother's favourite place,' he told Amma. 'We came here often and sat under this tree. 'It's been twenty-five years since your mother left you and me,' he said. He pulled Amma by her arm to the other side of the tree and pointing to a hump on the earth, he said, 'Mallika, this is where I buried Tara's ashes.' Then he let the birds out of the cage one by one.

I unscrewed the cap of the bottle and sprinkled water over Tara's grave. 'Wake up, wake up, Tara, come alive.'

Amma began to cry, wailing and howling. Tears streamed down her face. Then she turned and ran down the hill, the palav of her saree unfolding like batwings in the wind. She tumbled over the root of a tree and fell. Her body shook with the force of her heartache. Vishnu-thatha hurried to her. Holding her arm he took her down the hill. I followed close behind them.

On our way back Amma, who was sitting in the front of the car, suddenly pulled at the steering wheel and dashed the vehicle into a tree with a singular purpose. Amma's head slammed against the window; the glass cracked and it cut deep into her forehead and blood streamed down her eyes. Vishnu-thatha's right leg crashed against the dashboard. I was pitched forwards and my head banged against the seat in front of me. Tara screamed. Although I was unhurt, the terror I felt seconds before the car hit the tree instilled a fear in me forever – a fear of uncertainties. A passerby rushed us to a hospital. Vishnu-thatha's leg was broken; it had to be plastered. The doctor bandaged Amma's head and dressed the bruises on her arm. She smiled at her father awkwardly. A dimple dented her left cheek. I longed to touch the dimple. But I didn't. I was scared of her.

It was well past lunchtime when we returned home in a taxi. Patti was on the veranda, waiting, worried. When we stepped out of the taxi and she saw Vishnu-thatha's plastered leg and Amma's bandaged head, her hands flew to her mouth. 'What happened?' Patti cried aloud as Amma walked to the veranda. Amma hurried past Patti and into the house. Vishnu-thatha waved from the gate, and then got into the taxi and drove away. Patti slapped her head with both her hands, and asked me. 'What happened?'

I didn't reply. I walked up to my room and lay down in bed and thought about the day. I aged many years as I thought of the WHAT IFS. Appa had told me about the power of WHAT IFS in science, and how things could be predicted. Think out of the box, he would say. Think big, across history and geography, across the universe. So I thought about the bigger WHAT IFS.

What If there had been no Universe...
What If there had been no Earth...
What If there had been no England ...
What If there had been no English ...
What If there had been no Queen...
What If there had been no Georgie ...
What If...

Thinking big didn't work. It didn't let me know about the small things to come. Premonition: knowing that something is going to happen. I didn't have any premonition like Patti did. What was more, she had a host of superstitions and beliefs to help her, guide her, inform her well in advance: the twitching of an eyelid, the dog howling, summer rain and so on. If I had had even a pinch of premonition of the things to come, then I would have held my sister's hand, swallowed water and sunk to the bottom of Amma's womb. I covered my eyes with my hands and tried to sleep.

I was covered in sweat when I woke up. It was still early. I rushed up to Amma's room. She was sleeping with eyes halfclosed and her hair spread out on the pillow like a map. The room smelled of her, and of earth in the rains: scented, warm and moist. The diamond studs on her nose caught the morning light and the gold bangles on her wrist gleamed. She had not taken off the old wristwatch that had belonged to her mother. Unlike Appa and Vishnu-Thatha, Amma wore her watch with its face on the inside of her wrist as though she didn't want to face time. She didn't want to know if it had passed. Or stopped. Time, for her, didn't have a future; it only contained a long gone past.

The kohl had crept out of her eyes, and her lips pressed together were frail. The bandage on her head had spots of dried blood on it. She looked like a broken flower; I wanted to protect her. I lay down close to her, breathing her breath. She moaned and muttered in her sleep: *Amma. Ma.* Was she calling out to herself? Was she calling out to her mother? I touched my finger to the dimple on her cheek. She smiled. I would never forget this.

She turned on her side and wrapped her arm around me. 'Ma, Amma.' Her voice trembled. 'Please don't go.' Every muscle in my face contracted and a loud sob escaped from deep in my throat. Amma opened her eyes; they were wide open and yet asleep – an empty stare, one that didn't include me. 'Amma, look at me.' she said, 'it's me, your Malli.' She sat up on the bed and started to sing in a high-pitched voice. My stomach churned; I snivelled and coughed. 'You've got a cold,' Amma said at once. The concern in her voice warmed me. She stepped out of bed and hurried out of the door, down the stairs. Minutes later she walked into the room holding up a halved papaya like a trophy. 'I got it for you. You like papaya, don't you?' Her eyes grew misty. 'It's good for your cold, ma.'

'Amma,' I said. That's all I said. 'Amma.'

'Amma,' she repeated. And then the feelings shackled within her seemed to break free. 'Why did you go? Why did you leave me.'

I felt a sadness I had not felt before. I tried to understand Amma's pain and, overcoming my fear, I sat up in bed, reached out and held her face in both my hands and saw her smile; her eyes turned brighter and her dimple quivered. But only for a moment. A moment, and then gloom swelled in her eyes, filled them with fresh tears.

I pulled her face towards me and kissed her on her cheek. The touch of my lips on her wet skin startled her. Her eyes seemed to wake up and then fill up with cold fury. She covered her mouth in horror as she gaped at the fruit she held in her hand. She hurled it across the room. Orange blood of the fruit stained the floor where it had landed. She froze. Minutes later she walked to the window with purpose. On the windowsill she had set small piles of pebbles. She had started to do this frequently: she would collect stones from the garden in the evening and arrange them on the sill. Come morning they would be gone. She now picked up the pebbles one by one and threw them out at the tree trunk. One, two, three, missed, missed, missed... Then she threw all the pebbles at once outside the window. Raising her hand to her chest she patted her heart where her ache resided, mumbling gently to it, 'Why did you go, Amma?' She started to rock to and fro. 'Did you not love me?'

'I love you, Amma,' I said. That's all I said.

Next evening I went to see Vishnu-thatha. We sat in the garden at the back. The paving stones were covered with a film of evening dew. The flowerbeds were arranged with bushes that blossomed in the right places and the trees around them grew to the right height, flowered in the right colours. The cicadas in the trees made tuneful sounds. Everything was tidy and solemn. The bowl of Queens Mosquito Repellent Powder shone luminescent red in the shadows. Vishnu-thatha played a melancholy tune on his violin to match his mood and the surroundings.

I reached out and touched his plastered leg. 'Does it hurt, Thatha?'

The old violin screeched on a particularly sad note and he put it down. It was too sad. 'Don't blame your mother,' Vishnu-thatha said. 'She has gone through a lot of pain.'

'Is that why she crashed the car?' I asked.

'Whenever I was miserable I went to the hill with flowers and a cage of lovebirds. I sat under the parijat tree for many hours, sometimes most of the day. I took your mother with me once. She was only ten; I wanted her to feel my pain. Your mother died, I said. She said, okay. I buried her ashes under the tree, I said, and she said, okay. She picked up pebbles from the grave and threw them at the tree trunk: one, two, three, missed, four... She didn't feel any pain. This pained me even more.

'On our way back that day, I brought my foot down on the accelerator and crashed the car into a tree. The tree was dead and it toppled over. Your mother was unhurt. But she screamed – a long piercing, painful scream. I can still hear her in my head.'

He sighed deep and long. 'I tried to kill myself. I tried to kill your mother. It was because of her that my Vatsala died. I'll never forget that night when your mother was born. Your grandmother was in terrible pain. I could see the pain in her eyes: dark, spreading like an inkdrop in water. She gave your mother her name – Malli, jasmine. Call her Mallika. And then she closed her eyes forever. Mother and child: one dead, the other recently born. Your mother cried all day. I did not want to look at her. I locked myself in my room and did not come out. I sat in my rocking chair, consumed by grief.

'When your mother was eight years old the maidservant dressed her in your grandmother's saree. She coiled her hair into a bun and stuck parijat flowers in it. She smeared red pottu on her forehead and lined her eyes with kohl. I saw your grandmother's face in your mother's face, her eyes in her eyes. I seemed to come alive. The same day I retrieved the violin from its case and began to play. I sang late into the night. And the next day, and the days after. I taught your mother music and song. I did this with patience and affection at first. I was thrilled to hear her sing so well: she had your grandmother's voice. But later I became irate and demanding. I insisted that she wear a string of parijat flowers in her hair, kohl in her eyes and a large red pottu on her forehead just as your grandmother had done. Then I demanded that she wear a saree although she was only eight. I woke her at dawn to sing, or late in the night, whenever I needed to hear your grandmother's voice.'

His brow cleared for a minute. 'I remember it all so clearly. Your mother had a bad cold. I came home with a papaya. I had brought one for your grandmother whenever she had a cold. It was a hot fruit, she would explain to me, and the heat would melt the phlegm in her lungs. I cut the papaya into halves, a small one and a bigger one. I put one half on a plate and walked into your mother's room. Leaving the fruit plate on the bed, I sat beside her and shook her awake. "You like papaya, Vatsala, don't you? This is good for your cold." I held up the fruit.

'She took it from me. "I am Mallika. I am your daughter," she said and hurled it across the room. It was the smaller half. For some reason I remember this.'

Vishnu-Thatha looked far away and his eyes were fixed on a yellow leaf on the tree before us. As though burdened with sadness, the yellow leaf trembled in the breeze and fell to the ground. On that signal, Vishnu-thatha covered his face with both his hands and wept. 'Please forgive me, Siva. I caused your mother a lot of pain.'

'Is this why she is sad?'

'Sadness is like a monsoon cobweb,' Vishnu-thatha said. 'Sticky, damp, something that lurks in a dark corner and reappears each time you think it's gone. She can't forget what I did to her. She can't forget her dead mother. She can't forget your dead sister.'

My heart felt cramped as I walked back. I walked to the end of the mudpath, past the trees to the lake in the woods. I sat near the water and threw stones at a distant tree: one, two, three, missed, four.... I don't know why I was replaying the scene. As though by doing so I would find an altered end to it all. As I threw the stones I let images of Amma's unhappiness flash in my mind like the slide projector at school. They click-clicked, whir-whirred like slides projected on the screen in an illfated sequence. Whirr: Her mother died. Whirr: Her daughter died. Whirr: Appa was preoccupied. Whirr: Rukmini-aunty had arrived. There was no one to love Amma and for her to love back. But I was there. I was *there*.

I felt alone and sad. I looked up at the moon, lonely and grey, without a face. A bird flew across and for an instant split it in two. Another bird chirped in its sleep; I felt consolation in its voice. The sound deepened the spell and everything quivered and rustled with life. I was not alone. I had Tara; she was always there with me.

11

Oilseed plants grew around the compound and, here and there, chakka trees with their trunks painted in red-and-white stripes. The George Gibbs institute was a large rambling house with many rooms. In them were scientists and their assistants dressed in long lab coats. They greeted Appa as we walked past. One of them came up to Appa. 'Have you heard, sir, the Malaysian scientists are now trying to grow female mosquitoes in the lab. When they release them in the atmosphere they hope that these mutant mosquitoes will reduce the real mosquito population because no babies will be born to them.'

'I read about this.' Appa shook his head. 'However, I am sure that the outcome of this experiment is still a grey area.'

When we were in Appa's office I asked him, 'What is a grey area?'

Appa laughed. 'A grey area is a place which exists between two extremes, where things can be one or the other, and everything is a probability.'

I didn't quite understand much of what the scientist had said about mutant mosquitoes but I liked the idea of Grey Areas. I was grey. I was a probability. For Patti, however, there was no grey; everything was black or white, right or wrong, good or bad. White was good and black was bad. She followed Gandhiji's dictum: See No Bad. Hear No Bad. Talk No Bad. Patti tried to be purely white. She had been a good daughter, wife, mother, grandmother and a widow. She lived by white rules. She dressed like a white widow, talked and thought like one, prayed like one, and hoped to die like one: pure and white. Hence, tonsuring her head was an act of whiteness, and Tuesday was the designated white day of the week. The barber came every other Tuesday to shave the stubble from her head.

It was Tuesday. Patti was on the veranda, her eyes fixed to the tarred road. Illusory heatsmoke rose from it and the sweet smell of ripe jackfruits clung to the hot air and curdled the heat. Patti fanned her face with a coconut leaf fan; the breeze it gave off was warm. I was on the floor not far from Patti, colouring a sketch I had drawn. Tara kept muttering in my head. I slapped my head with both my fists to keep her quiet.

'Why are you hitting your head like that, kanna?' Patti asked.

'I want it to stop thinking.'

Patti laughed. 'Thinking is good, kanna. Ghandiji said: your thoughts become your words. Your words become your actions.' Just then a loud shout came from the gate. 'There you are, Thambi,' Patti said, 'I have been waiting all morning. Hurry now.' Patti stood up from the floor and sat down on a low stool.

The barber walked in with a bag of tools. Patti shut her eyes as Thambi touched the blade to her scalp. The barber giggled. 'Not that I have any reason to complain, ma, but tell me what do you eat that your hair grows so quickly? I will give you a free head shave if you tell me your secret.'

'You idiot! Why are you giggling like a donkey?' Patti grunted. 'Have you opened a barber shop to get rid of hair or grow it?' There was a rattling at the gate. Rose-aunty and Rebecca were coming toward us. 'Go now,' Patti said to the barber. She quickly covered her freshly tonsured head with the end of her saree, moved the stool against the wall and sat down on the pai. The barber packed his tools in the bag, claimed his fee and left.

Rose-aunty was tall and lean and had a quiet voice. She wore oversized black spectacles as though she needed to hide behind them. Despite being a widow she wore a bright-coloured cotton saree and pearl ear-studs; her face was madeup. She sat down beside Patti and held out a plate with four large wedges of cake.

'It's eggless lemon cake. I made it this morning,' she said. 'It was Rebecca's mother's favourite cake.'

Patti set the plate on the floor and wiped the sweat that had collected on the tip of her nose with the end of her saree then tucked her breasts under it.

Rose-aunty said, 'It must be so uncomfortable. Why don't you wear a blouse?'

Patti frowned. 'I am a widow. I can't wear a blouse. It's sin. And my Gods will punish me.'

'I would like to face Jesus as a woman and not a widow,' Rose-aunty said.

Rebecca stood before me hopping from one foot to the other. 'See Siva, Daddy got me this new dress.' The frock had layered frills of soft chiffon and lace, pure white, with mother of pearl buttons and a broad white satin sash. Tara's heart beat loudly in my ears. I looked down at the T-shirt and faded shorts I had on.

'Daddy got me other things too,' Rebecca said. 'Come to my house and I will show them to you.'

'I can't.'

'Ask your Mama.'

'She's not well.'

'What's wrong?'

'She feels sticky and moist and cobwebby.'

Rose-aunty said, 'Becky, let's go home. I have to get lunch ready.'

'Can he come to my house?' Rebecca asked Patti.

Patti had never let me go before so I was surprised when she said okay. Rebecca's mother having been a vegetarian had possibly done the trick.

**

Rebecca's house was smaller than ours. It had a pitched roof and wooden pillars all along the veranda. The living room was large and airy and on the far wall was a picture of a young woman. I guessed it was Rebecca's mother. The picture was freshly garlanded with jasmine buds. Their scent had permeated the room making her absence present. There were three more photographs fixed to the adjacent wall. In the first one, Rebecca's mother was wearing a long white gown that hid her entire body from neck-to-toe, and a flowing veil. The veil was seethrough and didn't hide much. Rebecca's father had on a black suit with a red flower stuck into the lapel. Both of them had happy-smiles on their faces. Rebecca was with them in the second photograph. She wore a happy-smile but her parents were not smiling anymore. Between these photographs was one of Jesus Christ. He was not smiling either. But given the life he had had, I understood.

The tops of all the sofas, chairs, and even the centre table were covered with white lace sheets. On a corner table was a glass vase with roses: stem, leaves and all. In my house we had unstemmed flowers, and only in the prayer room. And here, plants were everywhere: in the corners, on windowsills and even in old whiskey bottles. At home all the plants were in the garden. The dining table was round and on top of it was another disc, which went round and round. Rebecca later told me it was called Lazy Suzy. I didn't get it: it did most of the work, so why would it be called lazy? And I learned that they had Coca Cola in the fridge. Real Fridge. Real Coke. The only drink we had in my house was buttermilk. We had no fridge.

Rebecca and I went out into the garden at the back. Rose-aunty brought two wedges of watermelon on a plate and two glasses of Coca Cola. She left them on the table on the veranda and went back into the house. Rebecca reached for a wooden box under the table. She opened it and removed a thick glass object with a steel handle. 'This is a magic glass. Daddy gotitforme.'

Rose-aunty called out, 'Don't jumble your words Becky. Speak properly.'

And Rebecca said: 'Look. Through. It. It. Makes. Things. Bigger. Nearer.'

I looked at the glass of Coca Cola through the magic glass. I could see droplets of water jumping above the foam of the Cola Sea. I drank up the Cola Sea in one long swallow. I looked at the watermelon wedge through the glass. I could see its pink skin and thread-like flesh that held the red juice. The seeds looked like big beetles with a white moustache. I ate up the juicy flesh, spitting out the beetles. Then I lay under the peepal tree and looked at its bark. It looked like crocodile skin. The tree trunk looked bigger and closer and I could see the greenbones of the big leaves. I looked up at the sky.

'Siva! Don't do that!' Rose-aunty came rushing out and snatched the magnifying glass from my hand. She took a piece of paper from the table and placed the glass over it until the sun's splinter went through and made a glowing dot on the paper. The dot turned yellow, and then brown and then *whoosh*, it caught fire. 'Don't play with the magnifying glass in the sun,' Rose-aunty said, 'it will burn you.' Rose-aunty set the glass on the table. 'Come and help me in the kitchen,' she added and went back into the house.

When Rebecca turned to go Tara put the magnifying glass into my pocket.

In the kitchen Rose-aunty was dicing chicken into cubes. 'Here Rebecca, you do this,' she said, 'and Siva you chop the onions and tomatoes.' I had never chopped onions before. I had only chopped one half of the onion and tears were streaming down from my eyes. Rose-aunty laughed. 'Let me do that,' she said. 'You chop the tomatoes.'

When the chicken, onions and tomatoes were cut and the ginger and garlic had been ground into paste Rose-aunty brought down a bottle of curry powder. She heated oil in a pan and fried the onions with ginger, garlic, curry powder and the tomatoes. Then she added the chicken, a pinch of salt and water, and let it cook. Rose-aunty and Rebecca ate the chicken curry with rice dyed yellow by turmeric. I had the gravy with rice. I didn't eat the chicken: Patti had told me it was sin to eat meat.

Up in her room Rebecca emptied a plastic bag on the bed. There was an assortment of things: hair clips, a fancy brooch, a box of felt pens, a sketchbook, a doll with shiny blonde hair, a sky blue frock, a big atlas. Then I noticed a big fat pen. I picked it up; it had no nib or a lead point.

'It's a pointer,' Rebecca said. 'Daddy uses it to point at the board when he is giving a lecture.'

'Why doesn't he use his finger?'

'Daddy's finger doesn't glow, stupid.' Rebecca took the pointer from me, twisted the top and pointed at the corner of the ceiling. I watched the red light dot wriggle updown on the ceiling. Then she put the pointer in her mouth and grinned like a redmouthed demon. 'Look, I am my mother,' she said.

I grabbed the pointer and shoved it in my mouth. Tara yelped with glee. 'Where did your father get this?' I asked.

'LA.'

'Where's that?'

Rebecca opened the atlas and flicked the pages. She pointed to a map. 'Here. In. U.S.A.'

I took the atlas from her and pretending the pointer to be a plane I flew dot-dot-dot through it from Machilipatnam all the pages away to LA. 'Can I keep the atlas and the pointer for some days?' I asked.

'You can't. Daddy will be angry,' Rebecca said. She snatched the pointer back. 'The light will die.'

'What does your father do?'

'He's a specialist. He works for a thinktank.'

I imagined a large fishtank with multicoloured thoughts in it. 'Where is his thinking tank?'

'U.S.A. And granny works for a NGO.'

'En-Gi-O?' I spelled the word.

'No, stupid. N.G.O. It's an office that does all that the government pretends to do.'

Rebecca picked up the doll, held it to her chest. 'Let's play Pretend,' she said. 'You're the boy and I'm the girl. We get married and this is our baby. You go to office and I'll cook and clean the house. And when you come home tired in the evening I'll feed you nice food, okay? And then one day I'll die and you will be left alone. So you will go to office and come home in the evening and cook and clean the house and look after our baby.' She pointed to two corners of her room. 'This is our home and that will be our office. Come, let's play. It will be fun. I'll get some food from the kitchen.'

No sooner had Rebecca left the room than Tara pulled the blue frock over my head and slipped my arms through its sleeves. She buttoned the frock and tied the sash tight around my waist. She pirouetted round and round, her arms stretched above my head like a dancer.

Rebecca rushed in through the door with a plate of leftovers. 'Why are you dressed in my frock? Takeitoff. Takeitoff.' She set the plate on the bed. 'Takeitoff right now.' She clutched the frock and tried to yank it over my head. It ripped. 'Now look what you made me do.'

I took the frock off. 'I don't want to play,' I said.

'If you don't want to play, then go to your home.'

'Okay, we play. What do I have to do?'

'I'm the mother and...'

'Do you miss your mother?'

'No. I didn't like her.'

'How can you not like her?'

'Cos she left me.'

'But you told me it was an accident.'

'Mama could have stopped it.'

'You can't stop accidents. Patti told me. They are waiting to happen.'

'Mama's accident was not waiting. She made it happen.'

'Come down both of you,' Rose-aunty shouted from the bottom of the stairs, 'I have to go to Sunshine Home. I'll buy you ice-cream.'

Soon we left for the market. The ice-cream parlour was not far from Ranga's flower shop. The old tables and benches outside were painted in bright green-and-red watermelon stripes. The sign on the shop read:

Pinto's
Juice / Ice-Cream Centre

And below, underlined:

No Water Pure Juice Only and
No Ice Pure Ice-cream Only.

Rose-aunty got us chocolate ice-cream cups. 'Now wait here,' she said and walked down the street towards Sunshine Home.

'Look, there is half-and-half,' Rebecca said. 'The girlboy.'

'Girl-boy?' I looked down the street and saw Sweetie-Cutie.

'Yes. She is both girl and boy.'

'How?' I remembered asking Munniamma but she hadn't told me.

'Cos she was a boy first but became a girl.' Rebecca held my hand and pulled me across the road to Yusuf's Pet Shop. It sounded like a forest come alive: birds chirped, a lone eagle let out a cry, a parrot tapped its beak against the cage, tak-tak-tak, kittens and puppies whined, mice scrambled, and the fish, soundless, made squishy movements in the water. Yusuf-uncle was nowhere to be seen.

Rebecca opened a cage, and one by one the birds flew into the sky. 'Birds should be up in the sky, flying, not in cages,' she said. 'Look, they're so happy.' She looked at the fish in the large tank. A goldfish made fishmouths at her. 'They seem happy. Let the fish be. Let's go.' Rebecca held my hand and ran down the street.

'Where are we going?' I asked.

'To the palmreader. There he is.'

'What's a palm reader?'

'He can tell what's going to happen to us.'

'I thought only God can do that.'

'He's the Playing-God man then. Come on.'

The Playing-God man was matchstick thin and his face was worn-out. Coloured charts were fixed on the wall behind and on the ground in front of him were charms of many kinds. He looked up at us and exhaled with a hiss. He seemed to me as though he was dying.

Do Gods die? It was an important question and it needed to be addressed. For the sake of the flowers, trees, insects, animals, Amma, Appa, Patti, Vishnu-thatha, Rebecca and Tara. Tara was dead on this earth but alive in Para-dies. If God died what would happen to her? Miss Lobo, my schoolteacher had told us what B.C. and A.D. meant: Before Christ and Anno Domini, which is Latin for the year of their Christ. She also told us that Christ was born in the year 4 B.C. How could He be born four years before He was born? Christians weren't good in maths. More importantly, was there an ADC? After the year of Christ? However, this was for the Christians to worry about. I should be concerned with the fate of my Hindu Gods. But theirs was a complicated life: they kept being born in different avatars. What would happen when all the avatars were over? Patti said: *what is gained depends on the path followed*, which meant if you lived your life properly you would forever stay in heaven and not be reborn. Did the Hindu Gods not live their lives properly? Miss Lobo always said, Practice before you preach. But the Hindu Gods seemed only to preach, preach, and preach. As to the Muslim God, Allah, I didn't know much about Him since I hadn't seen any pictures or idols of Him. He must be shy. He didn't Himself preach, perhaps for the same reason. He had a messenger, Mr Muhammad, who did all his talking for Him. Gods should belong to the world of Grey Areas, since nothing definite is known about them. But for them everything was either right or wrong; things were one or the other. They sat in judgement and made drastic decisions and for Them there was no question of a probability.

'Tell me who I'll marry.' Rebecca's words interrupted my thoughts. The Playing-God man sneezed; he pinched his nose between his fingers, blew hard and wiped his fingers on the sleeve of his shirt. Rebecca held my hand and pulled me down beside her. 'Him? Will I marry him?'

The Playing-God man looked at me and smiled, showing all his crooked teeth. 'I am sure you will marry him.'

'See, I told you,' Rebecca said, 'I'll marry you and we'll have a baby. And...'

Behind us Tommy-uncle laughed out loud. 'Well, well, well, little Miss Coelho. You do have plans for your life!' Then he turned to me. 'Young man, don't ever forget what Yul Brynner once said: Girls have an unfair advantage over men. If they can't get what they want by being smart, they can get it by playing dumb.' Tommy ruffled my hair, 'Confucius,' he said and walked away.

I saw Swami crawling toward us with great speed. Rebecca stood up urgently, and holding my arm, ran out into the street. Swami screamed after us: Bastard. Bitch.

Rose-aunty was waiting outside Pinto's. 'Where were you? I told you to wait here. What were you both doing?' she asked.

'The palmreader said I'll marry Siva,' Rebecca said.

Rose-aunty laughed. 'There's a lot of time for that. Come on, let's go home.'

I could not get the question off my mind. 'When will the Gods die?'

'Gods don't die, child.' Rose-aunty patted my head. 'They live in our minds forever.'

'What happens when we die? Do the Gods die then?'

'Of course not. They wait for other children to be born and then reside in them.'

'Like a ghost?'

Rose-aunty laughed. 'Maybe.'

I inscribed a cross upon my chest. Now I understood why Miss Lobo said 'In the name of the Father, the name of the Son and of the Holy Ghost, *Amen.'* I must remember to address my letters to Tara as Georgie (Holy Ghost), I decided.

Mani was waiting for me at the gates. Rebecca turned to me. 'Willyou cometo myhouse tomorrow?'

Rose-aunty said, 'Don't jumble your words, Becky.'

'Will. You. Come. To. My. House. Tomorrow?'

'Yes,' I said. 'And. We. Will. Play. A. New. Game. Of. Pretend.'

'Who. Will. We. Be?'

'God.'

Rebecca screwed up her nose. 'But. I. Don't. Know. How. To. Be. God.'

'It's easy,' I said, 'first we will make people and then decide which people should live and for how long.'

12

The Gods had other plans for me. They had a great sense of timing: Perfect. Machilipatnam seethed with dark, uncontrollable forces. A dry wind raged across the land. Red dust, dried leaves and bits of paper flew up in the air. Birds flew in loops and for one split moment a frozen silence hovered over Victoria Villa. Then the wind seethed once more, and the windows flew open like bookpages in the wild wind.

I stepped out onto the veranda. Two squirrels scurried across the porch. A crow crashed into a windowpane. Its beak fell open and for a moment I could see the deep hollow of its throat, freshpink. Then it fell to the floor, dead. My ears buzzed, my head spun and I fainted. When I came to I was curled in bed, my knees pressed against my chin. I trembled and sweated profusely. Dr Kuruvilla was feeling my pulse. He was very tall and, despite the heat, as always he was dressed in a loose suit and a narrow tie. Patti and Appa were standing behind him.

'He's been sick all week,' Patti said. 'So much vomiting, poor boy, he can't keep any food inside him. Not even water.'

'Did he eat anything outside?'

'Only ice-cream from the market,' Patti replied, 'and that a week ago.'

'Wholly possible.' The doctor shook his head to and fro. 'He's hot and he's shivering. He's vomiting. Perfect symptoms.'

Appa intervened. 'Do you think what I think it is?'

The doctor nodded. 'It's wholly possible.'

'So it is malaria.'

'Yes.' The doctor took some medicines out of his bag and gave them to Appa.

'Go, work with your mosquitoes and fill the house with the parasite,' Patti screamed at Appa after the doctor left. 'It's because of you that Siva is sick.'

Mosquitoes whined in chorus around my room. Moonlight stroked Patti's darned mosquito net under which I lay trembling. Appa rubbed my forehead with eau de cologne, pressed a cold towel on my forehead and made sure I had my medicine. Appa was home early every evening. Vishnu-thatha came to see me, and so did Rebecca and Rose-aunty. Rebecca gave me her atlas and the pointer. I put them under my pillow. Tara was with me, now and then. I pointed at her with the pointer. Red in my eyes.

Are you goin to die?

Maybe.

Then come here.

Are there fairies with lights in their eyes?

No.

And the Gods?

What gods?

Patti said you are with the Gods.

Didn't see 'em.

Not even Jesus?

Who?

He is the God who speaks English.

***

Tara, are you there?

I moved the pointer across the room. Red dots, but nothing else. I got the magnifying glass from my desk drawer and tried to look for Tara with it. She was gone, like she had gone away the first time at the lake. She swallowed water, more water, sank to the bottom and closed her eyes. She had left me once more. I was half of myself again. I left the pointer on until all its light was gone.

***

The fever had gone down but I was still weak. Munniamma gave me all the news in town; Vishnu-thatha and Appa did too. Kuttan had gone to Dr Kuruvilla with high fever, almost 104 degrees. The chakka-man was covered in sweat, his eyes were swollen and he was barely conscious. Some days later Kuttan was found dead under the chakka tree. Flies swarmed all over his face. The jackfruit that he had cut in the morning lay exposed on the cart. Its sweet smell clung to the hot air mixed with the foul smell of death. Within a week of Kuttan's death, Dr Kuruvilla's clinic was full of patients complaining of high fever, nausea, vomiting, sweating and fatigue.

Already, in the other parts of the town there were reports of 140 deaths due to malaria; an epidemic had broken out in some of the villages in the district. The newspapers reported the numbers of the dead, but not their names. Each day the numbers increased on the front pages under the simple heading: Malaria Victims. The deadly plasmodium falciparum malaria parasite was the cause. In the 80-bed Civil Hospital in Machilipatnam, there were more than 400 malaria patients from all over the district. They lay on mattresses, reed-mats and sheets on corridor floors, verandas, under stairways, and on landings. Surveillance workers went house-to-house and field-to-field, spraying DDT. The district administration called for special medical teams from Madras equipped with microscopes and rapid diagnostic kits. They too went house to house, to collect blood samples. Health officials gave out free malaria drugs.

Vishnu-thatha made insecticide-treated nets at the Victoria Dyes factory, dying them with natural pigments, and distributed them for free. Appa toured the district with his team. In every village he visited, chimneys belched carbon-coloured smoke into the air and open sewage drains gushed into the ponds nearby. Buffaloes waddled through the slush with crows perched on their backs. Mosquitoes fed on swampy waters and bred. Invisible to the naked eye, the new parasites simmered. Appa brought samples back with him.

Each day Patti boiled turmeric roots in a large iron pot with sea salt, and at dusk she sprinkled the yellow brine inside and outside the house. One evening, when the fever had gone, I sat on a stool on the veranda watching Patti carry out this routine. It was still early but surprisingly Appa drove through the gates. He stepped out of the car and asked Patti what she was doing.

'Turmeric keeps mosquitoes away', Patti said.

'Rubbish', Appa retorted. 'If it were that simple there would be no need for scientists, would there?' Appa came up to me and ruffled my hair. 'You should be resting, Siva', he said. Just then the phone in the hall started ringing. Wearily Appa walked through the doors to it. 'Good evening David. I was expecting your call', he said into the phone. Appa often talked to him. His name was David Stevenson and he was the head of the malaria research team in London. 'Artemisinin and curcumin isolated from the roots of Curcuma longa?' Appa asked, his eyes round OO's. 'David, you don't mean turmeric?' Appa laughed as he ended the call. Then he shut himself in the study.

Appa laboured day after day, week after week. He submitted a report to the District Health Department, who set up clinics in every village and town in the region. They were a success and the lethal parasite was soon brought under control. The District Collector's office organised a special ceremony at the George Gibbs Institute to commend Appa's work. Patti and I were present at the function. Rose-aunty and Rebecca were there, and Dr Kuruvilla in a suit and tie. Tommy Gonzalves came in late. He looked about him and said, loud and clear, 'Confucius.'

The main hall was full. There were rows and rows of chairs, all of them occupied. There were journalists, bureaucrats, doctors, local people and surviving malaria patients and their relatives, and *their* relatives. People sat on the aisles and along the walls. Patti and I sat in the front row in the chairs reserved for us. There was a hush of anticipation all around; only intermittent coughs and the shuffling of feet could be heard until Tommy-uncle sneezed like a pressure cooker once-twice-thrice: Confucius. Confucius. Confucius. It set off some people laughing, and then all was quiet once more.

The District Collector and Appa walked into the room and occupied the chairs on the dais. A photographer took pictures of them, then he turned around and took another one of Patti and me. Patti covered her face with her hands. The District Collector rose from his chair. He turned to the wall behind him and switched on the electric lamp above the picture of George Gibbs. He garlanded the frame with fresh jasmine buds and then turned around to address the crowd. He talked for a long time. He took us on a journey through the country's history and its problems: British India, George Gibbs' struggle with malaria, freedom struggle, partition struggle, unemployment and poverty struggle, illiteracy struggle, communal struggle; and the ongoing struggles with floods, drought and disease.

'I am happy to say,' he said after he had finished his speech, 'I have seen a lot in my life, been through a lot, but I've not had malaria, and with able scientists like Dr Raman Iyer here I hope to never contract the dreadful disease.' There was deafening applause. The District Collector sank down in his chair, breathless.

A young man stood up, mentioned the name of the newspaper he represented, asked, 'Dr Iyer, are some people more prone to malaria than others?'

Appa stood up and spoke into the microphone. He adopted a different voice, confident and authoritative. 'Pregnant women attract malaria-carrying mosquitoes twice as much as non-pregnant women. Why? Because women who are at an advanced stage of pregnancy exhale 21% greater volume than non-pregnant women. Mosquitoes are attracted to the moisture and carbon dioxide in their exhaled breath. And the abdomens of pregnant women are 0.7°C hotter and they release more volatile substances from their skin surface, allowing the mosquitoes to detect them more easily. Malaria in pregnant women is the main cause of stillbirths, low birth weight, deformities and early infant mortality,' he said, 'and here at the George Gibbs Institute we are looking into the use of bactericidal soap to reduce the chemical signals produced by skin bacteria, which help mosquitoes feed on human blood.'

There were more questions; more answers. An old man stood up. He was weak and frail and looked like he was ninety. 'My wife was ten years younger than me,' he said. 'She was not pregnant, no,' he shook his head, 'and she had asthma so she could hardly breathe, in or out. Her skin had lost its warmth; it was cold. She died of malaria last month.' His voice was shaky. 'Why?'

'I am so sorry,' Appa said.

A hush fell through the crowd and stretched until Tommy Gonzalves in the back shouted: Dr Raman Iyer! Hip Hip Hooray! People clapped. Appa and the District Collector stepped down from the dais and walked toward Patti and me.

'This is my son,' Appa said.

The old man ruffled my hair. 'So are you going to become a mosquito genius like your father?'

'Yes,' I said. 'Just like Georgie Gibbs.'

***

Amma's body was covered in sweat and she shivered in the heat. A glassy look came to her eyes. She did not eat much; there was a knot of pain in her stomach, she said. Her breathing was short and laboured, and her skin had gone pale and dry. Munniamma was terribly worried, Patti too. That evening Munniamma found Amma sitting in bed staring fixedly at the window. She rested her chin on her knees which were pulled up to her chest. When she turned to look at Munniamma there was a little scowl on her face, but underlying it was infinite sadness. Her eyes were dark and heavy. Munniamma had never seen such loneliness in a face.

'What's wrong ma? I hope you are not coming down with malaria too.'

'A shadow is following me.' Amma pointed to the little shadow on the sill. The tamarind tree waved its fingers in the breeze.

Then the little shadow came to her, or so Amma said, lay next to her, holding hands, touching eyes, breathing the same breath.

Don't be afraid, the shadow said, '*walk to the water, into the water. More water. More water. Sink to the bottom, landscaped by deep shadows and silence, more water, more water until your heartbeat will rise and fall like a leaf detached from its tree. Then it'll be over.*

'It is over,' Amma said to Munniamma.

***

Two months after I had come down with malaria I was better, although weak. I had lost a lot of weight. Appa took me to Dr Kuruvilla. There were no patients in the waiting area so we walked straight into the consulting room. The doctor signalled us to sit down. He referred to some papers on his desk and then made notes in a pink file. Dr Jeevan Kuruvilla was the most reputed doctor in town especially because he was foreign-educated. He had long ago returned from Chicago.

I moved uncomfortably in my chair, pressed my knees together and secured a stray lock of hair behind my ear. The bookshelf in front of me was stocked with thick volumes of medical records. But one of the shelves had novels and children's books. I read the names: Dickens, Hardy, E.M. Forster, Rudyard Kipling, Sir Arthur Conan Doyle, Roald Dahl. Then I turned to the sidewall on which were fixed two large coloured illustrations of the male and female anatomy. The adjacent wall was adorned with several certificates, all neatly cased in gilded frames:

M.Sc. in Dietetics and Physiology: *A study of the relationship between physical activity, dietary factors and physiological disorders in a group of active young men and women.*

D.Sc. in Biochemistry: *a study of the nutritional content of rice and its link to physiological and psychological dysfunction.*

Dr Kuruvilla looked up from his papers, and coughed into his fist. 'I have to present a paper in Chicago next month,' he said to Appa. 'It's about diet and mental illness.' His smile widened into a grin. 'Psychosis is often induced by imbalance in blood sugar level and this is wholly due to our diet. Too much sugar – refined carbohydrates are bad for the brain.'

'Did you know that meat eaters are more prone to being bitten by mosquitoes?' Appa rubbed his hands together. 'Mosquitoes are attracted to lactic acid. Meat eaters are more acidic than vegetarians.'

A smile of discomfort came upon the doctor's mouth. When he spoke his voice had taken on a degree of sharpness. 'That may be so, but fish, chicken and eggs provide essential fats to build our brain's membranes,' he said. His eyes focussed on a spot on the table. It seemed as though he was attempting to extract something significant from his memory. Then he turned to me and his eyes grew small and intense under bushy eyebrows that he now twirled with his fingers. 'So how is he?'

'He is much better now,' Appa said. 'But he is very weak.'

'If you ask me, it's all because of the food he eats,' the doctor said shrugging his shoulders. 'Too much rice. And too many gourds and pumpkins. And no garlic? Wholly incredible. And all those idlis and dosas.' The doctor shook his head and clucked, tch tch tch. 'He should have no rice. He must have lots of milk, cheese, butter, eggs, and of course chicken and juicy fish steaks would be nice. All excellent sources of Vitamin B. But you are vegetarians so the last ones on the list are out. He must eat spinach, tomatoes, peas, cauliflower, and yes, sweet potatoes, excellent source of Vitamin C. Fry them, boil them or roast them, he must eat sweet potatoes. Not rice, not dosas, but sweet potatoes. And eggs, at least two a day.

On Patti's orders, Munniamma mixed two eggs in milk and forced me to drink it every morning outside the kitchen; Patti had said, No Eggs in the House. She asked Mani to boil, roast or fry sweet potatoes and she insisted that I eat them all day long. Despite consuming sixty eggs in a month I was still thin as a reed.

But Patti tweaked my cheek and said with a smile, 'Chubby-chiks, rozy lipss, dimple cheen and tith witteen. Aiyes not so bloo, lavaly too, Patti's pet, is zat eyu.'

13

Not everyone believed in God. Appa did not. When you are older and can think for yourself, it is up to you to believe in God or not, he had told me. Vishnu-thatha didn't believe in God either. Early tragedy had robbed him of his belief. Appa and Vishnu-thatha had taught themselves to be unafraid. Science was on Appa's side, and on Vishnu-thatha's, wisdom of many years. But unlike Appa, Vishnu-thatha was not a practical man: he believed in superstitions.

So did Sister Phyllis, my General Knowledge teacher. She had a lot of knowledge about general matters. She told us about the miracle of Five-Loaves-and-Two-Fish. Jesus had gone on a boat ride. He stopped at some place called Beth Saida. A big crowd of people followed Jesus there. It was a remote place. There were no restaurants and there was nothing to eat except five loaves of bread and two fish. People were very hungry. So Jesus did a miracle. He made the bread and fish into lots and lots of breads and fishes.

Sister Phyllis had then asked us to write an essay about miracles. Remember, she said, coincidence is when God wants to remain mysterious. Miracles are when God reveals Himself. So I did some homework.

Vishnu-thatha: a miracle is when the impossible happens. The impossible rarely happens.

Tommy Gonzalves: It's like missing the woods for the trees. C.S. Lewis said that the story is written in big letters across the world but some people can't see it. However, when the same people see the same story in small letters they think it is a miracle.

Appa: The inexplicable to people is a miracle. They don't have a questioning mind. Science can't accept miracles.

I had written the essay in four lines: Miracles happen only when you see God. It is impossible to see God. And the impossible is impossible. So miracles can't happen. People believe in miracles because they can't read big letters and because they don't ask questions. Science can't say Yes to miracles. It knows too much. It has most of the answers.

I thought it was a good essay. Sister Phyllis gave me 1/10. But when I showed it to Appa he said it was good. It was concise, precise and To-the-Point. He gave me 8/10. But I wanted the impossible to be possible. I wanted to believe in miracles. I hoped some day Amma would love me. Miraculously. No big miracle happened, but there were small miracles. At least, I believed they were. Like the old English coin I found in the attic. I showed it to Vishnu-thatha when I went to his house.

'Keep it safe. Old coins bring good luck,' he said. 'They make your wishes come true.'

'How?'

'It is an old superstition.' He held my face with both his hands. 'Superstitions are necessary,' he said. 'They let us Time-Pass our lives. The main thing about life is to know how to pass the time.'

A lot of Time-Passed. Superstitiously:

I didn't cut my nails at night and I turned away when a cat crossed my path. I tried not to have bad dreams in the mornings. When I sneezed I said, Shiva, Rama or Krishna. I liked to say Krishna since the sound was similar to the sound my sneeze made. I did not hold my hands behind my head, and I didn't do anything important on a Tuesday. I didn't bang the door, and when the lizard made a tch-tch sound I tried to think of only good things, as they were meant to come true. I tried to think I was Tara, and then miraculously Amma would love me.

But Amma had reserved her love for others. She had started going to Sunshine Home. It was Rose-aunty's idea, actually. Rebecca and I had gone to Sunshine Home with Rose-aunty several times. There were a number of handicapped children there amongst the destitute ones. Four of them couldn't see, and two couldn't hear. One was crippled, another deformed. Rose-aunty had given the children new names when they arrived so they would have a new beginning. She allotted new birthdays to the children, as they didn't know their old ones. She celebrated their birthdays with potato bondas, cakes and sweets. She collected all the children together with or without their eyes, ears, legs and fingers. She talked to them about things, places and people. She played music to them. Rebecca and I danced and sang songs for them. Rose-aunty told us that in this way we could soothe them of the fear that arose from being different, which made them feel sad and unwanted.

Priya had come to the Home only some weeks ago. She was an orphan. She had incredibly thick eyelashes, and her eyes were deep and distant, made me think of an entire universe enclosed in a small space. Her given birthday was in a week. She would be five then. On Priya's assumed birthday Rose-aunty took Rebecca and me to the Home. Amma was at the Home that day. She sat down on the floor in front of Priya and held out a box of pink sweets. 'Happy birthday Tara,' she said, looking into her universe eyes. Then she pulled the girl close to her bosom and started humming softly. She held Priya's finger and put it on the top of her forehead, then slowly ran it over the ridge of her nose, down its tip, over the lips, the chin and all the way down the neck to the hollow under it. Then she curled Priya's finger into the hollow, sheltered and safe.

I watched them, Tara's finger curled at my throat.

Time-Passed.

***

It was the Tamil New Year. Tendrils of morninglight, shiny and new, crept through the window of my room. A rooster announced the new morning that set the sparrows chirping. I heard Patti calling out to me, and minutes later she rushed in through the door. 'Wake up, it's Chitirai Vishu,' she said. 'Wake up, kanna, but don't open your eyes yet. Keep them shut tight.' Patti pulled me out of bed, as she did every Vishu, and holding my arm she led me down the steps to the prayer room. She pushed me down on the floor in front of a large mirror. She said, 'Go on open your eyes, kanna.'

I opened my eyes to see, reflected in the mirror, a silver bowl of rice, bowls of payasam and sweetmeats, fruits heaped on a silver plate, gold necklaces on a silk cloth, a bowl full of silver one-rupee coins and a pile of books.

'Now look at all the things here, one by one, and soak your eyes with them,' Patti said. 'You will be blessed with an abundance of food, wealth and wisdom.' I remembered Amma speaking the exact same words. It seemed so long ago that she had. Patti held out a parcel of brown paper. 'Here, take these,' she said. 'Appa got you new clothes. After you bathe, wear them. And don't make a noise. Your father is sleeping. He came back very late in the night.' She walked to the door and then looking back she said, 'Now pray to God. Ask him whatever you want.'

'Him? I pray to him too?' I pointed at the photograph of Gandhiji.

'Yes-yes, you must pray to Gandhiji. In a hundred years he will become God.'

So dead people became God? Impossible.

'And this?' I pointed to the Vacuum-Cleaner-God.

'Why not?' Patti said. 'God resides in everything.'

Things are God? A miracle.

In the light of the lamp I made faces at my reflection. This is an iiii face; this is a yeeee face and this is an oooooooo face. When I was finished with facemaking, I closed my eyes and sent a pictureprayer to Jesus. He was more accessible. *I am Tara and Amma's arms are around me, and she whispers, I love you.* Then with my eyes open I prayed to Jesus with my thoughtwords. *Let me be Tara. And let Amma love me. Amen.* I filled my pocket with coins, stuffed my mouth with the sweets, and then tore the parcel open: a pair of grey shorts and a pale blue shirt. I shut my eyes tight and tapped my brow with my finger. I concentrated hard and imagined my new clothes to be Rebecca's blue frock.

Up in my room I stood in front of the mirror dressed in my imagined frock. Tara's eyes stared back at me. Then, willed by her, I ran up to the spare room. Amma was standing by the window. I dashed to her and wrapped my arms around her thighs. I buried my face in the folds of her saree. Ammasmell. 'Amma, Happy Vishu.' Strangely my voice was shrill. Was it Tara's?

Amma's eyes, bright as ever, stared back at me with a peculiar, fixed intensity. Then she seemed to shudder. 'Don't touch me.' She plucked my arms off her one by one and pushed me away. 'Don't call me Amma. I am not your mother. I don't know who your mother is.'

I started to cry and Tara put her finger on my lips and said ssssh. Then she walked me out of the room, out of the house, out of the gates. Runrunrun – all the way to the lake. I saw someone swimming in the water. The new sky above, above the trees, was rapidly filling up with new morning light. I hid behind a bush and watched.

Sweetie-Cutie hoisted her masculine body out of the water and climbed out, a loincloth wrapped around her waist. Her long hair was loose and her face was without the usual makeup. She walked to the old chakka tree, picked up the towel under it and dried her body with it. Then she plucked her saree and petticoat from the branch where she had hung them, and tied them around her waist. She put on her blouse and adjusted balls of cloth in the cups. She shook out her hair and rubbed it dry with her hands. Then she saw me peeping from behind the bush. 'How long have you been standing there, princess?'

Princess?

Sweetie-Cutie pulled out a knife and a watermelon from a bag. She sat down and holding the fruit between her feet she cut it in half, then slowly sawed a disc, and then another. She held out the fruit disc to me. 'Come here, princess.'

I walked up to her and took the fruit from her hand. I lay under the chakka tree and raised the fruitdisc to my eyes. Tara watched the sun. The rays looked like tiny lights caught inside red teardrops. Tara licked the juice that trickled on my face; she stuck my tongue out and made a hole in the fruit disc, eating chunks of fruit as the hole got bigger and bigger, and finally there was only a ring left. Sweetie-Cutie lay close to me. We looked through the hole and the sky grew small and round and belonged only to us. Sweetie-Cutie-Tara-Me. Our own Para-dies.

'How did you become a girl-boy?' I asked.

Sweetie-Cutie arched an eyebrow. 'When a baby is a tiny little thing in the mother's womb it is always a girl first. Then as the mother's belly grows, the baby grows in it and if it has to be a boy then it grows as a boy but only bit by bit. But some babies take a long time to fully become boys and the mother gets terrible pain and so the baby is born even before it is fully a boy. His heart is still a girl's. So the girl inside him feels trapped and very sad.

'I was born a boy like you,' she said. 'But I was not fully a boy. One day I was looking into the mirror I saw the face of a little girl. I could hear her in my ears talking to me. I could think her thoughts. I had memories of her. I wanted so much to be her. I knew I would be happy if I could be her. So I became her.'

***

Patti sent me to Vishnu-thatha's house with a plate of New Year sweets. We sat on the steps of the veranda looking up at the setting sun. Sweetie-Cutie was very much in my thoughts. She had memories of a little girl, she said. How far back could memories go?

Vishnu-thatha asked, 'Why the serious face?'

135

'I was remembering,' I said. 'Thatha, how far back can we remember?'

'Some memories go far back, which is why sometimes we feel as if we know something even before we know it. It is called déjà vu.'

'Deyjhavoo?'

'Correct. Our remembrance of old things is stored on a special shelf in our brain. It is called the subconscious shelf.'

'What are memories?'

Vishnu-thatha asked me to get sheets of paper and the box of colour pencils from his desk. 'Memories are a library of feelings,' he said as I sat down beside him. 'You remember something because of what you have felt about it. There are four feelings.' He drew two perpendicular lines on the paper. Along the standing line he wrote Y and along the sleeping line, X. He wrote down numbers 1 to 10 along the Y line and along the X line he wrote down the words: anger, sadness, fear, happiness. 'The Y-axis measures your feelings. The X-axis tells you what you feel.' He held up the coloured pencils one by one. 'Red is for anger, black for sadness, yellow for fear and green for happiness. Now think of a person and using the colours make bars to measure how you feel about them. Let me show you.' On top of the page he wrote Vishnu-thatha. He wrote *Siva* along the X-axis and made a green bar reaching 10 on the Y-axis and a black bar reaching 3. He said, 'See, I feel very happy and a bit sad about you.'

'Why do you feel sad?'

'Because your sister died. You would have loved her and your mother would have loved you.'

'What colour is love?'

'Love is like a rainbow,' Vishnu-thatha said smiling, 'it has all the colours in it. And lots and lots of green happiness.'

I made two graphs: one for Tara and one for me. I coloured them from Amma's point-of-view. On Tara's graph I made tiny bars of red, yellow and black, and a long bar of green reaching

10. On mine I made black and red bars shooting beyond 10. This was it: the hopeless graph of my life. I wanted Amma to love me in all the colours of the rainbow. Her love was what I most missed, and what I needed most. So I cancelled Tara's name on her graph and put my name on it. I played Pretend. I was Tara. I was fully her. In a Mind-Over-Matter way.

That night I stood in the balcony of my room. It was my favourite Alone place. From here I peeped out at the world, outsidein, and deep into myself, insideout. I asked questions to myself that I dared not ask anyone else. Not even Tara. I had a lot of questions:

> Was I a girl when I was in Amma's womb?
> Was I born before I could become a boy?
> Is my heart still a girl's?
> Am I a girl?
> I am Tara?

14

I was ten years old and everything that could possibly go wrong began to do so with me. I had the sensation that I was in someone else's house, in someone else's clothes, in someone else's body, and my mother belonged to someone else. My desire to please her, for her to love me back, was crushed each day. For Amma I could be a wall, a pillar, a chair or table, or a potato that she was peeling, or any such inanimate thing: as a person I seemed not to exist. Even if I was in the same room she completely ignored me. Her aloofness, her contempt for me was hurtful, but there was something about being in her presence that I liked. I smelled Tara in her.

But when Rebecca was with me I forgot my despair, momentarily. She was often in my house in the summer holidays. Cocooned in my room, or up in the attic, we played Snakes and Ladders; we read aloud from storybooks; we spun stories out of stories we had read. We surrendered ourselves to fantasy worlds and believed every aspect of our creation. I waited for her to come each day.

So did Amma. The sticky, moist cobwebs in her head had disappeared. She hummed as she dusted the house; she was often in the kitchen making savouries and sweets, and she had cleared the weeds in the garden. She had even planted saplings of fruit trees – guava, custard apple, chikoo, mango, pomegranate – and she arranged the pots of flowering shrubs and creepers according to the colours of their blooms. She knew each one intimately, by their botanical names: allamanda cathartica, thunbergia grandiflora, gloriosa superba, ipomea palmate, and more. With the love and care bestowed on them they bloomed madly: white, pink, yellow, blue, purple, and orange as red as the setting sun.

It was early evening. Amma was in the kitchen steaming jackfruit. She had promised Rebecca she'd make chakka payasam for her. I liked chakka payasam a lot. I was on the floor with Patti, helping her clean rice. It was infested with lice and cobwebbed with maggots. Only that morning Patti had spread the grains on sheets of newspaper on the rear veranda. The sun's heat had flushed some of the maggots and lice out from the rice and crows had pecked at them, but not all the wiggly-wiggly things. I carefully looked over the rice for the black lice. Patti slurped her spit every time she found an obese maggot and crushed it on the floor. She grabbed a fistful of grains and smelled it. She wrinkled her nose. 'Aiyoo, this rice still smells of maggots. Tch tch, I will have to give away all the rice to Munniamma.' The thought didn't seem to please her much. 'Where is that Mani?'

'You sent him out only ten minutes ago,' Amma said laughing. She was in a good mood. She pulped the fruit with a wooden ladle, tossed it in a large vessel over the stove, and then added jaggery and ghee. The room soon filled up with the aroma of ghee, jaggery and the sour-sweet smell of jackfruit. When the mixture had reduced Amma poured in coconut milk. I got up from the floor and stood behind Amma, a stone pillar, watching the sweet concoction squelch and pop. My tongue popped and my saliva squelched. Rebecca stepped in through the kitchen door and at once Amma's eyes lit up. She switched the stove off and filled a small bowl with payasam and gave it to Rebecca.

'Thank you, aunty,' Rebecca said.

Amma said, 'Call me Amma.'

Patti's eyebrows shot up and she made a sour grimace with her mouth.

'Amma, I want some payasam too,' I said.

Amma covered the vessel with a lid, put the ladle down and walked out of the kitchen.

'Mallika, your blood is thinner than tap water.' Patti shook her head. 'I'll give you some, Siva. Let it cool before you eat it, or it will burn your tongue.'

'I don't want any, Patti,' I said. I rushed out of the kitchen and up the stairs to my room. I picked up the Snakes and Ladders board from my desk and set it on the bed. Rebecca came in with her bowl of payasam and sat beside me. Blowing on the spoon of payasam she fed it to me, and then had a spoonful herself. Between us, between spoonfuls, we finished the payasam. Then we played Snakes and Ladders. We had given names to all the snakes on the board: Appa, Amma, Akka, Mama, Mami, Kanna and so on. Amma was the longest snake on square 98 – the mother of all snakes. I was almost winning the game but Amma snake swallowed me and I landed all the way to the bottom of the board.

It was Rebecca's turn and she threw the dice. We heard footsteps on the stairs. I wondered if it was Amma. She always came to my room when Rebecca was with me. But Appa stood at the door, waved out to us. 'You should be out playing some sort of sport, or doing something more constructive. Go on,' he said before he turned to go to his room.

We ran down and out of the gates. Rebecca held my hand as we crossed Gibbs Road. Her fingers were warm and firm. We walked past the market, a warm breeze on our faces. I looked around and everything seemed so fine: colours were brighter, sounds were sweet and the sun felt like it had donned a soft silk scarf. We walked past the Shiva temple and toward the beach. Vendors had put up their stalls: corncob, peanuts, channa, coconut, lemonade, watermelon and cucumber. We sat on the dry sand not far from the sea, eating corncobs. Now and then I felt Rebecca's thigh brush against mine. Every time she leaned toward me to say something, each part of my body came alive, separately, continuously, like in the musical medley we had learnt at school. I studied her face. I hadn't noticed before but her cheeks had filled out, and twin dimples dented the left cheek when she smiled. Her hair was gathered into a tight ponytail. Strands that had broken loose curled on her brow and neck. When she looked at me her gaze held, unwavering. My heart beat in my throat and I looked away. Gulls flew in the air, gliding, plunging, and squawking. At a distance a family of monkeys called out to one another. I raised my face to the evening sky. Tara felt the breeze in my hair.

Then a shout:

HOW'S THAT!

Some distance away a team of boys were playing cricket. The stumps had fallen and new batsman was taking his place at the crease. I watched the bowler take an extra-long run-up, and he delivered the ball at high speed.

FOUR!

The bowler tossed another ball into the air. The batsman took his position and then:

SIX!

I saw the ball soaring in a wide arc across the sands, catching the wind, turning, and coming down at me with great force. Cold fingers ran up my spine: I remembered this incident from a long time ago; it had happened before. It was Deyjhavoo. I knew what would happen next. Just then Rebecca pushed me and the ball dashed inches away from my head and sank into the wet sand. One of the boys yelled out to us and, muttering, Rebecca picked up the ball and threw it across.

High tide had now set in; waves licked at our feet and bits of paper, plastic, flowers, floated around us. Rebecca walked further into the sea. The waves thrashed against her groin, sprayed all over her chest and fondled her face. Her frock was wet, her face oiled with seasalt and sweat. She called out to me but I didn't go to her; I was afraid. The muezzin's voice could be heard over a loudspeaker from the old mosque. It wailed into the moist atmosphere – la ilaha ila allah. Not far away, the bells in the Shiva temple clanged. Fifteen minutes late. To make up for lost time, the devotees chanted in one seamless voice:

ShivaShivaShivaShiva...Church bells pealed, quietly, softly. And through the clamour for the Gods, from a fisherman's boat an old film song played from the radio, *Ajeeb dastan hai yeh, kahan shuru kahan khatam...*

The sky turned orange in the sunset. Wild orange. Red dancing. Yellow dancing. Rebecca called out to me again. As I walked to her the wind made Tara shudder and the salt spray hit my eyes. In the water I stood still, not daring to breathe. Tara was breath-less too. The sand beneath my feet shifted and sifted away. I felt the sea wind slaver. Tara licked the breeze. Rebecca scooped water in both her hands and threw it at my face. She tossed her head back and her body shook as she laughed. I laughed with half my heart. With the other half Tara laughed. I looked around me: the wind, the water, and the trees. They appeared to me to be laughing in chorus.. It was unusual for me – all this laughing. All this joy: green, green, and more green of pure happiness.

OUT! A yell rang out.

I bent down, scooped the water in both my hands and filled my mouth with the brine. Rebecca did the same and hand in hand we spat at the setting sun.

***

We were together all the time, Rebecca and I. The small town gathered us in its arms, shared its inner secrets, its quiet places, its meandering lanes: Gibbs Road, the market, Tommy's Garage, Victoria Dyes factory, Eros Cinema, Good Morning Café, the beach, the fields in between, the lake in the woods, and the hidden cluster of bamboos on its shore that seemed to me like a womb. It was the only town we knew, Rebecca and I, and in our minds we shared a map of it, a coloured atlas that was our very own, in which green-green trees sprang out of the red soil, dwarfing the homes around, and the hills soared into the blue-blue sky ending in mountain peaks, and the rain fell incessantly, flooded the blue-blue sea, and here and there the lush paddy fields went sis-sis in the breeze. And above, the rainbow arched in all the colours of our days. The town had its histories; we had ours. I could not imagine being anywhere else; I could not imagine being with anyone else: only Rebecca.

We were often at Victoria Dyes factory or Tommy's Garage – Doing Something Constructive. Tommy-uncle had put up a new sign: it was midnight blue and it listed in small, neat running-hand letters all that was done at the garage:

dry wet servicing
car repair
painting
polishing
remodelling
bodywork
car interiors.
Old, imported cars also.

At the bottom of the list of jobs, boldly painted in black and underlined was the quote:

I hear and I forget. I see and I remember. I do and I understand.

Tommy-uncle was tall, with a great hooked nose like an eagle and an incredible moustache. He looked frightening but he was a kind man. He kindly let us watch the workers as they ripped a car apart. The skin and bones of the dismantled car lay in heaps: foamheap, leatherheap, clothheap, metalheap and partsheap. At the back of the garage Rebecca made wire flowers. I assembled metal junk and learned to weld and fabricate. I made a small brown lizard, its limbs three-quarters of its body, its tail twice its length. I painted it green and showed Tommy-uncle the green lizard.

'Jolly good!' Tommy-uncle said, scrutinising the reptile with lizard eyes. 'But not the right proportions.' Then he launched into a discourse on the Golden Ratio – the magic rectangle of Pure Proportions. 'Remember everything fits into a pattern,' he said. 'The arrangement of branches, veins in leaves, skeletons of animals, patterns on shells, the geometry of crystals, human structure and perhaps even thought. And the Golden Ratio is the pattern. It is Universal Religion.' He pointed a finger to the sky. 'In fact it is the only religion.'

'Who is its God?' I asked.

'It has no God,' Tommy-uncle said seriously. 'But it has a bible, a tool. The Great Divider.' Tommy-uncle helped me build the Great Divider: two tiny metal strips secured at the top with a small bolt and nut. I used the divider as a measuring device, because Tommy-uncle told me the most important principle:

Everything in life is Proportional.

So with the Great Divider I made animal sculptures in Pure Proportions, making all the parts first and then assembling it into a whole. I made small animals, a crab, a crocodile, a tortoise, and a large beetle with green button eyes. Rebecca liked the beetle the most, because its little green eyes were the best. She gave me a large rose made of copper wires and petals of pink upholstery. They were our keepsakes, the rose and the beetle, hers for me, mine for her. Forever.

At the Victoria Dyes factory Vishnu-thatha taught us all about dyeing. Soon we learnt to extract the dye pigment from plant fibre and wheat husk. We mixed crushed limestone, ash and toddy with it in a large vat to make a liquid dye. After a week when the dye had fermented, we soaked squares of cloth in the dye twenty times to deepen the colour. We dried the dyed cloth in the room with the skylight so that the dye impregnated the fabric and deepened in its veins. The walls of the room were stained with indigo. I called it the Blue Room. The room smelled moist, woody and strangely tart. Endless yards of cloth were hung from the roof to get rid of the folds and creases. Light from a glass tile above shone on the dyed cloth and gave the room an ethereal feel. I sat in it and dreamed of floating in the blue sky.

Amma came into the blue room one afternoon. She picked up a length of chiffon from the stacks and stepping up to Rebecca she wrapped it around her, round and round, until she was cocooned from neck to toe. Then she held the end of the cloth and spun Rebecca around like a top and then hugged her. 'My sweet Tara.'

'I am not Tara,' Rebecca said.

'You are Tara,' Amma said, her eyes gleaming. 'And I am your Amma.'

'You are not my mother,' Rebecca retorted. 'My mother is dead.' She pushed Amma with such force that Amma stumbled and fell. 'Look what you made me do,' Rebecca said and ran out of the room and out of the gates. She ran rather fast and I could catch up with her only close to Novelty Store. I held her hand. I could feel our breathlessness on my palm.

'Why does your mother call me Tara?' Rebecca asked, close to tears. 'And she's not my mother. My mother is dead.' She made a crazy face: eyes large and rounded, her mouth twisted. She looked scary. 'You mother's crazy,' Rebecca said.

'She's not crazy,' I said. 'She's just sad.'

***

It was a hot afternoon. We were by the lake, dangling our legs in the water. Rebecca threw stones into it, as far as she could. All of a sudden she shed her skirt and blouse and dived into the water. She swam across and in a circle, then back to where I was, and grabbing my feet she pulled me in the water. My shorts swelled like a gas balloon. Tara spluttered in my head. She swallowed more water, more water, and then she screamed. Rebecca held my arms and hauled me up to the shore. I scrambled out of the water and ran to the chakka tree, crouching under it. There had been a strong wind through the night and the ground under the tree was covered with leaves. The earth smelled odd – a mixed up stormsmell: the ground smelled nutty and the leaves smelled of flowers. The dead insects stank; a bitter smell.

Rebecca put her clothes on and came to me. 'I didn't know you couldn't swim.'

'I am scared of water,' Tara whispered in my ear.

Rebecca pushed me down on the ground, and then lay down close to me. She crossed her legs, and with her hands behind her head she looked through the leaves at the blazing sun. 'Daddy says if I study hard and do well at school he will send me to LA,' she said.

'You are going to LA?'

'That's where all the rich and famous people live. Granny says I have a good voice. I will study music and become rich and famous too.'

'I will become a scientist like Appa,' I said, 'and work at the Georgie Gibbs Institute.'

'No. You should come to LA. You could become famous too. Then we'll get married and have children. And we'll play the piggy game with them.'

'What piggy game?'

'Rebecca sat up and took my hand in hers. The she bent each finger and said:

One piggy went to market.

One piggy stayed at home.

One piggy had roast beef.

One piggy had none.

And one piggy ran all the way home.

She scrambled her fingers over my arm and tickled my armpit. I giggled. Tara giggled a lot. Rebecca started the piggy thing again and I stopped mid-giggle.

'Will it cost a lot to go to LA?' I asked.

'Daddy will give me money,' Rebecca said. 'And when I become famous and make lots of money I can get you there.'

'Promise?'

'Promise.'

'Cross your heart and hope to die?'

'Cross my heart.'

All Good Things Must Come To An End – This was Sister Phyllis' favourite proverb. She was pessimistic. She was somebody who always expected the worst to happen in every situation. For many, it didn't; for me, invariably it did, as it did now by pure happenstance. Happenstance was a new word I had learnt. It was a sandwich word, two words stuck together: happening+circumstance = Happenstance. I liked sandwich words. Now by happenstance Amma stood looking down at us bringing an End to All Good Things.

'Rose-aunty told me I would find you here.' She held Rebecca's arm and pulled her up. Rebecca tried to free her arm but Amma held on to it, tightly. 'You hair is all wet, Tara.'

'Letgo,' Rebecca said. 'I am not Tara. Let. Me. Go.'

With a compelling look in her eyes Amma put her arms around Rebecca and held her as though she would never let her go. Never let Tara go.

I stood up. I held my breath, pressed a hand on my heart to stop its loud beating. I doodled a crazy head in my headbook. I gave it big red eyes, a crooked mouth. I scribbled wiry hair all over the head. I drew a heart fluttering out of the body and into the air. And arms flapping like wings, and flying away.

15

Summer flapped its wings and flew away, and then another, not very different from the previous one. But there was one noticeable difference: at school the girls clung together; some sort of exceptional glue cemented them to each other. They giggled and laughed and spoke in whispers. They did not mix with the boys as casually as they did before, though they couldn't stop talking about them. They talked about each one incessantly. Mostly they talked about Cyril Ricardo. He was the headboy. He was handsome. Tara liked him a lot. I was with the girls most of the time; they didn't mind me. They shared their secrets with me. I was thrilled by their friendship and trust. But later on, it occurred to me that their ready acceptance was probably because my presence didn't bother them. I was not dissimilar. I was almost like them.

Although the older girls were rapidly turning into little women: they had grown dumplings of flesh on their chest, which they flaunted like trophies. They began to sprout hair on their arms, legs and in their armpits. Their cheeks and foreheads were oily and broke out in a crop of pimples and whiteheads now and then. The boys too were changing: soft coconut fuzz lined their upper lips and their cheeks. But at eleven I remained as I was before. No breasts, no pimples, no fuzz. Of the pimples and fuzz I didn't care, but Tara was very curious about breasts.

What are breasts made of?

Flesh I think.

All flesh?

Maybe they're hollow bags filled with air. Like a gas balloon. Or filled with liquid.

How'd they feel?
I don't know.
Are there bones in them?
I don't know.

We would soon find out. It was raining hard that day though it was not even the monsoon season. Rebecca and I were drenched when we returned to her house from school. Rose-aunty was on the veranda. 'You are all wet,' she exclaimed when she saw us. 'Becky, go up to your room and change your clothes at once. And Siva, you go and dry yourself with a towel. Or you will catch a cold. And when it stops raining, you had better go home.'

We ran into the house and raced up the steps to Rebecca's room. She peeled off her wet clothes and stood by the cupboard, almost naked. I stared at the pink bra she had on and felt my own flat chest with my hand. Tara's hand touched mine. In a quick movement, Rebecca shed her bra and panties on the floor and faced me. The spread of her hips was different from mine, rounded and shaped like a large peepal leaf. Tara guided my eyes upwards from the fuzz-lined plump triangle above the thighs, over the soft pucker of the belly around the navel, past the broomsticks of the ribcage to soft mounds peaked with nipples. Now I walked to Rebecca in a haze, my footsteps echoing Tara's heartbeat: thud-thud-thud. With a nervous finger I poked at Rebecca's breast. It felt soft and firm, like a juicy fruit – a ripe mango. Clasping my hand Rebecca pressed it to her breast. Tara curled her fingers around it and squeezed hard. No bones. No air or liquid. Just flesh. Tara's heart throbbed in my chest.

Rebecca bent down and kissed my cheek. 'Loveyou,' she said breathlessly. Then she turned around, took fresh clothes out from the cupboard and started to put them on. When her back was turned Tara picked up the discarded bra lying on the floor and stuffed it into my bag. I darted down the stairs, and then ran all the way home. It was still raining.

Behind locked doors, in my room I got rid of my wet clothes and stood before the mirror, Rebecca's bra clutched in my hand. I pressed it against my cheek; it smelled of moist husk. I felt Tara's heart beating hard. She wrapped the bra around my chest and clasped the hooks in front, then she turned the bra around and slid my arms into the straps. The bra hung on my shoulders like a pair of collapsible tents. I bent closer to the mirror and peered at my face, as though I was examining an exotic insect. A few strands of wet hair hung down over my forehead, sticking to the skin. Then puckering my lips I kissed my reflection in the mirror. 'Loveyou,' I said.

***

Tara was all over my body and mind. I felt I was doubled and halved at the same time. I was deeply confused because of this. A large portion of my confusion was simply because of not knowing precisely why I was confused. An incident was waiting to happen that would only make me feel worse. It happened at school. I was in the girls' room with Rebecca and her friend Radha. The girls were going to a movie and to Good Morning Café. I wanted to go with them.

'Only girls,' Radha said firmly as she changed out of the uniform and into a frock.

Rebecca pulled out a frock and a pink pouch from her bag. She dressed me in the frock and fastened the red belt tightly around my waist. She tied my hair into a ponytail with the red ribbon from her hair. From the pink pouch she plucked eyeliner, rouge and lipstick. She brushed two rounds of rouge on my cheeks, lined my eyes with the liner and put lipstick on my lips. 'Now you're a girl,' she said laughing.

Sister Mary Edwards, who was passing by, peeped into the room. She froze. She was the Head of the Secondary Section. She had a long, straight nose, which made her look severe. She was a severe Catholic. She chewed on her lower lip indecisively, and then making up her mind she rushed in and picked up my uniform from the floor. 'Pick up your bag, Siva. At once!' Yanking my arm Sister dragged me out and down the corridor. The boys whistled and laughed. Sister pushed me into her room, sat behind her desk and looked at me with scorn. 'What were you doing with those uncouth girls? Explain!'

I looked away and saw Rebecca and Radha by the door. Cyril stood behind them.

'Look at me when I am talking to you!' Sister Mary Edwards shouted, and she went to the door and shut it.

I looked up at the statue of Jesus Christ nailed to the cross on the wall. The plaster of Paris figurine was naked except for a bit of cloth around his groin and the headdress of thorns. He seemed sad and weak compared to Patti's Gods. He should eat more eggs, I thought. Dr Kuruvilla would have made Him eat 'More Eggs' had Father Joseph consulted him. I sent a silent prayer to weak Jesus nevertheless. *Amen.*

While I was preoccupied with Jesus and the terrible state of his affairs, I didn't notice Sister walk towards me, until I felt the steel ruler on my back. Once, twice, three times. She yanked me by my arm so I faced her. She used her morning assembly voice: 'Do you not know what will happen when you die? The devil will make you remember all the sins you have committed in your whole life. He will make sure you don't go to heaven. And if you don't want to go to Hell you must pray to our Virgin Mary for your sins. Now repeat after me.'

Sister joined her hands.

'Hail Mary, full of grace.'

Hail Mary, full of grace

'Our Lord is with thee.'

Avur lord is with thee.

'Blessed art thou among women, and blessed is the fruit of thy womb, Jesus.'

Blessed art thou...

Unwittingly, a shrill laughter arose from the pit of my stomach and resonated in my ears. Tears streamed down my face. Laughter and tears -- like the sun shining in the rain.

'Holy Mary, Mother of God, pray for us sinners...

'Amen.'

Amen.

Sister looked into a register. 'I am going to call your father. Until he comes to fetch you,' she pointed to the storeroom door on her left, 'get in there, stand in the corner and say your Hail Marys.' She smacked her hands. 'Go!'

The storeroom was tiny with a large steel almirah in it. On one wall were wooden shelves stacked with notebooks, textbooks and stationery. On another wall was a picture of Mother Mary in a white dress, the sun shining behind Her head. With both Her hands she pointed to the glowing heart in the centre of Her chest. I knew this much, for people the heart was to the left side. If the heart was in the centre, I decided then, It must be God. Next to Mother Mary's picture was one of Joseph holding Baby Jesus. Joseph didn't have a glowing heart or the sun behind his head, and he hadn't shaved. The photoframe perched on a small table by the corner had another picture of Baby Jesus in Mother Mary's arms. This time Mary was dressed like a Superman Queen: blue gown and a red cape, a crown on Her head. Baby Jesus was dressed as a pure-white saint. He had a crown on His head too. He was plump. I imagined Mother Mary carrying Fat Baby Jesus in Her arms, zipping through the sky, Her red cape flying. In front of the photograph was a picture book: Ring O' Roses Nursery Rhymes. A notepaper stuck out of it; it had these words in Sister Mary Edwards' slanting rounded handwriting:

Goosey, Goosey Gander is a nursery rhyme with a historical undertone rooted in religious intolerance.

'Are you saying your Hail Marys?' Sister's voice rang out.

'Yes Sister,' I shouted back. With my hands joined and my eyes closed I muttered:

Goosey goosey gander,

Where does thou wander,
Upstairs and downstairs,
And in my lady's chamber.
There I met an old man
Who wouldn't say his prayers.
I took him by the left leg
And threw him down the stairs.

'Siva is a brilliant boy,' Sister Mary Edwards said to Appa seated in front of her.

'Is this about donations?' he asked. The last time parents had been called to school it was for a fund-raising drive to build a small auditorium, which could be let out for weddings to raise more money.

'Oh no, but donations always help, sir.' Sister looked under a stack of books on her table and retrieved the receipt book. She filled it out. 'How much, sir?'

Appa took two hundred-rupee notes and gave them to Sister.

'Thank you very much.' She put the money in an old biscuit tin, and then said, 'Siva is really a brilliant boy...'

Appa looked at his wristwatch to emphasise that he was a busy man. 'Is this about clothes for the poor?' Only a week ago I had given Appa a flier requesting old clothes.

'No, no, no.' Sister shook her head. 'We have been able to collect a large quantity of old clothes and we have distributed them to poor Christian families in the neighbouring villages. As I was saying...'

'Yes, I know,' Appa said, 'Siva is a bright boy.'

'That's right. A bright boy,' Sister Mary Edwards repeated. 'And I have no complaints about his schoolwork.' Sister leaned forward and whispered in a conspiratorial tone. 'I don't know sir, if you Hindus believe in sin or not. We Christians believe in Heaven and Hell. We believe in the devil and sin.'

Appa looked at her in silence. Then he said, 'I am a man of science. God and science cannot coexist.'

'Oh my Lord Jesus!' Sister inscribed a cross upon her chest. 'You are an atheist, a non-believer? Are you not afraid?'

'Gods are for those who are afraid.'

'That's rubbish, sir. We believe in our Lord Jesus because we love Him and He loves us back.' Sister put on an expression of disgust and betrayal. 'Do you mean to say that your wife and son don't pray?'

'Oh yes they pray.' Appa said looking out of the window. 'You need to acquire a level of intelligence to abandon Gods from your mind. Let me say, they haven't arrived there yet.' Appa turned his head and stole a glance at Sister Mary Edwards and asked with a melancholic smile, 'Why did you want to see me?'

Sister responded with a menacing edge to her voice. 'Because your son has abused our Lord Jesus. He has sinned.'

'Sinned?' Appa's eyebrows shot up. 'How? What has he done?'

'It's terrible, sir. I have reprimanded Siva many times. I have told him he should be with the boys, playing cricket, cycling and all that. He spends too much time with the girls. Particularly that Rebecca. She is a wayward, motherless child and I think she's a very bad influence on Siva.'

'I don't see anything wrong with her,' Appa said. 'And she is Siva's friend.'

'But she's not a decent girl.'

'I don't understand. What has she done?'

A foul look came on Sister Mary Edwards' face. 'It's horrible. See for yourself.' Sister clapped her hands. 'Siva, come out, your father is here.'

I stepped out into the room. Appa's eyebrows arched and his eyes widened, a nerve twitched on his temple. Creases of a smirk showed on his face. He then opened his mouth in an unrestrained laugh. 'I thought it was something serious.'

'It is serious. Very serious and it's no laughing matter, sir. And it is that Rebecca who dressed him like this. I am telling you, that girl is no good.' Sister's face was stern. 'Look at him, sir. See your son. Look at him. See him.'

'I see him.' Appa said chuckling.

'What do you see?'

'What do I see?' Appa's eyebrows knit together; on his face was a scowl of annoyance. 'I see Siva.'

'See, that's your trouble, sir.' Sister thumped the desk with her hand to prove her point. 'That's not who you see.'

'I don't? Who do I see then?' Appa's face turned from amused to serious. Sister clasped her hands in front of her chest and looked at Appa condescendingly. 'You see Jesus, sir. That face does not belong to your son, it belongs to our Lord Jesus. How can Jesus wear cosmetics? And if he does then His face will become a lie. And Jesus does not want it like that. Remember, Jesus is watching all of us. You may not believe in Jesus, but for Him you are His son and He believes in you.' She used her Punishment voice. 'Your son should be what Jesus made him. A boy. This is what Jesus wants him to be.' She held out the uniform. 'Siva, change into these, clean your face and then you can go home with your father.' She raised her forefinger and shook it. 'Now don't forget to say your Hail Marys for a whole week.' Turning to Appa she added, 'You should have his hair cut, sir. Look how long it is.'

In the car Appa burst out laughing. Then he gave me a playful wink. 'Did you hear what the teacher said, Siva? She said you are brilliant. Very good, son, I am proud of you.' He turned his head and looked at me. 'But let us give her the benefit of doubt. She may be right you know. You should play with the boys, not girls. Don't be with that Rebecca all the time, kanna. Did you not hear what your teacher said? You should be with boys, play cricket, football, and bicycle... do something more constructive.' He leant across, put his arm around me and pulled me closer and kissed my head. 'Tell you what. We'll get up early in the morning and go to the beach, you and me. We will play cricket.'

'Promise?'

'But you must promise not to spend all your time with that Rebecca. Don't ask her to come home and you don't go to her house. Promise?'

At school when we made promises we crossed our chest and said aloud, Cross my Heart and Hope to Die. This sealed the promise but without saying it the promise remained open and could be broken.

'I promise,' I said and did not cross my chest.

Appa couldn't keep his promise, however. He had an urgent phone call that evening and he left early the next morning. I didn't have to keep my promise to him. It was unsealed. That night I went to Appa's study and took down the big fat dictionary. Whenever you don't understand a word, look into this book, Appa had said, you can also find the roots of words here. I called it Wordtree. I imagined words growing into a big tree, its roots digging deep into the earth. I wanted to know more about sin. But first I needed to know more about God. They went together God and Sin. I looked up – *God*.

God is the indescribable, uncreated, self-existent, eternal, all-knowing source of all reality and being.

I looked up each of the words and simplified the definition:

indescribable – God had no characteristics
uncreated – God was not born
self-existent – God was alone
eternal – God didn't die
all-knowing – God didn't need to study
source – God was the beginning
reality – God was real
being – God was a living thing

God was a real living thing with no characteristics as He was not born and He was alone since He didn't die and He didn't need to study because He was only at the beginning.

God didn't make sense to me. I looked up the word *sin* and its roots. Sin came from Old English *synn*. The word's older root was *es*, which meant *to be*. *Esse* also meant guilty in Latin. The oldest root meaning of sin was: *it is true*. Sin in the New Testament meant: *to miss the mark*.

So I had missed the mark. How?

***

Patti had got to know about Appa's visit to my school. 'Why did your teacher call Appa?'

'I don't know.'

'Tell me, what did you do?'

'I don't know, Patti.'

'Don't lie. I will give you a slap and the truth will come out of your stomach.'

'I missed the mark.'

'Mark? What mark? Did you fail?'

'No. Teacher said I was a clever boy but I had missed the mark.'

'How?'

'Because I sinned.'

'What did you do now?'

'Nothing.'

'Don't lie to me now. I will hit you so hard the truth will come out of your mouth.'

'You said stomach before, Patti.'

Patti whacked my head. 'Now tell me the truth.'

'I made Jesus angry.'

Patti snorted. 'Jesus has no right to be angry with you. You are a Hindu.' Patti frowned. 'But why was Jesus angry with you eh?'

'Because I wore Rebecca's frock.'

Patti laughed. 'What's wrong with that eh? Our Lord Krishna wears women's clothes sometimes. Nothing wrong. And our Lord Shiva is half man and half woman – ardhanarishvara.' She stood with her hands on her hips. 'Next time ask your teacher to call me and not your father. Then I will teach her one or two things about our Gods.'

'So I don't have to say Hail Marys?'

'No Hails and no Mary's. Our Gods are not as old-fashioned as Jesus. They are very modern.'

16

Jesus was not just old-fashioned but older than all the Gods. I learnt this from Fernandez Sir when he had come to school for the Exceptional Class. This special class was introduced a year ago when the government banned compulsory catechism classes for non-Christians, who were now required to attend the Exceptional Classes compulsorily. Fernandez Sir was tall and thin as a reed and his beard was long; he looked somewhat like a younger brother of Mr Moses, except he wore a suit. He was called Suit-n-Boot Moses. He came every few months to talk to us about the Exceptional things in science and religion. And for him religion always won since science couldn't explain everything. This time Suit-n-Boot Moses talked to us about the Big Bang.

According to him, in 1927, someone called Georges Henri Joseph Ed-ou-ard Le-mai-tre set out the theory of the Big Bang. All matter in the universe was pushed into a tiny dot, he said. This dot spun faster and faster and faster and then Bang, it exploded. Little parts of it flew into space – these became the universe. Suit-n-Boot Moses asked questions to Georges Henri Joseph, as if he was there: where did the matter come from? How did it become a dot? What made it spin? What made it explode? Of course there were no answers to these questions, Suit-n-Boot Moses told us. The Big Bang was not the absolute answer for creation. It only distracted people from the larger picture of the Creator, Jesus Christ. Christ created everything in the beginning. He gave different kinds of physical senses to all living things. The best sense was spirit, which Jesus gave only to humankind. Because of this man had the ability to reason.

Then Jesus wound up the universe like a big clock, so it started working: Tick-Tock Tick-Tock. But because of man's lack of reason, because of his sins, the universe stopped ticktocking properly. Everything in it was growing old, going slow and wearing out. Jesus said: "Heaven and earth shall pass away." Matthew 24:35...

I wasn't paying attention to what Suit-n-Boot Moses said or what Matthew had said in 24:35 or worrying about how matter became a dot, started spinning and then exploded; or about the ticktocking universe. I tried to reason a more important matter: why hadn't Rebecca come to school?

***

Rebecca had pulled her knees up to her chin and resembled a lying-down apostrophe. 'Why didn't you come to school?'

'Granny told me not to go,' Rebecca said. 'And your mother said the same thing when she came here yesterday. She went to the market and got me a saree. My. First. Saree. Candy pink, so pretty. And your mother made me wear it. She fixed flowers in my hair, a pottu on my forehead and she made me wear glass bangles on my wrist. She said. I. Was. A. Big. Girl. Now.'

'Why?'

'Because I got my periods, silly.' She stuck her hand between her legs, 'Every month blood will come from here. Because of hormones.'

'Hor-Moans?'

'Yes. Granny said they're telephone lines between our organs and cells. They carry messages from one to the other and tell them what to do.'

'When will I get it?'

'Get what?'

'Periods.'

'Only. Girls. Get. It.'

'Only girls have Hor-Moans?'

'Maybe.' She made a face. Then Rebecca leapt out of bed. 'I will show you something I found in Daddy's cupboard,' she said. 'It's a secret. Don't tell anyone.'

I liked secrets. Secrets brought its sharers closer. So I crossed my chest and hoped to die. Rebecca lifted down a book from the shelf and from its pages she produced a photograph of a woman with golden hair, light blue eyes, and skin so white.

'Who is she?'

'She's American, I think. She must live in LA. She must be rich and famous. I think Daddy's having an affair with her.'

'Affair?'

'It's what divorceless married people have when they reach midlife.'

'When they reach what?'

'Midlife. About 40.'

'Your father is 40?'

'He reached his midlife two years early.'

'So what happens in an affair?'

'Love. Happens. Lotsandlots of forbidden love.'

'What happens in love?'

'Granny says when you're in love your head feels light and you can't think straight. Your heart trembles. You feel as if there are butterflies in your stomach. And your fingers and toes tingle and your eyes go zzzinnng.'

'Zzzzinnng?'

'Yes, zzzinnng.'

'But how do you know your father is having an affair?'

'He keeps disappearing.'

'Is he going to disappear forever?'

'Coursenot, silly. An affair is only a temporary bliss, Granny said. It doesn't last.'

'What are you doing out of bed, Becky?' Rose-aunty stood at the door. 'Go home, Siva. Rebecca must rest now.'

I didn't go home. Something disturbed me; I didn't know what it was. I walked through the woods. I looked up at the palm trees that waved their fronds in the wind; and the big fat trees that spread their arms on and on; and the flowering trees that smelled nice and the fruit trees that the birds liked so much, and the leaves that rustled in the breeze and sounded like a little girl in a starched silk skirt, running. Like Tara. I lay under the parijat tree and took the Hobbit storybook out of my schoolbag and began to read it. The Library Miss said I must finish it in a week and re-re-return it. She said this because I had already read it and returned it twice. I liked re-reading Hobbit. I knew it so well that I could read it from the end to its beginning. It was nice to know the end and learn how it all began. Reading forwards was like exhaling: you saw everything before your eyes. Reading backwards was inhaling: you could see all that you wouldn't see. But this was my reasoning. Appa and Sister Mary Edwards had their very own reasons.

Appa said: it's very Froy-dian, reading in reverse. Looking backward helps to uncover the most improbable things at its origin. The excitement of the Why and How is the pure joy of science. And Sister Mary Edwards said: this is how they found out that unlike the Christian God, the God of Islam is not a father. I didn't quite understand either of them but what they said about the improbabilities of origin and fatherlessness of Allah sounded important.

I started re-reading from the point when Bilbo meets Gollum and they play the Riddle-Game. If Bilbo won, Gollum would show him the way out of the underground lake, but if he lost, Gollum would eat Bilbo. After that I would read how Gollum got to the lake in the first place. Sweet flowers fell on the open page I was reading. I watched a row of red ants climb on the page – plump 'i's' with circled dots. They loafed letter to letter, word to word, and between lines, disfiguring words, sentences and punctuation. I dozed off. I woke up with a start when an ant bit my earlobe. I searched my mind for nagging thoughts. Suddenly I knew what it was that had been bothering me, and Tara even more.

Back in my room I took a pair of fresh underwear out from the cupboard and then locked myself in the bathroom. I slashed my finger with Appa's 7 O'Clock razor blade. Ouch-*ouch*! I let the cut bleed and smeared the blood on my underwear and ran up to Amma's room. I held out the stained garment to her. Amma sat up in bed. She stared at me with a mixture of alarm and excitement. Then a wild look entered her eyes. She seemed as though she had gone crazy. For a moment I thought she was going to hit me. Then as though in a dream, Amma pulled me into her arms and kissed my cheeks. Then she got out of bed, pulled an old trunk from underneath it. She looked through the silk sarees she had stored in the trunk and lifted out the cinnamon-brown silk saree with peacocks and parrots. She draped it around me. She combed my hair, gathered it into a ponytail. Then she plucked the string of flowers from her hair and pinned it in my hair. She lined my eyes with kohl and on my forehead she smeared red pottu. 'Oh Tara,' Amma said drawing me back into her arms. 'You are a big girl now.

I put my finger on the top of her forehead, then slowly ran it over the ridge of her nose, down its tip, over the lips, the chin and all the way down the neck to the hollow under it. Then Tara curled my finger into the dip. It was a temporary bliss, I knew, and it wouldn't last. It didn't last. It was more shortlived than Temporary. I heard Patti call out to me, and a few minutes later I heard rather heavy footsteps on the stairs. That was not Patti. Who was it? Appa stood at the door. What was he doing here? He was on a tour and not expected back until the day after. I gaped at Appa's face and registered the three capital O's. OOO. Appa ground his teeth, the muscle of his jaw twitched. It required no more than two long strides for Appa to be standing next to me. He pulled the string of flowers from my hair. With his thumb he wiped the pottu from my forehead. The colour stained his thumb and Appa rubbed it on his shirt as though it was infected with some incurable disease.

Amma grabbed Appa's arm in a swift movement of her hand and pressed it to his chest. For her size, she displayed substantial strength. 'Leave my child alone,' Amma said. 'Please leave her alone. Tara's got her periods. She is a big girl now."

Appa stood motionless for a minute as though he had been stung. It was as though a dam had burst within him. He held Amma by her shoulders and shook her as Patti would a pickle jar. Then he gave her his Bracket-look. With sadness in his eyes Appa raised his hand, stroked Amma's hair. 'Tara died, Mallika. Look at him, he's Siva, not Tara.'

I wanted to tell Appa that Tara was not dead. She was one half of me. But Appa walked out of the door, and rushed down the stairs. The floorboards of Victoria Villa heaved and creaked under his feet.

17

Victoria Villa was full of old stuff. Appa did not permit Patti to throw away any of the old books, magazines or other odd things. They don't belong to us, he would say, they belong to the house. They belong to George Gibbs. But Patti was distrustful of other people's old things. So now and then, whenever Appa was travelling Patti set out to clean the rooms. She garnered the support of Mani and chucked away old things, which according to her were not useful: Georgie Gibbs was dead after all. She would warn Mani not to breathe a word about the undertaking and he readily consented to her bidding. He was excited by the secrecy and sneakiness of it all. I was rather glad whenever Patti took on this task, as there was always something or other I found that had belonged to Georgie, or at least I assumed they had, and they were my keepsakes. The last time Patti had cleaned up Appa's study I had found an old tobacco tin and a small metal box.

Appa had left on a tour only that morning and when I returned from school I found magazines, newspapers and old books strewn in the hall outside the storeroom. Patti stood at the doorway brandishing a broom. Mani heaped rat poison on bits of paper and set it here and there in the storeroom. A family of mice had made their home in it and had gnawed away at the sacks of rice. Patti didn't like this. Patti didn't like mice at all.

I looked through the old things. I found an old pen-stand, which I set aside. I was sure it belonged to Georgie. I noticed a big ledger on the heap of old magazines. Its red spine was torn; only a part of it remained. I opened the cover carefully. On the first page were the words:

George Gibbs.
Victoria Villa
23 Gibbs Road
Machilipatnam

'Stop messing around, kanna,' Patti said.

I pressed the book to my chest. 'It belonged to Georgie Gibbs.'

'Put it down. You shouldn't keep other people's things,' Patti said. 'They store old memories, and they will seep into you and make you live their lives. Go up to your room. Go now!'

Clutching the ledger and the pen-stand I ran up the stairs. I set the pen stand on the desk, next to the toy hen, old tin, and the box and stones. Then I sat on the bed with the old ledger. It fell open on a page:

My memory is like an ant that halts at every obstruction and meanders down a less difficult path. I would never have been able to arrange time in a sequence of events since I was so much a part of it, and because I have no clear remembrance of the shape and continuation of my days. These are, therefore, nothing more than random fragments of my life.

George Gibbs
Machilipatnam

The pages following this were blank. I opened a page in the middle of the ledger. There was a date on top: June 1851 – August 1854. I read on...

The Victoria Dyes factory sweated and swelled in the heat. Inside its ovenlike womb I inspected the bales of silk, each with a tag: Kalamkari on silk – Tree of Life. Just then I heard voices of boys shouting in chorus: cri-cket, cri-cket. I stepped out. The local boys had collected in the open ground near the factory. The cricket bats and stumps were fashioned from branches of the chakka tree and the pitch was prepared by rolling a heavy drum on the ground. I had got the cricket ball all the way from England. It was a bright, sunny day. The boys were excited: the game was on. The batsman and bowler took their positions across the pitch; the fielders were in their assigned places: Short Leg, Mid-wicket, First Slip and so on. Each time the ball was batted, a cry: Six. Four. No ball. Every time the batsman was out, I shouted: How's That! And then the ball bounced off the bat, soared in a wide arc, caught the wind, turned, and hit me hard on my head. With a sour grimace I looked up. Low sullen clouds obscured the colour of the sky. Then the clouds burst. The sky whitened with explosions of electricity, and thunderclaps like gunfire made the air vibrate. The boys ran to the trees. I escaped into the factory.

Dense slanted masses of water slashed down in such quantities that within minutes the parched earth had turned to slush. A plague of geckoes descended upon the inner walls of the factory, and mosquitoes whined around the workers and fed on their blood. Crickets set up a chorus and large rats came squealing out of the shadows. Undeterred by the geckos, rats and mosquitoes, the workers packed the bales of silk in cloth and marked them. After they were done, and the rain had stopped I walked out of the factory, down Gibbs Road to Victoria Villa.

A young woman swept the water off the veranda floor. She was no more than twenty years old at most. She had on a green saree and a yellow blouse, with a string of purple flowers in her hair. The silver anklets that she wore sounded as she moved. Only a week ago Matthew had hired her to replace the old woman who had left. I eyed her speculatively as I walked up the steps. I inquired if she was done with my room. A look of confusion came into her large eyes. She spoke to me in Telugu, which I didn't understand. With a sudden movement she dropped the broom and rushed past me and up the stairs. I followed her. She was standing next to my bed. Then all at once she unwrapped her saree from her body and shed her blouse. She had golden taut skin, a delicate beauty of feature, and a fullness of breast and hip. Her hands covered her crotch. She looked down at her toes.

I stood still, trying to gain control over myself. My heart was beating wildly; my mouth was dry and my palms wet. Then I clapped my hands together to catch her attention, gestured that she should dress once more, and leave. She smiled and wrapped her saree around her body and put on her blouse. I plucked some coins from my trouser pocket and gave them to her. She put them inside her blouse, between her breasts and bending low she touched my feet before she ran out of the room. I went straight to the study cobwebbed with spiders and sat down at the desk. I opened the safe in which I secured, not money or anything precious, but a handsome timepiece, a box of cigars, a bottle of Spanish Sack, some papers of importance, and an old sketchbook I had got in a second-hand shop in the by-lanes of London Docks. I looked through the sketchbook. I gazed voyeuristically at the drawings of nude English women, touching them, scratching them, smelling them. They smelled of Englishness. Or old paper. Or of the spit of all those who had thumbed these pages before me. Loneliness crept into me. I had devised a method to defeat the aloneness.

That night, beneath flashes of lightning, I ran to the woods all the way to the chakka tree by the lake. I shed all my clothes in a great hurry and dived into the water. I swam ferociously until I was spent and then placing my hands on the bank I hauled my body out of the water. I walked to the chakka tree and rubbed my taut body against its trunk. With eyes closed, I clutched the voluptuous fruit in my hands, rubbed my cheek on its porcupine skin. I kissed the clefts in the bark and inhaled its aphrodisiac smell deep into my armpits and groin. I imagined the tree to be imbued with a surfeit of passion; I thrust myself against the tree, slick with sweat and swollen with desire, uttering obscenities in a language the tree couldn't understand. And then I gasped in pleasure. With a sharp stone I marked the tree with a 'GG', as *lovers are wont to do. I then put my clothes on, patted the tree with a co-conspirator's caress and walked away.*

***

At early dawn I stood on the docks looking up at the swarm of people on the East India Company ship's deck. It wasn't easy for the hundreds of people to disembark from a ship that had sailed the rough seas for many months. I watched the moving eddy of people and cargo as they snaked to the shore. Then I saw Elizabeth and called out her name.

Elizabeth turned, and then hastened past the seamen, luggage, agents and sunscorched porters into my waiting arms. I disengaged myself from her embrace to look at her. The gown she had worn was an unflattering shade of brown, much like dried earth. An equally drab cloak was draped around her shoulders. The ginger ringlets that had escaped from under her bonnet were untidy and rather sweaty. She looked terribly pale as compared to the velvety dark-skinned women of the land I had got used to seeing.

Back at Victoria Villa I took Elizabeth for a brief stroll around the garden and then I took her inside. She ran from room to room, exclaiming how wonderful everything looked, how pretty the mirror-frame was, how glad she was to have come, and then she disappeared into my study at the back. She took her bonnet off, and her hair, almost the colour of the local earth, swirled around her shoulders. She surveyed my table burdened with books and a hotchpotch of things: a box of cigars, snuff jars, fountain pens, papers and whatnot. Then she noticed the bale of cinnamon-brown silk with parrots and lotuses that Chotoo had brought home. It was evident from the expression on her face that she liked what she saw. She darted out of the room and up the stairs to continue her inspection of the house. She stopped at the door of a small room which resembled a construction site. She turned to look at me; she was smiling and I smiled back.

'I am building a dressing room here, princess,' I said. 'The backyard privy is not too convenient.'

'Then why did you build it?'

'I didn't think you would come.'

Elizabeth reached up and ruffled my hair. Her blouse fell open to reveal large white breasts. 'Well, I am here.'

'And thank heavens for that! I have ordered a chamber pot, washstand and a portable tin bath. They should arrive when the Company's ship calls at this port.'

'That will take months, Georgie.'

'It's worth the wait, don't you think? Will you stay?'

She leant towards me and kissed me on my cheek. 'I must say, I quite fancy your Victoria Villa,' she said.

***

The cinnamon-brown silk painted with lotuses and parrots had been stitched into a gown with trimmings of silver gauze on the skirt and ribbons that matched at the waist; it fitted Elizabeth very well. She wore it often, more so because I liked her in it, although it was most unsuitable for the local weather, which Elizabeth had not yet become habituated to. It had been five long months since she had arrived in Machilipatnam.

One evening I returned late from the factory and found Elizabeth in tears. I saw the expression on her face. She was as lonely as me. Sniffing loudly she blew her nose. I pulled her up from the chair. Hand in hand we walked out of the house to the lake at the back, as we were accustomed to do now and then when the day had been hot and stifling. The chakka tree cast shadows on the water and its leaves rustled in the light breeze. Elizabeth sat under the tree. A peculiar odour laced the air and she closed her eyes and collapsed on the ground and began to moan. The mushroomy scent of the earth infused with the aphrodisiac smell of the chakka fruit went to my head that night. It seemed to affect the moon, too, as it wandered out of the trees and cast its light on Elizabeth's face. A gust of wind tossed up her ruffled skirt. The moon moved hastily to illuminate her thighs, plump and white and waiting. The wind grew innumerable hands; a pair cupped her breasts, another kneaded her thighs, pressing upward until she parted her legs and the whiff of something quite else tickled my nostrils. I stroked her breasts, the furrows of her flesh, and her body arched in pleasure. When I heard her whisper my name in halfsleep I fell upon her flesh and consumed her. When our lovemaking came to its end, the moon moved away and it was dark all over again.

***

Real terror filled me when Elizabeth swooned in my arms; she was four months pregnant. Her temperature was high and her sweat-covered body shook violently. A glazed look came to her eyes and she withdrew into silence.

I did not know exactly what I should prepare for when Matthew told me that a mysterious sickness had come to many villages. Several people had fallen ill in the town, and some had died. I sent for a doctor from Madras at once. By the time he arrived Elizabeth was worse. She retched all day, her vomit sticky with mucus and blood. Her skin had crinkled like old parchment. Her eyes were wide and childlike with pain and distress, and she shuddered spasmodically with fever. The doctor was afraid Elizabeth's illness was none other than malaria, and was more fearful because she was pregnant and the disease could affect the child. He asked me to feed her well. She was anaemic and needed strength to fight the illness.

I fed her dried fruit, meat, rice and rotis softened in milk. Elizabeth could not eat much anyway, what with the knot of pain in her stomach and her increased weakness. When she looked at me her bulbous eyes failed to recognise me. Tears of fear filled my eyes. I was afraid she was going to die and I would carry the guilt all my life.

Matthew brought an old woman with him one morning. She had a long nose and obsidian eyes, a witchlike face framed in wild hennaed hair. The sun had blackened her skin, and her breasts inside her blouse had gone slack. Between her hands she carried a piece of burlap and piled on it were flat stones she had heated to redness in the fire in the kitchen. She wrapped each stone in a mesh of dried herbs and heaped them around Elizabeth's feet and hands, and on either side of her body. A pungent medicinal aroma rose from the stones. Elizabeth broke into profuse sweat. The old woman leant toward Elizabeth's belly and fixed her ear to it. She shook her head and frowned. Straightening up she retrieved a cloth pouch from inside her blouse. She pulled at the strings and plucked out of it what looked like seeds. With her thumb and forefinger she pressed Elizabeth's jaw so that her mouth fell open, then she pushed the seeds into her mouth. It will be a boy, she said to me, picked up her ragged piece of burlap and set off towards the door. I named my son then and there: John.

Elizabeth opened her very blue eyes and seemed to recognise me; I touched her forehead and found the fever high. For three long weeks Elizabeth was asleep or unconscious, dead silent or delirious. But when she came to, after those weeks, she was as well as ever, her fever gone, the shakes gone, the sweat had evaporated and brightness came back in her eyes. She looked up from her bed, caressed her abdomen and smiled, 'My poor Jane, I hope she's well.'

'It could be John, you know,' I laughed. My relief showed in my smile.

But Jane it was for Elizabeth. She made me get fabric from the factory and had it stitched into frocks of different sizes: Jane – 2 months. Jane – 6 months. Jane – 1 year. Jane – 2 years... And I got baby boy clothes all the way from England. I was sure her Jane was going to be my John.

I had ordered a sackfull of pyrethrum seeds from Africa. They arrived when the next ship called at the port some months later. I had the seeds sown in the fields between Victoria Dyes and Victoria Villa. Soon the patches of land were covered with short feathery plants clinging to the ground. Some of them had white *and yellow flower heads that resembled daisies and emitted a rancid smell. Mosquitoes were drawn to these flowers, but the smell choked the breath out of them.*

I built a shed not far from the Victoria Dyes factory and enrolled jobless workers to work in it. They ground the pyrethrum leaves to paste, its seeds to powders, flowers to essence, and roots to dust. They squeezed the dust and powders into pellets that could be burnt, mixed petroleum jelly with the paste, and soaked the essences in oil. The packets for these creams, powders and pellets were branded with the face of Queen Victoria and called Queens Repellent. They repelled the fiercest of mosquitoes and Queens became a household name in Machilipatnam.

I knew what I had to do. I set out to build a centre for malaria research: George Gibbs Institute.

***

It had been pouring throughout the month, although it wasn't the monsoon season. It was a curst ill fortune, this early rain. Suddenly, in the middle of a sodden April, Elizabeth gave birth to her baby. I breathed comfortably as the midwife lifted my child in my arms. I savoured the smells of the newborn – all milk and honey, and better than that, the pinkness of its skin. I walked to the window. Wild flowers of many colours grew in the garden below and the chakka tree outside rustled in the wind. A slight, delicate chill in the early morning air sharpened the fragrances of flowers and fruit. Somewhere off in the woods at the back a dog barked. I gazed at Gibbs Road skirting the house. This was the road I had walked down for years, troubled and alone. Now I had Elizabeth and the child in my arms. 'John, oh my little John.'

'Jane, it's Jane,' Elizabeth said, her voice weak.

'You are mistaken, Liz,' I said. 'It's John,'

'It's not John, silly, it's Jane,' Elizabeth cried.

'It's John,' I said firmly.

The infant set up a wail. 'Take the child away,' Elizabeth screamed. She refused to nurse her child. She was so distraught, and in the days to come her maternal milk dried up and her nipples cracked like parched earth. I handed little John to a wet nurse. The sight and sound of her pale child slurping at a brown bosom filled Elizabeth with such disgust that she locked herself in the spare room above and rarely ventured out of it except to go to the lake at the back of the house. Here she would sit for hours staring blankly at the water. Then when the moon came out Elizabeth returned home weary and spent. In the following months she became gaunt; she was unwashed and swaddled in filthy clothes. She stank of sweat and tears. Whenever I drew close to her I flinched from her stale breath.

Her eyes flickered redly as she screamed, 'It's your fault, it's all your fault. Now look what you have done.' Then, sobbing, she added, 'Everything has gone wrong for me. Each day feels like years, and there are shadows all around. They follow me.'

I felt helpless. I also felt very tired. I felt annoyed by the situation I had created. I was filled with sudden dread when Elizabeth's tears turned to laughter or her laughter to tears. What I feared most was when she sat still, quiet, inert, gone away in mind: gone out of her mind.

Matthew comforted me. The next day he arrived with a band of keeners; there were five of them. They knelt down in a circle around Elizabeth. They removed their ornaments one by one, and then the flowers in their hair. One of them took in a deep breath, and then she wailed. The others, slapping their chests with their hands and banging their heads on the ground, began to moan. Elizabeth sat in the chair, her hands covering her ears, her eyes vacant. Then she shut her eyes with certain finality.

It was over. OVER.

I suddenly felt that God was not on my side. I chose to forget that I hadn't thought of Him in a while. Now to make amends I prayed to Him feverishly, morning, noon and night. I donated a large sum of money to repair and extend the old Shiva temple. I knew little about the habits of Gods – unaware that ignored they could condemn. The Gods had made up their minds.

Three months later when the East India Company steamship called at Machilipatnam Port, Elizabeth Gibbs, clutching a suitcase, disappeared into the aft compartment of the ship.

I stood on the dock that morning looking up at the sky. It was overcast and resembled an English sky.

I stopped here. I flipped the pages backward and read from the beginning when Georgie comes to Machilipatnam. Was it true what Patti had said: old things store old memories, and they seep into us and make us live others' lives? I shut the ledger; I didn't want to read any more. I didn't want to know what happened to Georgie and his son after Elizabeth left them. I was afraid. So I bundled the ledger in an old cotton towel, round and round, and then put it away in my cupboard so that I would never need to read it again.

18

Rebecca had a secret: she was born in LA, and when she was three her mother left home and filed for divorce. Some months later she ran in front of a car just when the accident was waiting to happen. She died on the spot, divorceless. Rebecca's father returned to Machilipatnam with her because he couldn't bear to live in LA. Wifeless. Divorceless. When I asked Rebecca why her mother and father had wanted to divorce she said they didn't see 'Eye-to-Eye'. I wondered if Appa and Amma would get divorced. They weren't Eye-to-Eye, Ear-to-Ear or Touch-to-Touch.

I looked up *Divorce* in the dictionary. Beside the 'end of a marriage', it also meant:

1. A complete separation or split.

2. To separate or distinguish something from something else.

There was a complete *separation* between Amma and me now. We were totally *split*. So not only could Amma *divorce* Appa, Amma could also *divorce* me. In fact, according to the dictionary, we were already *separate*: I was *something else* for Amma.

Sister Mary Edwards told us that we should learn to get along. She harnessed the support of God to convince us: God helps those who help themselves. Friendliness is Godliness. Love thy neighbour and God shall love thee, and so on. Why did grownups forget to get along? I wished I knew, and then again I was glad I didn't. Being a grownup was complicated. Being Amma was complicated.

The more she turned away from me, the more Tara came to me. She was an older sister after all; she had maternal instincts.

Through summer, monsoon, after-monsoon and before-summer she was my constant companion: we were undivorced, except when Rebecca was around. Then we were separated. Temporarily. I kept them separate in my mind, Rebecca and Tara, concealed in two separate parts of it. Together they wouldn't work; by instinct I knew this. Like Amma and Appa. Rebecca and Tara were my armour, a soothing balm to my confusion, and without them I ceased to function. There was Georgie Gibbs too, hidden in the deepest part of my mind. So I blundered through the days, weeks, of each month knowing they were there for me. Absolutely.

It was summer again. Rebecca met me in the market. The air was awash with the smells of fresh vegetables and fruits, stinking fish, chicken feathers, roasted peanuts and pungent chillies. Flies buzzed over sacks of brown jaggery. Amidst an orchestra of bickering, haggling, shouting, voices sweet and harsh, dogs barked, cats mewed, cows mooed, and rats squeaked as they darted one behind the other through gaps in the walls.

Ranga had opened his shop. He held out a rose to Rebecca. Free-of-Charge. It was a day-old rose. Rebecca took the flower from him and as we walked on she tore the petals off one by one.

'He loves me. He loves me not. He loves me. He loves me not. Helovesme.'

'What are you doing?'

'Finding out whether he'll love me or not,' she said. 'He loves me not. He loves me. He. Loves. Me. Lots. Look, he is going to lovemelots.'

'Who?'

'He.'

'Who's he?'

'The one who'll love me lots.'

Women were complicated.

We stopped at *Mohan's Fruit & Juice* stall sheltered under a large banyan tree. Swami was at the stall as usual, and not far from him Sweetie-Cutie. She moved closer to Mohan and poked her long reddened fingernail into his side. 'I'll have two glasses today. I am so thirsty.' She leaned towards him. Mohan rode his hand over her thigh playfully. Sweetie-Cutie slapped the back of his hand. 'You won't spare a hijra even, will you?' Mohan handed over the two glasses to Sweetie-Cutie. She gave one to Swami. "Now drink this and not another word about Coca Cola,' she said, slapping his head.

Swami drank from his glass in a long swallow and, wiping his lips with the back of his hand, he jerked his head back in appreciation. He looked up at the pigeons drifting in the breeze like fluffs of soiled cotton. By some freak of nature the sky was clouded over; freakish for this was not the monsoon season. Then all at once, without notice, it began to rain. The birds flew up in a flutter and found shelter in the banyan tree. The aberrant rain cloud moved away and the rain stopped as suddenly as it had started. Swami stretched his arms above his head and squeezed the air with his fingers. 'Come on you impotent clouds,' he shouted. 'Rain, you dried up sisterfucker!'

Sweetie-Cutie clapped her hands. 'Come, come. Rain all over our parched red earth and wet me now!'

Rebecca laughed. Sweetie-Cutie turned around and stepped up to her. She surveyed Rebecca from head to toe. 'You're all grownup. How old are you now?'

'Fourteen,' Rebecca said.

Sweetie-Cutie turned to me and asked. 'And you, my princess?'

'Twelve.'

'Letsgo,' Rebecca said.

Eros Cinema was the only theatre in town that screened English films. It had a matinee show on – Alfred Hitchcock's *To Catch a Thief*. Outside the cinema house, Rebecca bought purple berries from the jamun-seller. I looked up at the poster on the wall: Cary Grant kissing Grace Kelly against the backdrop of the French Riviera. I ran a finger over the mouths trying to decide whose lips were which. Rebecca was looking at another poster of Grace Kelly in a short dress. She had blonde hair and light eyes and her lips were painted a dark maroon, almost purple. Rebecca hitched up her skirt to make it shorter, unfastened two buttons of her blouse, and tucked the collar in. She bit a jamun and rubbed its flesh hard on her lips. They turned purple. 'Look, I'm just like Grace Kelly,' she said.

'Beautiful,' a voice said from behind us.

I turned around to see Cyril Ricardo standing by the railing. He was dressed in jeans and a blue shirt. He had faint stubble on his face. He smiled at Rebecca. Her face turned as purple as her lips. Then he smiled at me. Tara smiled back at him.

'Are you going to the film?' Cyril asked.

'I'm going with Siva.' She clutched my hand in hers.

'Fine. I'll get tickets for all of us,' Cyril said.

Inside the hall Cyril sat between Rebecca and me. He whispered to Rebecca all the time and she whispered back. I didn't know what they were whispering about. Tara whispered to Cyril but her whisper came out loud. I put my finger on my lips and said, ssshh. Then Tara moved closer to Cyril, shoulders, arms and thighs almost touching. Cyril turned and ruffled my hair. Tara smiled.

After the film, we went to Pinto's for ice-cream. We stood under a tree and ate the cones. Tara liked ice-cream. But she couldn't eat it fast enough and the cream trickled down my arm. Cyril laughed as I licked my arm clean. Then we darted into Sunrise Studios next door. Bala showed us the three backdrops that he had. Plain white. For passport, he said. Another was of a blue Eiffel Tower in stormy Indian weather. The third one was of a tree with Japanese cherry blossoms and a full moon. It was for lovers, Bala declared with a wink. Bala had special clothes that we could wear. Cyril wore a red shirt and a cowboy hat, Rebecca a saree as blue as the sky. Tara chose a yellow skirt over a red blouse. They were too big for me. Cyril smiled and Tara smiled back at him and filled me with sudden warmth.

Bala handed Cyril a comb and a box of talcum powder. Cyril patted Rebecca's face with the powder and ran the comb through her hair. He twirled a lock of Tara's hair and pressed it behind my ear. Tara looked up at him with shining eyes. Then with his arm around Rebecca's waist and mine, Cyril stood in front of the pink blossoms and the full moon. Three copies. One for Rebecca. One for Cyril. And one for me.

Next to the studio was Glorious Me that, besides cosmetics, sold hair clips and ribbons, bras and panties. It had a show window with a buxom mannequin, its Plaster-of-Paris hair shaped into a bun. Its candypink body was dressed in a pointed bra and flimsy lace panties, and covered with a see-through nylon wrap. Inside the shop, Tara tried out hairclips and ribbons on my hair and glass bangles on my wrists. Out of the corner of my eyes Tara saw Rebecca pick up a tube of lipstick from the Mix-n-Match box and shove it into her pocket. Tara slipped a butterfly hairclip into my pocket. Cyril bought two friendship rings. He slipped one onto Rebecca's finger and the other onto his own. I felt a constriction in my throat and I wondered what it was all about. Inside my chest Tara's heart beat wild. Just then there was a screeching of tyres and a scream from the road and we rushed outside. A taxi had hit Swami, and he had fallen on the road. A mob had collected around him. It watched as Sweetie-Cutie pulled Swami up. There was a bruise on his arm and a gash on his forehead. 'It's a miracle,' she said, 'he is not hurt much.' The mob watched as Sweetie-Cutie pulled the driver out of the taxi and started to beat him up. She let out a stream of choice expletives, and then she lifted her saree up to her hips and exposed her sexless groin to him. The crowd rapidly receded. Rebecca let out a series of moans. She was shaking.

'I'll walk you home,' Cyril said.

Rose-aunty was on the veranda. 'Hello Cyril,' she said. 'How is your mother?' Then turning to me, she asked, 'How is your grandmother, Siva?'

'There was an accident in the market,' Rebecca said.

'Much better aunty,' Cyril said.

'Patti's okay,' I said.

'A taxi hit Swami,' Rebecca said.

'But he was not hurt,' Cyril said.

'Not much,' I said.

'It's a miracle,' Rose-aunty said.

'Ma didn't have a miracle,' Rebecca retorted and rushed inside the house.

'Miracles don't happen,' I said following behind her.

'As if you know,' Rebecca said.

I knew. But I didn't shed-light-on-this-matter since Rebecca had darted up the stairs and into her room. When I got to the door Rebecca was standing before the mirror lipsticking her lips.

'I'm Grace Kellying myself,' she said.

Cyril had walked in through the door. He laughed. He ran his fingers through his hair, puffing it up. 'I am Cary Granting myself.'

Then Rebecca played records of Beatles and Cliff Richard. Grace and Cary sang the songs they knew: words of loving and kissing you, tomorrow missing you.

Tara tried to sing-a-long; she didn't have the words. So I hummed the tune. Cary held Grace in his arms and they danced. As I watched them I felt Tara sliding downdowndown inside me. The constriction in my throat grew into a lump. It's all right, I thought. They were only playing Pretend. It wouldn't last. It was only a temporary bliss. Grace and Cary's singing voices rose in the air like smoke. The smoke caressed the walls, the curtains, the paper flowers on the desk, then trembled over the bed, and lay on the rumpled cotton sheet. There it remained soaking up all their singsong tenderness. There was too much of it. Cary sighed and Grace tried to sigh but instead she gulped down a word and it slipped down her throat and lay waiting in her belly, a flitting, a fluttering: a butterfly.

Suddenly Grace leant toward Cary and pressed her lips to his.

I was aghast. 'Why did you do that? Now you'll get pregnant.'

Cary held his stomach and roared with laughter. Grace giggled and her eyes filled up with tears.

'It's true,' I said. 'After a girl gets her periods, it is not safe to kiss.'

'Who told you that?' Grace asked.

'Munniamma.'

'What did she say?'

'She said if a girl kisses a boy, she gets a daughter. And if a boy kisses a girl then a son is born to her. And, and,' I clasped my hands and looked down at them, 'if a brother and sister kiss then she gives birth to a he-she.'

'A he-she?' Cary was laughing. 'Do you mean a hermaphrodite?'

'Her-ma-fra-dite?'

'A child that is both – a girl and a boy together?'

'Yes. Like that Sweetie-Cutie. Munniamma told me this was what happened when a brother did it to his sister.'

Cary said, 'Rubbish! A girl will get pregnant only when a man does that stuff to her.'

'What stuff?'

'You don't know?' Grace asked.

'What parents do?' Cary said.

I was confused. But Tara seemed to understand. She trembled with unknown, unfelt, delight.

'You will know next week in Philipose Sir's class,' Cary said grinning right at Grace.

But she was not looking at him. She had pressed her hands together with the palms facing up and the lines on them aligned. 'My boyfriend will be handsome,' she said.

'And how do you know this?' Cary asked, his eyes twinkling.

'Because I have a deep, curved heart line. That's why,' Grace giggled. 'Had it been flat I would have got an ugly boyfriend.' Then standing on her toes she plucked a hair from Cary's head.

He screamed. 'Stop screaming,' Grace said as she took off the ring from her finger. She tied the hair to the ring and held it over his left palm. 'Be still now,' she said as she watched the ring. It began to circle. 'Ah, you'll have a boy! Now do it for me.'

Cary held the ring over her palm. The ring started to move back and forth. 'I'm going to have a girl,' Grace squealed.

'So we'll have a girl and a boy,' Cary said looking intensely at Rebecca, 'and we will play the Piggy Game with them.'

Rebecca's face went red and she started to giggle. 'You know the Piggy Game?'

'Sure. Mummy played it with me.'

'My mummy too.'

Tara's heart was pounding in my stomach. The lump in my throat had become a hard knot.

I had a crazy dream that night, most wonderful: Cyril, Rebecca and I were on the beach. The sea before us was like a big field with cloud-like frothy flowers. Hand in hand Rebecca and Cyril ran into the blue field of flowery froth. He pulled at her hair and spread it around her shoulders. Clouds began to tumble and roll gently and they drizzled on Rebecca's face. She had rainstars on her skin and hair. The waves lapped at her body and her small breasts under the damp frock were pushed up. A knot of warmth quivered under my chest. Something stirred in me, a feeling I had never felt before: I felt as though the sand below my feet was sucked into my legs, swirled in the pit of my stomach, crashed against the walls of my heart, and then gently poured out from my pores, dribbled out of my fingertips. I spun around like a piece of paper in the wind, then ushered by the breeze, moistened by the seaspray, I ran to Rebecca. Water lashed up my thighs and spray splattered on my face. I licked my saltlaced lips. The colluding breeze blew Rebecca's hair all over her face. Thus veiled, I gathered her in my arms, even as Cyril stood watching us. I clutched her hair in my hand and yanked it back, and then reaching up to her face I kissed her on the lips. Just the way Cary Grant had kissed Grace Kelly in *To Catch a Thief.*

Why did you do that? Cyril said, and I woke up.

I trembled as I lay in bed. I caressed my face and my arms; I rubbed my chest, I stroked my ribs, my hand moved over my belly and beyond. I breathed hard. I felt giddy. Luminous colours swirled in front of my eyes: Zzzzinnng-Zzzzinnng-Zzzzinnng. And deep inside my body I felt the twinge of something. What was it? Was it love? What was love?

***

God is love, Sister Mary Edwards always said. But this was not the kind of love I was concerned with – all holy and so pure. I needed more practical answers. So I asked around. 'Love' could be very 'Questionable.' I gave marks and re-marks to each of their answers.

True Love is the only feeling which is its own cause and its own effect – Appa. (Not clear. 6/10)

Love is the answer to all our questions – Patti. (Not true. 5/10)

You will know love when you find it – Munniamma (Not bad. 7/10).

If you would be loved, love and be lovable – Benjamin Franklin (From a textbook. Nice. 8/10).

The road to self-discovery is paved with Love. (Don't know who said this. Vague. 6/10)

Can't Buy Me Love – The Beatles. (Interesting. 7/10).

All You Need is Love – Ditto. (Ditto)

When you're in love it's the most fantastic two and a half days of your life – Tommy Gonzalves. (only 2 ½ days! 4/10)

Love is a sickness. It eats away at your heart – Vishnu-thatha. (Really? 5/10)

Was love really a sickness? So I decided to ask Dr Kuruvilla. I chose an appropriate time to call on him: midday. The doctor didn't have too many patients then. I told the doctor

I was working on a school project and I needed a scientific explanation. This is what he told me, scientifically:

Love is nature's cunning plan. It is what keeps the human species alive and reproducing. Love happens because of chemicals in the body. Scientifically speaking, it takes up to 4 minutes to decide if you love someone. Love-struck people are affected by three main neurotransmitters: adrenaline, dopamine and serotonin, and two hormones: oxytocin and vasopressin.

Adrenaline: makes you sweat; your heart races, and your mouth goes dry.

Dopamine: increases your energy and helps you go without sleep or food for some lengths of time.

Serotonin: makes the loved-one constantly pop into your thoughts and gives you a rose-tinted view of him/her.

Oxytocin: increases the bond between two people – mother and child, and lovers. Mothers with low oxytocin could reject their own child.

Vasopressin: nourishes a long-term relationship.

Dr Kuruvilla summed up love as an exhilarating roller-coaster ride that could last for a considerable length of time with all the ups-downs, swings and turns, gasps and cries, and a great deal of rattling. 'Banana and dark chocolate are very good for love,' he said.

I drew my own conclusions: Amma had oxytocin deficiency as regards to me, and where Tara was concerned she had an overdose of vasopressin. I had a lot of adrenaline, dopamine and serotonin. I was sick with love.

I should eat bananas.

19

S tudents of class X were abuzz that morning as Philipose Sir was coming to talk to us. Sister Mary Edwards told us that the lesson was about evolution. But Rebecca had told me it was a lesson in You. Know. What.

WHAT?

We were all gathered in the assembly room. Sister ordered the students to close all the windows. 'You are going to be told a secret,' she said in her morning assembly voice, 'so you have to be enclosed.' Then she made the girls sit on one side of the room, and the boys on the other side. She ensured there was a considerable gap between the two sides. 'Today Philipose Sir will tell you the difference between a boy and a girl,' she said with a secret smile.

Philipose Sir was an old man, almost bald; a silver lock of hair flowed like a tidal wave from one side to the other, covering half of his forehead. He was dressed younger, in corduroy trousers and a bright blue T-shirt, to make up for his oldness. He was thin, tall, a deeper shade of brown, almost like burnt coffee. He clasped his hands before him and started: 'When boys and girls get older the season changes in them.' He stared at the floor for a moment, then picking up a chalk from the table he turned around and scribbled on the blackboard: XX and XY. Over XX he scribbled the word Girl enclosed in brackets (GIRL), as though clothed, and over XY, Boy, unbracketed, naked. He faced us once more. 'Who can tell me what a chromosome is? Anybody?'

Only a hush of collective breathing could be heard, like the hush before a secret is told.

'Chrome' means colour,' Philipose Sir said, 'and 'some' means bodies. Chrome + Some means – the colour of bodies. It is really a list of instructions for the reproduction of the body. For example: the colour of hair, eyes, skin, the shape and size of the body and a thousand other characteristics. Chromosomes are found in the centre of all our cells. They are like twisted staircases of D-N-A. DNA is like a workbook. It holds the instructions. Chromosomes come in pairs. Normally, each cell in the human body has 23 pairs of chromosomes. Half come from the mother; the other half comes from the father. Two of the chromosomes, the X and the Y chromosome, determine if you are born a boy or a girl. Girls have XX chromosomes and boys, XY chromosomes. Women's eggs provide the X chromosome. Half of a man's sperm will be carrying the Y chromosome and the other half, the X chromosome. Therefore, it is the father that determines the gender of the child.' Philipose Sir rubbed his hands together. 'Any questions?'

A boy stood up. 'Does the X sperm look different from the Y?' he wriggled his finger through the air and the boys laughed.

Philipose Sir said, 'they look similar, the X and Y sperms, but they are different in other ways. The Y sperms are faster, but tire more easily. The X sperms are heavier and slightly slower players, although they have greater stamina.' He crossed his arms and asked with a conspiratorial smile and a wink, 'Any more questions?'

I stood up. I started to speak but stopped when the boys began to giggle.

'Go on son, don't feel shy,' Philipose Sir said. 'Don't mind the others.'

'What about boy-girl?' I asked. 'What chromo-some do they have?'

'You mean hermaphrodites.' Philipose Sir clasped his hands together. 'Excellent question. Let me explain. In most cases, a person has a XX or XY chromosome but a mixup in the DNA causes abnormal results. Remember every person starts out as a hermaphrodite – the baby has both male and female parts while it is developing. Then depending on the overall chromosomal instructions in the cells one or the other parts are suppressed or cancelled. Then the baby becomes fully a boy or a girl. Sometimes the instructions are not so clear so the baby is then born as a hermaphrodite, a boy-girl.'

Somewhat like the Before After game, or reading Hobbit backwards, Philipose Sir started talking about the Beginning since he had already explained the End. He substituted for the word sex, words like intimate, intercourse, close, passionate, personal, communication, interaction, exchange and so on. He treated the eggs as though they were goals and the sperms were players running in the field. Intercourse was a heated, perspiring, passionate football match and if the players won they got a prize: XX, XY or in mixedup cases, otherwise.

I wasn't listening to all that he said, though. I had something else playing in my mind: in my body I felt like a boy; in my thoughts I felt I was a girl. I was mixedup. God was not responsible for who I was. Amma was not to be blamed for who I was not. It was all Appa's fault.

That night I took down the dictionary from the bookshelf and looked up the word *Hermaphrodite*: An individual having both male and female behavioural characteristics and sexual organs.

Is this who I was? Some sort of a hermaphrodite? A half and half?

***

It was the last week of the summer holidays. Rebecca had not been very well and she had been acting strange, like the other day when her eyes were far away.

'What's wrong,' I asked.

'Everything,' she said, looking away into the miles.

The next day, the day after, the-day-after-after that day, Rebecca was still unwell. Her stomach ached or her head hurt.

Her throat was sore or she was feeling faint. Each day she felt pain in different parts of her body. This is what she told me. Was she really sick? Was she trying to avoid me? I decided to put to use the Benefit of Doubt. Appa had told me about this on the day he had met Sister Mary Edwards. 'It is an important tool,' Appa said. 'For science to make progress we must give others the Benefit of Doubt, and then when you prove them wrong your victory is sweeter.'

I waited a week after giving Rebecca the Benefit of Doubt. During this time I felt dreamy and vague and I couldn't eat. At night I couldn't sleep. I tossed and turned in my bed, rubbing my fists on my chest; something inside it moved and it hurt each time it did. My throat was dry, with no moisture in it. Deep inside me the season had changed. Rebecca's seasons had also changed. I was getting worried about her. I was convinced that she was trying to avoid me. I went to her house each day. She asked me to go away. Or she was not even there. Where was she? Then a few days before school reopened I was surprised to see a cage of lovebirds in Rebecca's balcony, and a vase of red roses.

'Birds should not be caged,' I said. 'They should be flying in the air. You said so.'

'Not these,' Rebecca said.

'Why not?'

'Because Cyril gave them to me.'

The next afternoon I stole some money from the biscuit tin in the prayer room and from Yusuf I bought a glass bowl with a goldfish. On my way to Rebecca's house I stole a sprig of turmeric yellow Bougainvillea from someone's garden.

I found Rebecca in the balcony, huddled in a chair and looking gloomily at her feet. I held out the bowl and flowers to her. 'I got them for you.'

She looked up at me and then at the fishbowl and made a fishface. 'Don't want it.'

I thrust the bowl toward her. 'Take it. Take it.'

Rebecca grabbed the bowl from my hands and crashed it to the floor. 'I told you I don't want it. Look what you made me do.'

The goldfish twitched, gasped, its mouth opening and closing as I watched it die. Then Tara ran across the balcony and set the lovebirds free. She turned around and said, 'Look what you made me do.'

'Go. Away.' That's all Rebecca said. Go. Away. It was the tone in which she said Go. Away. that hurt me. So I went away clutching the branch of Bougainvillea. I ran all the way down the strip of bitumen and turned into the fields. The oilseed plants on either sides squeaked as the branches rubbed against one another. Bushes trembled with life: the flutter of a sleeping bird, zipping dragonflies and the scamper of mice. A large grey rat shot across from one field to another. I ran through the woods, past the bushes to the lake. I walked along the shore to a cluster of bamboo trees and enclosed myself in it, as if in a womb. The bamboo leaves went sis-his in the breeze. The water sloshed against the banks. A hum went off in my head: our wombsong, Tara's and mine.

Wazz wrong?

Everything.

Don' worry, am 'ere.

Go. Away.

Then I lay my head down on a clump of grass, the Bougainvillea next to me, and shut my eyes. I pressed my fist to my heart so it wouldn't move. And there, in the afternoon breeze I fell into a deep sleep. Until I was surprised by noises, voices I recognised and my heart moved again: it fluttered alive and then it sank. A chill spread right through to my chest, arms, legs, right through to my toes. There under the chakka tree, the orange setting sun on them, were Rebecca and Cyril. I looked away at the pond.

I started counting:

2 large lilies ...

1 toad...

Out of the corner of my eye I saw Cyril hold Rebecca's face in both his hands.

2 buds.

2 more toads.

Cyril bent down and kissed her cheeks.

1 more half-bloomed lily.

And 1 toad on a wet leaf.

Cyril put his arms around Rebecca's shoulder.

1 more lily in the corner.

Cyril pressed Rebecca to him.

And 1 more lily.

Then Cyril kissed her head.

And 1 more toad.

And kissed her eyes...

And another 1.

And kissed her forehead. And 1 more time. I lay still, still counting. Then Cyril kissed Rebecca hard on her lips.

14 full-bloomed lilies.

4 half-blooms.

6 buds.

And 7 toads.

Tara felt a fury knotted deep inside; it tasted sour on my tongue. Suddenly the typhoon in Tara's heart raged, the air in my head swelled, and a wail of despair escaped from my mouth. Then Tara felt the pain. I felt a different sort of ache.

***

Rebecca didn't come to school the next day and I was glad. She didn't come all week; I was worried. I tried not to think of her or the way her luminous eyes lit up, as though she held an inconceivable joy inside her. She was always laughing, even when there was no reason to laugh. I longed to touch the two dimples that appeared on her cheek when she smiled. And that earthy whiff about her reminded me of the rains; I longed to inhale her scent. I tried not to think of her.

My heart was pounding, as I thought of that afternoon by the lake when Rebecca had pulled me into the water. I had felt her body crushed against my chest as she had held me, helped me up on the shore. Then as I lay down on the ground she had bent over me, drawn a line with her finger from my brow to the tip of my chin, and then her finger had moved over my cheek, outlined my lips, and she had bent close and kissed me. Her lips were musky, moist, like the earthmusk of first rain. I had remembered this. I remembered this. She had rested her cheek on my chest and heard my heart pounding in her ear. All at once she stood up, scrambled to the chakka tree and with a pointed stone marked its trunk with the letters: R Loves S. I had remembered this. I remembered this.

I had wanted to take pleasure in that moment when she kissed me; I had wanted to live with it each day. But I couldn't, unless Rebecca returned to me. So I had for all these days locked this memory in my heart for safekeeping, trying not to let it escape into my mind. But it did constantly. Then her voice screamed in my head: Go Away. And then I remembered there had been *14 full-bloomed lilies. 4 half-blooms. 6 buds. And 7 toads* that day.

I couldn't stop thinking of Rebecca. I stood opposite her house to stop thinking of her. I went to the lake to our favourite spot to stop thinking of her. Everything seemed different now. The usual noises, the sound of the water, trees, birds, insects, collapsed into one long humming sound, like the wind in a tunnel. When a crow cawed, it did not disrupt silence, it added to it. Sound had a way of being very silent. Even the smell was unfamiliar: the sweet-pungent aroma of the chakka fruit, the sweetlysmelling flowers, they had all gone. Everything smelled dry. I felt dry. My stomach groaned and caved in. I knew this much: love was felt in the heart, but I felt it in my belly. Maybe it was not love, but something similar that had yet to be named:

Heartfelt – Bellyfelt
Heartrending – Bellyrending
Heartless – Bellyless
Heartwarming – Bellywarming

I had no idea how the week passed, ever-so-s-l-o-w-l-y on caterpillar legs. Now here I was again across the road looking up at the green shutters of Rebecca's house. They were all shut. Maybe she was out of town. Where had she gone? Had she Gone Away? Oh God let me not think of her.

Just then I heard voices screaming aloud. I ran up the road to see. A crowd churned around Tommy's Garage. The shop sign had been painted over in black. Tyres were all over the road, and nuts, bolts and all sorts of scrap. Men in saffron-coloured clothes shouted at Tommy-uncle, their fists raised in the air: no English names. Change your garage name. Swami sat on a tyre on the road shouting: Motherfuckers. Sisterfuckers…

Tommy-uncle stood there, his arms crossed across his chest, muttering: a rose is a rose is a rose.

Across the street Pinto's Ice-cream Centre, Good Morning Café and Eros Cinema were in a mess. Further up Gibbs Road, the glass window of Gracious Me was smashed. Ribbons and hairclips were strewn on the pavement. Cake and pastries were strewn inside Sweet Heaven Cake Shop, and piles of photographs lay outside Sunrise Studios. A large signboard had been rammed into the earth: *No English. Only the language of the soil. Only Telegu.* Ironically the sign was in English. At the bottom of the sign was a list of new names assigned to the old names.

Gibbs Road – Sri Krishna Road.

George Gibbs Institute – Mahatma Gandhi Institute.

Victoria Dyes – Vishnu Dye Factory.

Queens Hotel – Maharani Mahal.

Eros Cinema – Saraswati Talkies.

Tommy's Garage – Laxmi Garage…

Nearer home I saw a gang of saffron-clothed men walking away from Victoria Villa. They had fixed a cardboard sign on the gatepost over the old name: Ram Vilas.

That night as I looked up at Georgie's picture on the wall, the lightbulb was reflected in his eyes. He looked worried and sad.

I am so sorry Georgie, I said.

***

I was startled to see Rebecca with her father in school the next day. They were waiting outside the principal's office. Was there something wrong? I wondered if I should go over to her, then I thought maybe not. What would I say to her? So I turned away just as she called out to me. And then she was by my side. 'Can't talk now,' she whispered. 'Meet me by the lake this evening.' Rebecca's father called out to her as he stepped into the principal's office. '4 o'clock. Be there,' Rebecca said.

I went to the lake half an hour early and waited for Rebecca for nearly an hour. I wondered if she would come. What did she want to tell me? My head throbbed and I felt a dull ache in my belly. The chakka tree swished-swished above me. I rested my head on the ground and fell asleep in its smell.

I heard a sound and I opened my eyes. Rebecca was sitting on the shore. I crawled up to her and sat down beside her. The air was moist and heavy. The clouds looked like dirty rags hung on an invisible clothesline. Around the sweet hedge, fireflies danced and cruised the evening air in fine grains of light. I sighed, not because of the fireflies but because I could feel the warmth of Rebecca's thigh pressed to mine. A giant firefly stirred in my belly; it flapped its wings and forced my breath out in a whistle.

'Daddy's moving to LA,' Rebecca said.

'Moving?'

'Yes. He's going to live with that American woman.

'You said he was only having an affair.'

'He was.'

'You said it was temporary.'

'This is a different kind of temporary.'

'So why did your father have to meet the principal for that?'

'To get my leaving certificate.'

'Are you leaving?'

'Yes. I. Want. To. Go. To. LA.'

'For how long?'

'For. Ever.'

Desperately I threw my arms around Rebecca's neck and, pulling her closer, kissed her lingeringly on her lips. Her lips were soft and smelled of sweet flowers and spice and her breath was warm like the summer breeze. I felt an unfamiliar thrill. The giant firefly fluttered in my belly once more and a surge of longing consumed me. 'I love you,' I blurted out.

'Don't be silly,' Rebecca said pushing me away. I was afraid I was going to cry. To make matters worse she thrust a hand in her pocket and held out the beetle with green eyes. 'You keep it.' She shoved it into my hand. 'I am not taking it to LA.'

'It's yours,' I said giving it back to her. 'Take it.'

'I don't want it.' She flung it into the water. 'Now look what you made me do!'

I stood up, turned around and walked away. My head felt numb; I couldn't think. I walked and walked. My feet walked me to the beach and, squatting on the sands, I stared into the sea, darkblue as the sky. It seemed to me like a big hole, the sky and the sea together. I dipped my head forward, pushing it into the hole, further so that I could never see myself again. I tried to work it out backwards, Hobbit-like:

The kiss.

Lilies and Toads.

XX & XY.

The dream.

To catch a thief.

Loves me, loves me not.

Periods.

Hail Marys.

Breasts.

All good things must come to an end.

Ajeeb dastan hai yeh, kaha shuru kahan khatam.

Snakes and Ladders.

Pretend Game.

Butterfly & Caterpillar.

Before After.

Rebecca's hair floating out of the window.

We'd gone through a lot together. It didn't make sense. Perhaps there was more to it, but I didn't know any more. I didn't know how long I sat there. The sky had turned dark and the stars had come out. The light from the boats in the sea seemed to grow bigger and bigger. Then the light burst into flames. Or so I thought. My eyes felt as though they were on fire. I closed them and ended the pain momentarily.

Something ended in me.

20

An end in the end was no end. An end was merely a pause before change, an interruption. End was unnatural, Appa had told me. The end of the pupa was the beginning of the mosquito. The end of a caterpillar was the beginning of the butterfly. Changes in nature, of life, were ruled by patterns of cause and effect. Every effect was the result of a string of causes, and each cause had an effect. To prove his point Appa relied heavily on the Fibonacci sequence:

The sequence was formed by starting with 0 and 1, and then adding the latest two numbers to get the next one: 0 1 1 2 3 5 8 – what came after was the result of all that came before. It was endless. The Fibonacci sequence revealed the pattern of things: of things to be, and of things to come, not as ultimate law, but as a tendency.

I should have known therefore, that Rebecca's departure somewhat followed the Fibonacci Sequence. It was meant to be. I couldn't fight what was preordained. So whenever I missed Rebecca I spread her atlas on the floor and with a hope and a wish I flew my finger across the Indian Ocean, over Egypt and the Sahara, and then I submarined under the South Atlantic Ocean, skirted the bottom of South America, plunged into the South Pacific Ocean, headed north and swam all the way to the coast of California. There with my finger poised over the land I walked them to the cities: San Francisco, San Jose, Monterey, Santa Barbara, Los Angeles, Long Beach, San Diego. Where the hell was LA? Rebecca would let me know when she sent for me. She surely would.

Promise?

Promise.

Cross my heart and hope to die.

And with that hope in my heart I remained comforted.

Rebecca's departure seemed to affect Amma more than me. Her skin was pallid, notched with pain lines, and her eyes, those aubergine eyes, had turned muddy brown. Aches descended inside her head and stayed there: hurting, throbbing. Shrill sounds drilled into her ears. Sunlight pricked her skin, left it raw. Her eyes discovered darkness invisible to most. She could see shadows in the dark.

Amma walked stealthily, shadow-like, her body pressed against the walls, from room to room, up and down the stairs, her head bent low, her eyes tied with invisible strings to her toes. Sometimes she would shadow down the road, stop midway and wonder where she was going: she forgot things frequently. What was worse, she forgot the Sequence of Things. She would boil the vegetables in coconut paste before she added the tamarind instead of the other way around, and quite often she changed into fresh clothes before she had a bath, and on some days she forgot to bathe all together. It was not easy for her. The hours took months to make a day; the month sometimes collapsed in a minute.

On her better days Amma went to the market and returned with armful of old magazines and secondhand books, tattered copies of Georgette Heyer novels. They were her favourite. Her room was full of them. As she read them she would be transported to those old times and she was at once Leonie or Barbara, or Judith or Horatia, falling in love with the Duke of Avon, or the Duke of Wellington, the Earl of Worth or the Earl of Rule. She would read aloud from these books or sometimes talk to herself in a strange voice. No one understood her actions; neither did I. Only Munniamma did: Amma confided in her.

A little shadow came to her, she had told Munniamma. With little hands it opened Amma's eyelids one by one. Then it stood by watching Amma fall asleep.

'Your mother is not well,' Munniamma told me.

'What's wrong?'

'Shadows follow her.'

Sometimes Amma offered to go to the market with Munniamma to buy vegetables. But once she was there she didn't know what to get; she had forgotten the colours: tomatoes seemed blue to her, aubergine, red and the beans, a passionate pink.

And the little shadow whispered to her:

Red tomatoes.

Purple aubergine.

Green beans.

On her way home she walked close to the compound walls of houses, and now and then looked behind to see if the shadow on the wall was following her. Come on, come on, she would say to it, wondering why it always lagged behind. Sometimes she turned around to reprimand the shadow; the shadow disappeared behind her and lay flat on the road. When she turned towards the road the shadow crept up the wall. Don't play games with me, Amma would say, her index finger recycling the little air around it.

It had started with colours first, and then even brightness turned to darkness. Those were Amma's colour-confused days; they happened once in a while and then more frequently. Soon she would mix up sounds: the milkman's cycle bell sounded to her like a dog barking; gentle raindrops made the noise of an avalanche; birdsong became the shrill whistle of the new pressure cooker in the kitchen.

And the little shadow whispered:

That's the milkman.

Look, the rain.

The bird is singing.

On such days when confusion ruled her mind Amma remained in her room sewing: swish-swish-swish. She brought down the curtains, cut them into pieces and then sewed them all over again. She did the same with bedsheets, towels, her old sarees and anything else she could find. She did things in reverse. She started reading her books again. As Amma read them, she told Munniamma, it occurred to her that her own life, like those of the Leonies or Barbaras, or Judiths or Horatias, had been a long succession of acts of weakness and compromise. Amma felt sorry for them; she felt sorrier for herself. She was leading two lives, hers and *theirs*, and now she was truly tired and frustrated by this and the routine of daily tasks, daily thoughts, daily worries and concern that fitted into the everyday structure of living a daily life.

One evening Amma looked out of the window at the little shadow climbing the ladder against the wall. Amma said: you shouldn't be out. It is the time for mosquitoes. Now say mosquito. Mus-mus-ki-ki-toe. Mos-ki-toe. You must beware of the A-no-phee-lees mosquito. Repeat after me – Aa. No. Phil. Liss. Aa. No. Phil. Liss. The shadow moved down the ladder. 'Don't go,' Amma pleaded to the shadow.

I am not going anywhere. I am right next to you.

When Munniamma told me all this, I didn't know what to make of it. Something had gone terribly wrong with Amma's Fibonacci Sequence. If only I had paid more attention I would have known the pattern of things to be, and of things to come.

***

One night I heard Amma singing a sweet song, sadly. I crept up to her room and found her on the windowsill. She had on a petticoat and blouse and the moon on her face, specks of moonlight in her eyes. This would be the time of the day that Amma liked most, when cloaked by darkness she could travel in her mind and roam unshackled, to find the dearest one she had lost, the one she would think of again and again, forever, ever: innocent like the beginning of all things, blameless and pure like the moon that shared its light. The night would share its dark shadows with her. And the night would have gotten darker but Amma wouldn't notice this. All she would hear was the little shadow on the ladder singing to her in the glimmer of the moonlight.

Even as I watched from the door Amma lifted her legs one after the other and dangled them out of the window. I was terrified she was going to jump out. But I stood still; my thoughts still, Tara's breath still. Only the other day when I was in Vishnu-thatha's house and I smacked my hands together to drive away a pigeon, Vishnu-thatha told me I was never to do that, as it would scare the bird and it could die of a heart attack. That night I left Amma alone. But in my dream she jumped out of the window. Then with white wings, and silver bells on her ankles she flew *ting-ting ting*, with dreamlike purpose, feeling what she had never felt before: lightness, sudden release; the silence she so longed for. There was moonlight in her eyes as she flew all the way to Para-dies.

Next morning Amma had disappeared. Amma had taken to disappearing. It would happen in the morning or late afternoon. She would be in her room and then not in her room, not in the house, and not in the garden. She would disappear from the house sometimes for several hours, or go away in her mind for days. Was she having an affair? I saw her leave the house one afternoon. I followed her to the market. She stood at a bus stop. Buses arrived and moved away, but Amma stood still, waiting. Not far from her Swami was squatting on the ground eating a banana. Just then a man in a safari-suit, briefcase in hand, walked to the bus stop with a young girl. Amma rushed to the girl, grabbed her arm. The man reacted fiercely: he clasped his daughter's arm and yanked her to the other side of the bus stop. Swami turned to the man and snarled: Bloody Motherfucker. Soon a bus arrived and the man got into the bus with his daughter. Amma called out to him, and when the bus began to move she waved to the little girl. Then she sat down on the ground next to Swami.

The manhole in front of them leaked and smelly water had collected on the road. Swami picked up a stone and chucked it into the puddle. Whore, he shouted. Amma plucked a stone and flung it into the puddle. Whore, she screamed. Then again: Bloody Slut. Bloody Slut. Sisterfucker. Sisterfucker. Mother's Cunt. Mother's Cunt. A taxi sped down and shrieked to a halt beside the bus stop. A wave of dirty water curled up from its tyre and drenched both Swami and Amma. Swami let out a stream of abuse and Amma laughed. She laughed and laughed.

Then I saw Munniamma approaching from the market. She pulled up Amma by her arm. Amma pointed to the shadow in the puddle of water, and she said, 'Why did you have to go?'

The shadow replied: *One, two, three… count to a hundred and you'll have no after.*

And Amma counted aloud: one, five, nine, eight, eleven …

She had forgotten how to count.

***

People were saying a lot of things. Poor woman, she's gone mad, they said and when they saw me, you poor boy, they clucked and shook their heads. There was talk in George Gibbs Institute. Poor fellow, the fellow scientists said. Appa was totally bewildered. He was more so when he found Amma in his study one evening. A number of books lay open on his desk. She had on his spectacles and she rocked back and forth repeating the word, *Wolbachia*. She pushed the spectacles down her nose. Then she looked up at Appa and spoke these words in a gruff voice: Wolbachia is bacteria that infect fruit flies. The Wolbachia-infected mosquito can only make babies after drinking human blood. Because it needs fat for her babies and human blood has more cholesterol. Because the Wolbachia bacteria needs fat to grow so it eats away all the mosquito's fat stores. So the mosquito has to bite fat people for more fat. It's only for her baby mosquito.

Later that evening a man came to the house to talk to Appa. He was thin, tall and had on a slightly crumpled safari suit.

Under his arm was a black umbrella and held in his other hand was a cloth bag; drumsticks and leaves of spinach pushed out of it. Appa led him into the hall because the man had told him he wanted to have a private word with him. The man came into the room and stood silently even though Appa had signalled to him to sit down. He opened his mouth as if to say something, then closed it. Appa asked him to sit down again. The man remained standing, speaking in low tones. Appa hissed like a snake when he heard what the man had to say. I had never seen him so angry. The man shrugged and then walked out of the room. Appa rushed up the stairs.

'Who was that man?' Patti asked me.

'He was the man from the bus stop.'

'What bus stop?'

'39.'

'Which man?'

'The man in a safari-suit with the little girl.'

Patti held my arm and we climbed up to Amma's room. Amma was dressed in a blouse over two layers of petticoats. She had draped a silk saree around her shoulders and on her head was the old threadnet bonnet. She was standing by the window seemingly looking out of it. But the cut-and-stitched curtains were drawn.

Appa stood by the door. He said carefully, 'Mallika...'

Amma turned to face Appa. 'For the lord's sake what?'

'Mallika, don't go to the bus stop again,' is all Appa said.

It was then that Amma let it all out. 'Life's so easy for you. You go through each day as though there's nothing wrong. Nothing. The sun rises and the sun sets. You arise and you rest. There's nothing wrong for you. But everything is wrong for me. I can't go through a single day. There is no sun or moon. It is dark all the time and each day feels like years.'

Appa was bewildered. 'Nothing is easy. I have problems too, you know,' he started.

'Be it as it may,' Amma lashed out. 'It's because you are the cause of all the problems.'

'Now what have I done?'

'By Jove, of all the things to say, what have I done? You killed Tara.'

'How did I kill Tara? Tell me, Mallika.'

'Just like you killed me.'

'I killed you? How did I kill you?'

'I dare say the same way you killed my mother.'

'Why is Amma speaking funny?' I asked.

'It's all the funny books she reads,' Patti said.

The next day Amma disappeared for several hours. It was evening and she had not returned. Patti grew anxious and sent for Appa. We were on the veranda steps. It was getting dark; the stars were out. Appa sighed with relief when Amma walked through the gates. But he didn't go to her. He was afraid of how she would react. Amma walked up straight to him. The light shone on her face and I realised she looked different: her lips were painted red, like Rukmini-aunty's, and her cheeks wore a pinkish blush. Amma ran a hand through her hair. 'I cut it,' she said smiling. 'See, Raman, I look just like Elizabeth Gibbs.'

It was the first time she had addressed Appa by his name. Until now she had addressed him cryptically: *Listen. Look here. See.*

Amma turned to me. Her face was vacant: she didn't wince nor did she display any sort of recognition. I wanted to rush to her but a gush of fear locked my knees; I couldn't move. Amma reached out and ran her fingers through my hair. 'You should have a haircut, it has grown so long.'

Then Amma noticed the dead moth on the veranda floor. She watched the swarm of ants around it disentangle the insect's legs and pull it towards a hole in the wall. Amma spoke aloud to the lifeless moth: men are like ants. They will clip our wings so we can't fly anymore. Remember, it is a burden to be a woman.

Large rocks are tied to our back and we sink deep into dark waters. The shadows on the floor rippled like water. The wind howled: oowata-oowata-r-*wate-r*. 'I am coming,' Amma said to the shadows, 'wait for me. I am coming.'

'Is Amma mad?' I asked Appa after she had gone up to her room.

'She's not mad. She's like that old vacuum cleaner in the prayer room,' Appa said. 'From outside it seems okay but inside it there are a lot of little parts that are broken and so the machine doesn't work properly.'

'Amma is broken from inside?'

Munniamma who had come up behind us burst into tears.

21

She was enormously fat. Her reddened hair was knotted at the top and floweradorned. Several necklaces covered her ample bosom and her kohl-lined eyes were large and weepy. She was Savitri, the local keener. She chewed paan. 'Just twenty minutes is all she needs,' Munniamma told Patti. 'She will make Mallika-ma cry out all her grief and happiness will shine inside her like the sun.'

Munniamma and Savitri followed Patti to Amma's room. Amma was on the bed, her eyes fixed on the shadow on the windowsill. Savitri removed her necklaces one by one, and then the flowers in her hair. She let her hair down and spread it around her face. She stood still for several minutes, her eyes closed. And then taking a long and deep breath, she wailed – a long, single wail, like the opening note of an orchestra. Her shoulders grieved, her breasts drooped; she beat her chest rhythmically, again and again, gasping. Tears ran down her face with rivulets of kohl. She wailed. For half an hour she wailed. Amma still stared at the sill, tearless. Savitri knotted her hair and put the flowers back. She adjusted her breasts inside the cups of her bra, put on her necklaces one by one. 'It's no use, ma,' Savitri said wiping her face and neck with the end of her saree. 'Her grief is too deep. Only Lord Ganesha can help her now. He will destroy her grief and remove the obstacles in her life. Bring her to the prayer room.' When they were in the prayer room Savitri lit the lamps and burned incense sticks. 'Look at our Lord Ganesha,' she said to Amma, 'talk to him, tell him your woes and he'll help you.'

Amma looked at the idols of the Gods, fresh flowers surrounding them, and the bowls of fruits and milk set on the shelf. She stared at Ghandiji, the Vacuum-Cleaner-God, and the clay idol of the snake goddess that Patti had brought back from Chiroor. The Goddess's face was black, as was the snake coiled around her body. Her eyes were algaegreen and the tongue sticking out of her mouth was bloodred. The plaster of Paris idol of Rama, the Lord of selfcontrol, gleamed in the lamplight. His lips were postbox red, his teeth Colgatewhite; he wore a permanent holysmile, a somewhat mocking grin. Amma's body shook and her breath came out in a tiny gasp. She grabbed the bowl of milk and poured it over the idols and threw the fruits at them, one by one and with every throw she screamed. 'You killed Tara.' She banged the empty bowl hard on the idols. The clay and plaster of Paris idols cracked, crumbled bit by bit, and fell – a holy head here, a sacred hand there, the snakehead in that corner, the bloody tongue in another, and at Patti's feet, the permanent pious smile.

Patti grabbed Amma's hands. She gritted her teeth, swung her arm back and slapped Amma's face, hard.

That night Amma disappeared.

***

Appa and Vishnu-Thatha looked for Amma everywhere: the market, the bus stop, on the beach, in the woods. Two days later Appa filed a Missing Person report with the police. The police came to the house and questioned the rest of us: Patti, Munniamma, Mani and me.

When is the last time you saw her?

Did something happen in the house to upset her?

Does she have any close friends?

Has she done this before?

Did you notice anything unusual about her?

When the police asked me these questions I said 'No' to all of them except the first. To that I told the truth: Amma was in the prayer room. And I didn't tell them about the man at the bus stop. Not-telling was not lying. Had Amma gone away with him?

Patti was miserable. She bought a number of replacement Gods and prayed to them each day. She went to the Shiva temple each evening and offered flowers, a coconut, ten rupees, a bunch of homegrown rastali bananas, to Lord Shiva with light in His eyes. Appa was disconsolate. He would go up to Amma's room after he returned from work and stay there until Patti called him down for dinner. During the meal he would talk about Amma constantly:

'She made the best puliodhare. She was the Puliodhare Queen.'

'She liked only white flowers.'

'Did you know she was ticklish on her nose?'

'I could always tell when was going to be angry. Her left eyebrow would have a strange tilt to it.'

'Sometimes when she was fast asleep she didn't snore but she whistled a tune through her nose.'

'Why did Amma go away?' I asked.

Appa looked at me for a long time and then he smiled. 'Funny, your mother often answered a question with a question. Why did you go away? She would have said: why does the monsoon not stay?'

I was convinced that Amma had gone away because of me. So I prayed to God, week after week, in all the languages I could speak: English, Tamil, some Hindi, a spattering of learnt-by-heart Sanskrit. I even sent a silent thought prayer to all the Gods-in-One to bring her back. Patti had told me for important matters it was always better to address all the Gods at once. I waited until the end of the month, until the prayers would have reached Those addressed. Then in my dream one night Tara's voice was sweet like the note of a flute. Hand in hand, like two lost children, we wandered together in the woods. We stood on a cliff looking down at the sea. The rock cracked below Tara's feet. She tripped and fell; her voice cried out to me. I lunged towards Tara and grabbed her hand just before her body was pitched forward. I could see her face contort, horror in her eyes. I tightened my fingers around her hand, but I couldn't hold on. Tara fell into the sea. She swallowed more water, more water and sank to the bottom.

Amma came up behind me. She screamed. 'You killed Tara.'

I woke up. I felt an overwhelming fear. I had a memory of something soft and zigzaggy, like melted tar with tyremarks. My eyelids seemed to be glued together. I rubbed my eyes hard, opened them wide. The window was a square of light. I leapt out of bed and ran up to Amma's room. It felt empty even though it was full of things: trunks, suitcases, utensils and heaps of magazines. I looked in the steel almirah. Amma's clothes were still in it. I took a saree out of the shelf and buried my face in it; it was soft, as soft as Amma's skin, and it still smelled of her. I pulled out the trunk from under the bed and rummaged through it. At the bottom I found a photo album. I opened it carefully. On its first page were the words: *My Tara*. On subsequent pages were photographs of girls cut out from magazines and newspapers. Under each of them were written: Tara 6 years old. Tara 7 years old. Tara 8 years old... There were also pictures of flowers and food, captioned: Tara likes roses. Tara likes ice-cream. There was a photograph of a mother holding her daughter. The mother's face was not visible. Amma had captioned it. *Amma* and *Tara*.

Snakes of light fell on the floor. The tamarind tree outside had maps of morning glow on it. India, Australia, China, America... The birds were awake and busy flitting from one country to another. I walked to the window; I saw the ladder resting against the wall. Had Amma climbed down and run away? Suddenly it struck me how closely Snakes and Ladders represented life: ladders to climb up, only to slither down snakes, for every square of joy, a circle of misery: the Golden Ratio. Amma had been swallowed by the Amma snake and landed at the bottom square. There were ladders all around her but she couldn't see them. I now knew why Amma blamed me. It was as simple as the Snakes and Ladders game: snakes, you hate. Ladders, you love. Tara was the ladder. I was the snake. Amma had no ladder left.

**

I returned to my room with the album. I hid it in my cupboard under a pile of old clothes in the bottom shelf where I had hidden Georgie's old ledger wrapped in an old towel. I had forgotten about it. Did Elizabeth come back to Georgie and her son? This would answer the more important question: would Amma return? I took the ledger out, lay in bed and started to read from the page where I had stopped:

It was not, of course, to be expected that Elizabeth's departure was the only matter that disturbed the peace of Victoria Villa. My child wouldn't stop crying. It was late in the night and the ayah had gone home hours ago. It was the weekend and she didn't stay overnight. I rocked the cradle and sang the only rhyme that came to my mind:

> *Goose-a goose-a gander,*
> *Where shall I wander?*
> *Upstairs and downstairs,*
> *In my lady's chamber;*
> *There you'll find a cup of sack*
> *And a race of ginger...*

But my child wouldn't stop bawling. I was exasperated and worn-out. How was I to look after a child who needed its mother above all things? And then a thought struck me. I opened my cupboard and took out the leftover yardage of brown silk. I wrapped it around me and then went to the cradle and picked up my bawling child. The baby nestled its face in the folds of silk and let forth a series of gurgles. Holding the child in the crook of

210

my arm I rushed down to the kitchen, where I pulped a piece of ripe papaya in a small bowl with my free hand.

I continued singing as I fed my child:
Old father Long-Legs
Can't say his prayers:
Take him by the left leg
And throw him downstairs

***

A flock of brilliantly feathered birds descended from the sky to settle around the pond and under the trees. I was in the garden making a bird out of wood and metal wires. I had shaped the wings, a pointed beak and the claws. I measured each part. Perfect proportions: I was pleased. A gleam of silk caught my attention. The ayah had come to me with the baby in her arms. 'Good heavens! Why have you dressed him in that?'

'Lis-bet Memsab stitched it for her,' the ayah said.

I eyed her closely for some moments, deep in thought. Elizabeth had reached London some months ago. My mother had written to me that Elizabeth had gone completely insane. Poor girl. Then she had run away from home.

The ayah noticed me staring at her and drew her saree over her head and face. Then, as I reassembled my thoughts, my eyes moved to the child in her arms, slowly absorbing what I saw: my son, my daughter: a hermaphrodite – the offspring of two lonely, bored English people. The startling news about the abnormal child had spread all over the town.

The gates clattered and my eyes turned toward the sound. I saw a group of eunuchs clapping their hands and shouting. They had come before; they came every day. They had warned that they would come every day.

'Give us your child,' they now shouted from the gates, 'she belongs to us.'

I put down my tools and the hen I had partly made and stood up tall. I clutched the ayah's arm and dragged her into the house.

*Minutes later, I rushed out of house with a rifle in my hands.
I aimed my weapon at the eunuchs. 'Go away. Leave my child
alone,' I shouted, 'or I'll shoot every one of you.' I shot into the air.*

*'Why shoot us?' one of the eunuchs screamed at me. 'We are
not to blame.' The other eunuchs smacked their hands together
and ululated. 'It's your fault,' one of them said. 'We know Elisbet
is your sister. And this is what happens if you do it to your sister.'*

I stopped at this point. I turned the page back and read it once
more. Elizabeth was Georgie's sister? John was Jane? What
happened to John? I turned the page and read the account dated
October 1860:

*John was six. His skin was as soft and pink as an English rose,
and his smile so sweet. Even though he was dressed in boy's
clothes people mistook him for a girl. I had allowed myself to
accept the oddness in my son, though I ceased to understand
much of his speech and many of his actions. He seemed to possess
clairvoyant powers: he remembered things that had happened a
long time ago or knew what would happen in the future. I didn't
believe him but I was afraid to question him for fear I would
lose his love. And I loved him so.*

On a rainy day he asked me: 'What is rain?'
'Water.'
'What is lake?'
'Still water.'
'What is river?'
'Running water.'
'What is sea?'
'Tides in water.'
'What is ocean?'
'Biggest water with the sea in it.'

*I never left John alone at home with the ayah. He was a
wanderer and he frequently stole out of the compound. He
returned with a collection of stones, smooth round pebbles. Once*

he had walked alone for hours on end, until a neighbour had found him at the edge of the sea, crying his heart out.

'I look the sea in the ocean,' John told me that night. 'The sea a bad monster.'

'Why?'

'It swallow me. It swallow daddy.'

After that I took John to the Victoria Dyes factory each day. In the skylit room John noted down what he knew in a notebook I had given him. Sometimes he was in the backyard chasing butterflies.

One evening I was at the factory until late. I had to check the consignment of cloth to be shipped. Out of the corner of my eye I saw John playing with the yards of silk on the floor. He had coiled the cloth around him. A ruckus could be heard from the gates so I stepped out into the porch to see what the problem was. A group of eunuchs stood there, clapping their hands. For six long years they had harassed me.

On seeing me they shouted, 'Give us your son, she belongs to us.' In a mass, they produced a rumbling, menacing sound, like bees in a swarm.

I shouted at them, my voice gravelly and tired, and then yelled out a command to my workers. With sticks raised in their hands they rushed towards the eunuchs. The eunuchs held up their arms in protest.

'Our curse is worse than a snakebite,' one of them said. Then smacking their hands the eunuchs went away.

I stood in the porch watching them until they appeared as two dots at the end of the road. I looked up at the white radiance of an obese moon. Doubts and indecisions swayed me: the John I knew might be my private illusion. The Jane seen by the world might be the real thing. I returned to the dyeing room. My son had disappeared.

I looked for him everywhere in the factory. I looked in the dyeing room, in the storeroom, in the yard at the back. I studied the ledger where I had made entries of the consignment to be shipped that night. I searched in every roll of cloth but I couldn't find my son. Those bloody eunuchs had taken my son. With Chotoo, a few workers and my rifle I marched to the eunuchs' settlement near the sea. It was well past nine by then, pitch dark, and the wind wailed from the west. The ground was uneven and slippery with rubbish, and glittered with a coating of rain. I turned towards the huddle of mud houses. Scanty fires burned inside most of them. I smelled meat and fowl roasting, and felt acute hunger.

I shot a round of ammunition into the night air, which brought the eunuchs scurrying out of their huts. 'Give me back my son or I'll shoot each one of you,' I shouted, and fired more bullets into the air.

'We don't have your son,' the eunuchs shouted back. They looked deep into my eyes; I sensed the honesty in theirs.

Broken and tired, I walked away toward the sea. I stood on the warped planks of the old jetty. The air smelled of fish and salt. I could hear the tides slap and splash, swell and recede, and call out to me. The wind made its sound behind and around me. Like a hound on a trace, I focused all my senses, looked far into the water. My eyes bore me onward, further and further into the sea, because there was nothing else I could do.

***

It was only February and the Northeast trade winds brought, along with early dark clouds, bad news. Fires had broken out near Calcutta. They were believed to be the result of arson. The Hindus and Muslims were fighting again.

I was in my study when Matthew brought me my evening drink. He set the tray on the table and looked up at me. 'It's not being safe here, sar,' Matthew said. 'You must go back.'

I thought of the English countryside turned emerald by the rain, and yellow and blue flowers showing themselves in the thick grass. I thought of the English birds, throats full of music. I thought of English women's breasts, full and white. I thought

214

of dark fermented beer and the fragrant smell of apple pie with cloves in it. Surely then, I thought, it was time to leave this incomprehensible land where the Hindus disagreed with their fellow Muslims, and more, the English who ruled them.

Then I thought of my son. 'I can't go,' I said. 'For John's sake, I can't go now.'

Under this, scribbled in pencil, was a note, an afterthought:

(John, my son, I have written these notes for you so you will know exactly what transpired. Please don't blame me. I was helpless. And if you ever return and if you read these notes you will know that I never left. I loved you so.)

I looked up at the picture of Georgie on the wall; his eyes stared back at me. A muscle twitched at the back of my neck and my stomach turned. Georgie had written these notes for John and I shouldn't be reading them. Once more I wrapped the ledger in the old towel and put it away.

22

I started to feel nervous, strangely nervous. It wasn't something I could understand clearly, it was as though my body was too small; I felt hemmed in. I felt my heart convulse: it seemed to have a life of its own that had nothing to do with me. It seemed to me that I had grown shorter. I had lost height and weight. I felt sharp pangs in my limbs, so acute that I could hardly walk or sometimes even stand. I did not know where the pain came from nor why. I was in the clutch of some mystifying thing. But now and then the aches became numb; I couldn't feel them. I couldn't feel my hands or feet. I felt Tara's arms in my arms, her hands in my hands, her touch in my touch. My skin stretched and I filled up with her. Her blood felt warm inside me. Until now she had been one half of me and now it was as though I was she. Or she was me. Her feet walked me everywhere and through her eyes I saw everything. She talked to me; she told me what to think, what to do and how to do it; helplessly, I surrendered to her. Honestly therefore, I didn't know if it was Tara who decided to talk to Appa or if it was me.

Appa returned home and went straight to his study. Patti was in the kitchen making coffee. Moments later, I found myself at the study door. Everything in the room appeared solid and foreboding. On the desk was a heap of books, leatherbound, all gloomy and dark. The room was dark too. Only one light behind Appa spread a steady glow that illuminated the slight bald patch on his head and a portion of the paper he was reading. An elliptical shadow cast by his head fell onto the rest of the paper. He looked old.

I pushed my head against the door and Tara wrapped her arms around my body. I shook with convulsions of fear, anger, loneliness and the frustration of not knowing what was wrong with me. Appa turned and looked at me. I walked to the chair and sank in it. I felt a curious tossing in my stomach. I stared gloomily at my feet. I rotated one foot round and round and then Tara rotated the other.

'What's wrong, Siva?'

'I think I am Tara,' I said.

A deep hurt showed on Appa's face. His eyelids trembled with the *sorry* in his eyes. He walked around the desk, held my arms and lifted me from the chair and put both his arms around me. 'You're Siva, kanna.' His hands trembled as he drew me closer to him.

'I am Tara,' Tara said, her voice shrill and sharp.

Appa was a man whose life had been filled with the small activities of mosquitoes. They were his world. He would not have known that everything around him could break down, that he himself would break down. He did.

Patti stepped into the room with a tumbler of coffee. 'Why are you crying Raman?' she asked and then she looked at me. 'Is something wrong with Siva?'

Appa raised his hand to his eyes and closed them with his thumb and forefinger to stop his tears. 'I don't know.'

'What do you mean, you don't know? You usually know everything.'

***

The waiting room of Dr Kuruvilla's clinic was crowded and it was not any different from the railway platform. Entire families had accompanied their sick ones and they talked incessantly. The older men talked about politics and the problems of the country; each had different solutions. Middleaged men discussed the prices of land and petrol, and cures for balding. Old women talked about arthritis, and the cost of green chillies and onions – the poor man's staple food, and how cheap they were in their younger days. Young girls giggled over gossip of their favourite film stars. Some stood around the water cooler, filling small steel tumblers with cold water and drinking it with unexpected thirst. The water was free. My throat was dry and my lips stuck together.

The two tubelights on the wall flickered; clockticking, they flickered like the eyes of those people who waited: uncles, mothers, fathers, daughters, sons, perhaps a postman or bankclerk, a businessman. A priest, a lame man, a man with a golden tooth, an old man with an old heart, a woman with a baby in her womb. I turned my head with a jerk, sourness in my mouth, and a dull pain in my chest. I felt empty, like a carcass into which I would crawl again tomorrow, and the next day, and the day after. I waited.

Nearly an hour later Appa and I walked into the consulting room and sat down in front of the doctor. Black hair bristled up on one side of his head, which was otherwise full of grey. 'So who is the patient?' the doctor asked smiling. The doctor studied me. 'He's half his size.' He tilted his head and returned Appa's stare. 'What's the problem with him?'

'His mother disappeared three months ago.'

'I heard about it. I am sorry. It's wholly understandable your son feels terrible about this.'

'This is not all.' Appa looked at the doctor with a pitiful desperation. 'He thinks he is Tara, his twin sister who died at birth.'

The doctor leaned back in his chair and clasped his hands in front of him. He shook his head to and fro. 'Wholly understandable.' His eyes softened a little as he surveyed me. He leaned towards Appa. 'I would like to talk to your son alone,' he said. 'Please wait outside Mr Iyer.'

'Don't be afraid, son. Talk to me,' the doctor said when Appa had left the room. 'Tell me everything. Tell me your thoughts, your memories, your dreams, everything.'

My whole world shrivelled into a bookroom of memories. Thoughts moved in my brain, round and round, deep in all the shelves. When I spoke I couldn't stop; words, memories, voices spewed out of my mouth. I babbled on and on incoherently. The doctor's eyes grew small and intense as he listened to me.

'Wholly incredible.' The doctor stood up and pulled at the waistband of his trousers. He removed his spectacles, blew on the lenses, wiped them with a handkerchief, and then put them on. He walked to the door; opening it slightly he asked Appa to step in. The doctor went back to his chair and Appa sat down in the chair he had recently vacated. I stared out of the window. The stars had come out in the sky. Then I saw one fall. Appa had told me that the falling star was not a star falling but tiny bits of dust and rocks that left a streak of light across the sky. But Patti had told me that it was a sign. When a person saw a falling star it meant he had reached his ultimate destiny.

Appa rested his hands on the table and leaned towards the doctor. 'What's wrong with my son?'

The doctor coughed into his fist and I turned to him. He attempted to smile but only one half of his mouth curved into an arc. There was a glint of triumph in his eyes.

'It's the perfect case of the Twinless Twin,' the doctor said, a frown coming to his face. 'Let me explain. When two embryos develop together in the womb, they have a vague sense of one another, even in the earliest weeks of pregnancy. When a twin dies its imprint lies somewhere in the surviving twin's memory and it expresses itself in a coded message that the twins once shared in the womb. So the surviving twin develops dual personalities: one that he has inherited, and the other, his own. Some surviving twins feel guilt that they have survived and feel the need to live for two and do the things their dead twin cannot.' The doctor's eyes rested on me. The doctor fiddled with the oversized ring on his finger. It had a ruby the size of a one–rupee coin, the kind that is worn to ward off evil. 'It is wholly possible that Siva feels displaced,' the doctor said. 'He may also feel he is less than and not as important or special as his dead twin. And this leads to a lot of psychological problems. It is wholly understandable. But what I can't understand is the matter about George Gibbs. Siva talks of him as though he is his intimate friend. He seems to know a lot about him and his sister Elizabeth.'

'You mean his wife,' Appa said. 'There's a picture of her in my study.'

'According to your son she is George's sister. He told me a fantastic story about Gibbs, the dates, facts all a hundred percent accurate. Wholly crazy but wholly believable.' Then the doctor's eyes grew ponderous and he nodded his head a number of times as though he had recollected an exciting memory.' The doctor rose and walked around the table to Appa and pressed his shoulder. His eyes were serious. Suddenly he laughed out loud. His eyes were laughing as he looked at me. 'You had me fooled, son, you did,' he said with a chuckle. 'I believed what you said about Tara. Medically speaking it is wholly understandable. Until you told me all that nonsense about George Gibbs.' He turned to Appa. 'There's nothing wrong with your son, Mr Iyer. He has an amazing imagination. It is wholly possible that your son's loneliness makes him fantasise, invent invisible companions.' The doctor returned to his chair. 'Let me explain, the type and potency of chemicals in our brain is dependent on the food we eat. In the end everything boils down to diet. Too much carbohydrates can induce a dream-like trance, an inactive phase in the mind. They make one daydream even when awake and make one imagine the unreal. What is worse, they sometimes bring on a touch of clairvoyance and this can be disconcerting, as one could lose the sense of the present world around.'

Clairvoyance. Clairvoyant. I repeated the word in my mind. I had read it in Georgie's diary but I didn't know what the word meant.

'Are you saying he's making all this up?' Appa asked.

'Wholly fertile imagination,' the doctor said, scribbling on a piece of paper. 'I have prescribed anti-anxiety pills but what your son needs is a healthy protein-rich, fat-rich diet. Good for the brains. No rice, no potatoes. He should eat fish.'

Appa drove home in silence. He swerved when a cyclist shot past the car and then braked hard to avoid Swami scuttling across on his hands and leg.

'Motherfucker,' Swami screamed out. 'Are you blind? Are you mad or what, you sisterfucker?'

A taxi driver who had pulled alongside sniggered. He leant out of the window and said to Appa, 'This country is full of sightless, mindless people, sir. The blind people call others blind. The mad people call others mad.'

'It was my fault actually,' Appa said.

'This is the problem with this country, sir. Everyone blames themselves. They don't blame the others. All Gandhi's fault. When somebody slaps you, Gandhi said, show your other cheek. Why get slapped twice eh?' The taxi driver stamped hard on the accelerator and sped away.

Patti was waiting restlessly on the veranda steps. She ran to Appa as we got out of the car. 'What's wrong with Siva?' she asked, tugging at his arm.

Appa shrugged. 'There's nothing wrong with him, ma. The doctor said he should eat fish.'

'Rubbish,' Patti retorted. 'Gandhiji's diet was vegetables, nuts and goat's milk. Great men don't eat fish.'

***

I sat at my desk and looked in the dictionary.

Clairvoyance – 'clear seeing'. Having the supposed ability to see objects or events that cannot be perceived by the senses.

I was a half-and-half who could see beyond the senses.

23

Dr Kuruvilla came to the house a few weeks later. Appa had sent for him. Patti was unwell. 'You must drink milk and eat a lot of spinach,' Dr Kuruvilla said after checking Patti.

Patti drank a glass of milk each night. Mani got different kinds of spinach and sautéed them: Patti ate them with rice, which turned green or red depending on the colour of the leaves. She developed stomach cramps and was horrified when her stools were black. She told Appa her liver was malfunctioning, her kidneys had hardened, and she was going to die of kidney failure.

Dr Kuruvilla, who had come to check on her, asked her to cut down the spinach, drink coconut water and be active. So Patti drank coconut water and walked updown updown in the garden. Then, when she felt reasonably content, she burst into tears suddenly without any provocation; she continued to cry for days. The doctor attributed such behaviour to age and sorrow. 'Wholly understandable,' he said patting Appa's shoulder. 'Loss is a terrible thing. Have you heard anything about your wife?'

'I put several notices in the local papers,' Appa said, 'but I haven't heard anything yet.'

'It must be terrible for you,' the doctor said, 'but try to understand your mother's moods. You are young and you have the strength to sustain, conceal your pain. But your mother can't. So talk to her about the aches of grief. Now and then, humour her.'

Appa did, but Patti never ceased to complain about her ailments. For no reason at all, she explained to Appa, a sort of pouring fire from hell oozed through her body and swelled her blood. Sometimes a hardened chill from the Himalayas rattled her bones. She was dying, she said. She made arrangements for her imminent death. She packed all her clothes in a trunk except the one she would wear each day.

I tried to humour her. 'When you go, are you taking your trunk with you?'

She laughed. 'When you go you must not leave behind a mess, kanna. You must leave everything tidy.'

I imagined my room: sparkling clean. The bedcover tucked smoothly under the mattress, books lined tidily on the shelves, all my clothes packed neatly in a trunk, and Georgie looking out with sad blue eyes, as I lay on the floor, dead.

'But I don't want to die here,' Patti added. 'I must die in Madras. I was born there. I have eaten my first grain of rice there. I have to die there.'

Patti's trademark logic again. It contained in it the evidence of the simple rule of life. Dust to Dust, Boiled Rice to Boiled Rice: that Sort of a Death. Reap what you Sowed: that Sort of an End.

Patti had made lists – she made a list of 10 things TO DO and 20 things NOT TO DO. Then a list of 10 important things and where they were in the house, and yet another of names of 10 most important people who must attend her funeral. She tried to count these people on her fingers; she could count only 7. She kept trying to think of the remaining 3. She was adamant.

10 must be an important number for her, I thought – like the 10 commandments that God gave Moses. God had written them Himself, Sister Mary Edwards had told us, with His Godly finger, double-spaced on two stone tablets.

'Because 10 is a holy number?' I asked Patti.

'No, kanna,' she said. 'Because it is a round number. Nice and round.'

Patti was always good with numbers.

She held long dialogues with the death-god who for her was a kind of saviour: he delivered special people from the evil world. First her husband, then her granddaughter, and soon it would be her. I realised she was serious about dying. 'Are you really going to die Patti?'

'Everyone has to die someday, kanna,' she said, 'and it is good to Be Prepared.' She stressed the B and P.

'Should I also be Be Prepared?'

'Don't say that, kanna.' She placed her hand on my head and blessed me. 'May the remainder of the years of my life come to you.'

'But you said you didn't have much time, Patti.'

'I don't. But whatever I have left is now yours.'

It wouldn't make much difference, unless I was 99 plus. Then with some more time I would live to be a hundred. Nice and round: 100.

While Patti was preparing to go, Appa was preparing for London. His experiments using genetically altered mosquitoes to create new strains capable of delivering anti-malaria vaccines had been successful. His research had brought him considerable prestige in the UK and was called the *Raman Technique* and, what was more, Rukmini-aunty had called Appa to give him the good news: Appa had been made an Honorary Fellow of the Royal Society. His old institute in London had organised a ceremony to honour his work.

Patti would have been happy for him had she not been unwell. She got breathless while talking, and when she cleared her throat it made a wet sound like a death cough.

'Look after Patti, Siva,' Appa said to me the day he was leaving. He scribbled on a piece of paper, gave it to me. 'This is my phone number. Call me if there's any problem.'

I promised him I would. Besides Mani I was the only man in the house. Of course there was Georgie Gibbs but he was something else, really. And Munniamma was always there; she didn't go home in the evening like she previously did. She was more than a man. She was Superman. It would be all right.

Vishnu-thatha came every day to check on Patti. One evening we were out on the veranda. Munniamma got Vishnu-thatha a tumbler of coffee and sat down on the steps, not too far from us. Patti rubbed balm on the soles of her feet and sighed. Her face was covered in a cold sweat of pain. 'Any news of Mallika?'

'Wherever she is I hope she is happy,' Vishnu-thatha said.

'Why have the Gods troubled us like this?' Patti asked.

'The Gods have nothing to do with our troubles,' Vishnu-thatha replied. 'Gods exist only in our minds, because we are afraid, and They keep us afraid.' Vishnu-thatha looked up at the sky. 'Can you see those seven stars? At the beginning of this world there was only a big round of white light. It was much bigger than the sun. Around it everything was dark. Then the light exploded into seven large bits. The western scientists call it the Big Bang, but we know it as the *saptarishi*, the seven stars – the seven minds of the universe. Out of the light energy of these seven stars people's minds were made. And out of people's minds the Gods were made up because people were afraid. Remember this, the mind existed even before the world was created, or the Gods were. So as long as you feel fear, create your own fleet of Gods. Bribe them with flowers and coconuts; yes they like coconuts but money they like even more. Then when you are no longer afraid, let all the Gods go. Release them. Like this.' He clapped his hands thrice. 'Po, po, po.'

Patti stood up and darted into the house. Concerned, I ran after her. In her room she rummaged through her trunk. She took a silk saree out of it, an old blouse, a blue velvet jewellery box and a silver container in which she kept jars of kohl and pottu. She slipped her arms through the sleeves of the blouse, draped the saree around her and then she put on her jewellery piece by piece. She smeared kohl round her eyes and dotted her forehead with red pottu. I gawked at her, openmouthed.

We returned to the veranda. 'I am going to a new world shortly,' Patti said. 'Munniamma, you make certain I don't reach there dressed like a widow.' Patti sat down on the steps, looked up at the moon. She clapped her hands and in a loud and clear voice she said: Po. Po. Po.

Victoria Villa was quiet that night. The streetlamp cast shadows on the ground. The branches of the neem tree sounded tick tick tick in the wind. Patti breathed heavily and her heart raced, until at dawn it stopped.

***

Munniamma dressed Patti in a red silk saree and all her jewellery. She smeared pottu on Patti's forehead and poured drops of Ganges water into her mouth. She tied a piece of white muslin under Patti's chin and around her head. She joined her hands at the chest and with strips of cloth she tied Patti's thumbs together, and then her big toes. On a whim, I applied Amrtanjan Balm on Patti's forehead and the soles of her feet. She would like that. Then, with Rose-aunty's help, Muniamma lifted Patti's body, smelling of the heat and spice of balm, on to a palanquin.

Appa, when I called him to tell him the news, was totally shattered. He asked me to carry out the funeral rites. It would take him two full days to return from London. The garden that afternoon was filled with neighbours and friends who sat on coir mats laid on the grass. Rose-aunty, Vishnu-thatha, Munniamma and Mani sat amongst them. Including me there were only six most important people instead of ten. It was not nice and round. Three eager crows sat in the neem tree and I counted them on my fingers: 7, 8, 9. They could be Patti's ancestors. Beneath the tree, a purple flower bloomed on the plant potted in an old rusted milk-powder tin. The tin, I remembered, was nearly as old as me. Patti had told me this. Sweetie-Cutie stood outside the gate smacking her hands. I counted her. 10 – nice and round.

The pundit lit the ritual fire and I sat in front of it. Mani presented me with a large vessel of boiled rice, and I emptied it on the ground. The pundit directed the steam from the boiled rice towards heaven, pushing it with his hand: Go. Go. Go. He coaxed it in Tamil: Po. Po. Po. He blew after it phonetically: phoo phoo. Phoo. The steam rose, moistened the neem leaves, and soaked the air above; then, with a loss of spirit, it spread downward, wrapping itself around the people who had gathered. The pundit slapped the rice into a perfect square, cut it into three horizontal sections, sprinkled rice, sesame and water on it, and offered it to three generations of the deceased.

When the funeral rituals were over at the house, Vishnu-thatha and the other men carried the corpse to the cremation ghat along the river. I followed them with the pundit who was carrying a clay pot filled with water. At the ghat the corpse was set on a heap of firewood. The pundit made a hole in the clay pot and raised it on my shoulder. The water dripped from the pot as I circled the pyre. Once. Twice. Thrice. On the pundit's signal I crashed the pot on the ground and then lit the pyre. The smell of smoke and balm filled the air above us.

I felt a deep ache, not in my heart, but deeper, in my belly. I looked up at the sky. Then I clapped my hands. Po. Po. Po.

***

Appa had framed a black and white photograph of Patti and set it on the shelf in the prayer room. It was the only photograph that he found amongst Patti's things. She had been very young. Every morning Appa lit a lamp and a bundle of joss sticks and hoped that her soul would find rest. He didn't address the replacement Gods directly; he seemed a bit awkward with this. I took down the bottle of rice and sesame seeds from the shelf and set it near Patti's photograph. On the floor I arranged Patti's small khaki-covered suitcase, the tiffin carrier, the old English holdall, the lantern, the jar of Amrutanjan balm and the mosquito net that had been darned in a number of places. These six items had comprised Patti's life: food, clothes, sleep, light, no-pain and no-bite.

Appa seemed lost without Patti. It was as though he had misplaced his timetable. He was frequently late for work; on some days he didn't eat his breakfast and surprised Mani by turning up for lunch. Appa had always been meticulous about his clothes and the way he wore them. But now he didn't seem to care. His shirt would often be buttoned wrong and once he had worn different coloured socks on his feet: blue on one and black on the other. When Mani pointed this out to Appa, he shrugged and said, 'Did you know mosquitoes are attracted to the colours blue and black?' Then Appa stopped going to work. He would wander aimlessly, room to room and finally he would retreat into his study and be in it till late playing solitaire. Mani would have left his dinner on the dining table. A few bowls of this and that covered with steel plates. Appa, who was very particular about the food being piping hot, ate it cold or didn't eat at all. One evening Appa sat on the stone bench near the pond, his head slightly bent, staring vacantly at the water. Mosquitoes swarmed around his feet; many of them bit him and sucked his blood most certainly, but he didn't seem to care.

'*Tisstime tomorrow, reckon where I'll be, downinsome lonesome valley, hangin froma quite ol' treeee. Hangdown your head Tom Doooley...*'

The next day, sufficiently restored and resigned to fate, Appa dressed up in office clothes, ate hot idlis for breakfast and left in time for work. Everything had returned to almost normal for him. But not for me: Rebecca had gone. Amma and Patti had left me. But Tara was Ever Present.

***

Tara had appropriated my soul, my innerness. She had become a bigger part of my conscious, and she orchestrated my life with obstinate precision. There was nothing much I could do about this except confine Tara deep inside and Timepass one day at a time until all time passed. The countdown clock was ticktocking the seconds away. So I set a routine to my days. After school I didn't return home: there was no one there to return to. I wandered about in the market or I was at Tommy-uncle's garage. I could talk to him about Rebecca. He listened quietly. But once, when I asked him how much it would cost to go to LA, he gathered me in his arms and surprisingly he had nothing to say.

It would be late evening when I came home. Then Appa and I ate dinner together, but neither one of us spoke much. There didn't seem to be any use for words. Loss sufficed. Each night as I lay down in bed I felt as though someone's hands were pulling the quilt away. Tara always felt hot even when it was cool. This routine continued until one day I didn't go to school. Tara didn't want me to go. She was resolute.

The morning air smelled of salt and moist earth. It tasted salty in my throat where the Tara-feeling nestled deep. She walked me out of the gates; the peepal tree outside went sis-sis in the breeze. The clouds were dark and heavy. The grey folds of the sky resembled the waves in the sea. Tara walked me through the woods in a hurry as though someone, something was waiting for her. And there under the chakka tree was Sweetie-Cutie. I knew she would be there. Clairvoyantly.

'Hi princess.' Sweetie-Cutie dried her hair with a towel. 'It's so hot, I wish it would rain.' Then she sat down and began to cut a watermelon. I sat down beside her and raised my hands to my eyes. A deep hazy look came into Sweetie-Cutie's eyes. She caressed my face with her fingers; they felt warm and sticky against my skin. She curled a lock of hair that had fallen on my cheek. Her face was so close I could feel her breath. 'Is there something you want to tell Sweetie-Cutie?'

Tara opened my heart as if it was a small but full purse with a tiny clasp ready to burst open. It burst open and all her troubles spilled out.

'Oh my sweet Tara.' Sweetie-Cutie held my hand. 'I know how you feel, my princess. I have known for some time. You are different from other boys.' Sweetie-Cutie pressed my hand against her chest. 'You are one of us.' She had tears in her eyes.

The falling star had fallen, silently. I had reached my destiny. I had grown from Siva to Sivatara to Tara. My own Fibonacci sequence. Suddenly a dusty haze darkened the sky. The trees threshed the wind and made a dry, rasping sound. I watched Sweetie-Cutie's face soften, as large drops of rain fell from the skies and seemed to wash away her sadness. Soon, rivulets of rain streamed over the ground and the soil bled with reddish sludge. The rain stopped as suddenly as it had started. It was just a passing cloud. Sweetie-Cutie clasped my hands. 'You can't live in your house anymore. You are not Siva. You are Tara. No one will understand this. I will look after you from now on. I am going to Madras in two days. You must come away with me. Meet me at the station at 7 pm. And don't tell anyone.'

Tara, who I had shackled deep inside me, surfaced and floated as if on water, uncontrolled and flowing free.

***

The evening light cast an eerie stain on the wall in the room; it shuddered, full of life. Tara felt restless and inadequate. She undressed and looked at her reflection in the mirror. She stroked her arms and felt her skin, her flesh: soft, supple. She took out Rebecca's bra and Amma's saree with peacocks and lotus flowers that she had hidden deep inside the cupboard. She dressed up. A warm feeling spread through her and her toes and fingers quivered. She spread her arms out and spun round and round, and round. She could hear her heart beat in her ears.

Mani stood at the door with a large sweet lime and a knife. He raised one eyebrow and whistled. He tossed the fruit in the air; he caught it but it slipped out of his hand and rolled towards Tara. Mani walked over, picked the fruit up and cut it in half. He pulled down the blouse, and stuffed the fruit cups inside the bra Tara had on. He pressed the sweet lime halves against her nipples, moving them slowly in circles. Citrus juice trickled down her bare stomach and her body went taut and her breath burst out of her nostrils. She shivered with an unfamiliar thrill; it was like standing on the edge of a cliff. Every moment seemed drawn out and electric with meaning. A door banged shut downstairs. Mani ran out of the room. Tara caught her reflection in the mirror and giggled.

This is how Appa found her. Giggling. With fruithalves inside the bra cups and juicestains on her belly. He opened his mouth then closed it rapidly. A thin wail erupted from his throat. He rushed to her side, pulled the saree off and then the bra. He flung the fruit halves on the floor. Then he turned on her and hit her, hard. 'Why didn't you die?' he said.

'I did,' Tara said, giggling.

24

The late night train to Madras rocked with the rhythm of iron upon iron: turum turum turum. Tara rocked with the train. Front-back-front-back, like the small movements of pigeons when they made those sounds in their throat: guturu guturu guturu. Her stomach made sounds: buru buru buru. She inhaled the smell of the evening. Somewhat scorched, as though the train was burning through a bale of hay. She looked at her toes: they were edged with black dust. Beside her, Sweetie-Cutie had nodded off. Tara pressed her back to the seat and shut her eyes. Soon she was fast asleep.

The train rushed out of a tunnel; morning light felt warm on her face. Tara looked out of the window: all around the land swelled with clusters of coconut palms, guava and chickoo trees. Here and there, the ripe fruits on the pomegranate trees glistened like jewels. Buffalos waded kneedeep in water and the canals were swathed with mauve lilies. Then there were villages with brick houses, temples, mosques, lush fields around; brightlyclothed women and children who waved at the train; trees, birds, flowers, and cows with garlands round their necks, their horns painted blue, green, red – all drenched by the morning sun. The train squeaked to a stop at a roofless station. Brownfaced men stood on the makeshift platform, squinting as the sun swelled overhead. A frail dwarf swept the ground. Smoke rose from cooking fires in the thatched huts nearby. Vendors with baskets of fruits balanced on their heads went by the train windows shouting out their wares. A woman stood before Tara's window. Sunlight flashed from the many silver ornaments that she wore; she had on a mustard yellow saree. She held out a bunch of rastali bananas toward Tara. Mustard yellow.

Tara remembered the plantain tree at the back of the house. The bananas would be ripe now. She heard a familiar drone and she slapped her cheek. She scrutinised the squashed mosquito on her palm. Its palps were not as long as its proboscis, and its wings didn't have black and white scales. It was not an Anopheles mosquito. She thought of Appa and felt remorse. With her thumb Tara flicked the dead mosquito off her palm, and with it her brief regret. A young boy stood outside the window shouting: coffeetea, coffeetea...

Sweetie-Cutie woke up. She stretched her arms wide and yawned. Then she leaned across Tara and stuck her head out of the window. She bought two glasses of coffee from the boy and gave one to Tara. 'Drink up,' she said, 'the train will be leaving soon. We have to return the glasses.'

'It's hot,' Tara said.

'Fill your mouth with air,' Sweetie-Cutie said puffing up her cheeks. 'Take a sip of coffee and swirl it around. It will get cooled.'

Tara filled air into her mouth and took a sip. The coffee was still hot. Sweetie-Cutie gulped down her coffee in a number of puffing-up, swirling-around actions. She looked funny doing this. I wanted to laugh but I couldn't. Tara had pressed her lips tightly together. The train began to move. The boy outside the window started to run alongside the train. Tara puffed up her cheeks, took one long sip and handed over the glass to the boy. The coffee scalded her tongue. I felt the raw taste of it.

The train picked up speed and more villages, temples, mosques and fields shot by. In the midday heat, the carriage filled up rapidly with dust and the smell of sweat. The train shot past forests and hills, past waterless rivers, through dusty towns where peeling walls were decorated with paintings of Gods and men pissed between them.

'When will we reach Madras?' Tara asked Sweetie-Cutie.

'By evening.'

'Where are we going to stay?'

'In Krishnapuram. My home.'

'Your mother and father live there?'

Sweetie-Cutie looked away. There was a trace of redness on her cheeks and her nostrils flared. She told me her story:

She was a boy. Her name was Kamal. He was thirteen. His mother was a whore. His father brought home his friends – taxi drivers, petty traders, shopkeepers – and took money from them. Kamal watched each night from where he slept. Men came and went and he wondered if some fucking stranger could have been his father. Who was his father? Even his mother didn't know! Then one morning when Kamal woke up he saw his mother's feet first, not on the floor but dangling midair. Her head was several inches below the fan. His father walked into the room and screamed. Kamal could never forget that nerve-racking scream. After that things became really bad. There was no money in the house. His father didn't have a job. He kept cursing Kamal because he was not a girl. Kamal could not do what his mother did. His father nonetheless forced Kamal to wear his mother's clothes and made him sing and dance for the customers. But they never came back. So Kamal had to find another job. Not far from his house was a taxi stand. Kamal washed taxis in the morning; during the day he had to do his mother's chores at home – washing, cooking and cleaning. And in the evening he worked in a cheap hotel. He cleaned utensils and plates until midnight. When he came home his father would be drunk, passed out. One evening Kamal returned home early, when his father was still out drinking. Kamal dressed up in his mother's saree. He put on lipstick that smelled of stale oil, and kohl that had hardened like rock. He felt good. His father returned stinking of sour rum and sweat. He put his arms around Kamal's waist and pushed him to the floor, pulled the saree up and began to touch him. Then like a raging beast he brought his body heavily on top of him. All of a sudden it started

234

to rain. Kamal was confused but he distinctly remembered the fermented smell. Rum? Kamal opened his eyes. In the old mirror against the wall in front of him Kamal saw the motherfucker pissing on him. And then the mirror seemed to merge with the floor, until it faded. Several minutes later Kamal thought he smelled something else: pungent and aromatic. He was not wrong. His father had brought mutton biryani. He was stuffing the rice into his mouth as Kamal watched. It must have been expensive biryani: it had black kismis in it. Kamal didn't know why he remembered this, but he did. This was how it started. After that day Kamal often dressed up in his mother's clothes. He felt relieved every time he did. His disgust for his father took on another shape. Kamal realised that his misery was not entirely because of his father, or his mother. They were but two festering boils filled with foul pus, whose smell reminded Kamal he was not an orphan. His ache was deeper. It was connected to the core of him that had misgivings about who he was. Or was not. Then Kamal knew. He was not a boy. He was meant to be a girl. This new knowledge made him happy, but life wasn't simple anymore. Kamal met Sita-Gita some months later. They were an inseparable pair of hijras. They became his friends and Kamal told them everything. He left home with Sita-Gita. They boarded a bus to Krishnapuram and Sita-Gita took him to Laxmi-amma, their guru. With her help Kamal became Kamala. But she was the youngest, the sweetest, the cutest, so everyone called her Sweetie-Cutie.

***

It was late evening when the train reached Madras. After a hurried meal at a wayside stall Sweetie-Cutie and Tara took a bus to Krishnapuram, far away, almost where the city ended. Tall arecanut palms veiled the slum. Sweetie-Cutie and Tara walked into a narrow lane. On either side, the huts were huddled close and they smelled of old leather – a pungent-musty smell. Women with rugged faces were everywhere, peeping out of

235

doors, leaning over fences, gossiping, laughing and scratching their hair. A radio blared a film song. The lane was strewn with debris: wood fibres, stone dust, and metal bins, garbage oozing out of them. Tara pinched her nose with her fingers and walked on. I could smell the stink. Sweetie-Cutie stopped before a large house made of bricks; it had a tiled roof. 'This is Laxmi-amma's house,' she said. Holding Tara's hand she walked in.

It was dark inside. Laxmi-amma was reclining on a mattress. She was short and fat and her thick, pouting lips were painted a ruby red. Fake diamond studs glittered in her nose and ears. Her teeth were yellow-stained with tobacco and pan. 'Ah there you are Sweetie-Cutie,' Laxmi-amma said. 'You have forgotten poor old me, eh? It's been almost a year.'

'Have I ever missed your birthday?' Sweetie-Cutie pushed Tara forward.

Laxmi-amma sat up and surveyed Tara with piercing eyes and a solemn pout. She held her chin and tilted her face then ran her hands over her body. She shook her head at first, then her eyes filled with pleasure. She slapped her forehead. 'Sweetie-Cutie, take this creature away and feed her. Fatten her up. She must have something to call hips if she is to be a beautiful woman. Even goats are fed and fattened before they are slaughtered. And it's a tough life for people like us. Make her understand this.' She shoved her hand under the pillow and pulled out a red cloth purse with bells attached to its strings: *Ting ting ting.* She took some money out of it and gave it to Sweetie-Cutie. 'Get her a nice skirt and blouse tomorrow. Now go.'

Sweetie-Cutie took Tara to a hut not too far away. It was bare except for the three reedmats spread on the mudfloor. Sweetie-Cutie had bought a dozen rastali bananas at the station. Tara had six of them; she was hungry. She was tired. I slept.

They took a bus to the city the next morning and got off at the market near the station. From a shop nearby Sweetie-Cutie bought Tara a long red silk skirt with gold motifs on it, and a green blouse. It cost her nearly two hundred rupees. Then from a vendor she got two plates of idlis, which they ate. Sweetie-Cutie bought strings of jasmine from a flower-seller, then they returned to the bus stop. It was late afternoon when they reached Krishnapuram. Sarojamma, an old hijra, was waiting for them in the shack. She dressed Tara in her new clothes. Sweetie-Cutie combed Tara's hair and fixed the jasmine flowers in them. 'My beautiful princess.'

Sarojamma clasped Tara's hand and walked her to a solitary hut at the end of the lane. Inside, in one corner, was a basket of bananas, a jug of water, and on the floor, a reed mat. 'You will have to stay here alone,' Sarojamma said. 'You must have no other thought except that you are Tara. You need time, silence and darkness to get used to the new you.' She pushed Tara into the hut and locked the door.

The hut was so small and low that Tara had to crouch. She couldn't lie down straight or stand up. There were no windows and it was dark inside, except for the sliver of light that came from the edges of the door, until it was deep night. I was afraid but Tara didn't seem to mind at all. She was used to the dark. Sarojamma let her out next morning to wash and eat. Then she locked her in the hut again for two more days.

On the morning of the fourth day, when Sweetie-Cutie opened the door, a crowd of hijras greeted Tara. Laxmi-amma stood before her. 'Are you Tara?'

'*Ya*,' Tara said with my mouth.

The hijras smacked their hands together and hollered, loud and shrill. 'Welcome home sister,' Sarojamma said.

And then, one by one, each of the hijras hugged Tara. They gave her gifts: trinkets, flowers and sweets. Sweetie-Cutie kissed her cheek. 'You are now one of us,' she said.

Being one of them wasn't easy. All day long Tara had to work in Laxmi-amma's house with a boy named Arun who shared their shack. He was dark and skinny; upon his upperlip was a scraggy moustache. He was dressed in a saree though. He had come to Krishnapuram a few weeks ago. Arun and Tara swept the floor, swabbed, cleaned utensils, washed clothes, fetched water and, in the afternoon, massaged Laxmi-amma's legs. By nighttime they were completely worn out. They slept side by side in the shack. Tara couldn't sleep because of the pain in her arms and the throbbing in her legs. She couldn't think; her thoughts were tired too. The weeks passed, and each day was no better.

'Don't you want to run away from here? Tara asked Arun one night.

'I ran away and came here,' he said matter-of-factly.

Nothing was matter-of-fact about Tara. When she had the chance, she decided, she would run away. Where? That was the second question. The first, and the more crucial one, was: where would she find the money? She found the chance a few afternoons later. Laxmi-amma had sent Sweetie-Cutie and Arun on an errand into the city but before she did this she took some money out of her red cloth purse. *Ting ting ting*. She tucked the purse under her pillow then lay back and asked Tara to rub her legs. Tara kneaded them with all her strength. Soon Laxmi-amma was fast asleep. Tara stood back, waiting. When Laxmi-amma didn't move Tara crept toward the top of the bed and very carefully slid her hand under the pillow. She grasped the purse and pulled it out. *Ting ting ting*. Laxmi-amma opened her eyes. In a fit of rage she slapped Tara repeatedly, shouting crude abuse. Tara covered her face with both her hands, but this didn't help much. Laxmi-amma thumped Tara on her head again and again until hearing her shouts Sarojamma rushed into the room.

That night as Tara lay on the mat Arun put his arm around her and pulled her close to him. Arun grabbed Tara's hand and pressed it to his bulging crotch. Tara pulled her hand away and crawled to Sweetie-Cutie on the far side and lay down next to her. She couldn't sleep that night. She screamed loud and shrill in my head.

I don't wanna stay here. Am goin.

There was utter silence. Even the wind had paused. I didn't know if it was the failure of my imagination, but Tara had gone, like she had long ago by the lake, bit-by-bit-by-bit.

***

Sweetie-Cutie's red saree was tied across the window bars and a gust of wind tossed it up and morning light seeped into the room. It was early. The moon was still in the sky, almost full. 'Wake up,' Sweetie-Cutie shouted, 'we must get ready. It is Laxmi-amma's birthday.'

Sweetie-Cutie dressed me in the red silk skirt with gold motifs and the green blouse, which was too big for me. She combed my hair into a tight ponytail then twisted a string of jasmine around it. After she had patted my face with talcum powder she smeared bright pink lip colour on my lips and rubbed rouge on my cheeks, pinching them to soak the blush in. And then with her middle finger Sweetie-Cutie stained my eyes with kohl. She pushed me in front of the small mirror on the wall. 'See how pretty you look, my kanmani.'

I stared into the mirror. Was this really who I was? One half of me was silent but the other half despaired. I studied my face. I touched my nose, and my eyes, ears, my cheek, my neck – all mine. A wiry hair grew out of my nostril. I pulled at it hard.

Aooou.

The hair stuck to its root so I pulled harder.

Aachooo.

I heard the voice in my head sneeze. Was Tara back? I was terrified. At that moment however, another feeling overwhelmed me. 'I am hungry,' I said, bunching up my skirt.

'Stop crushing your skirt, Tara,' Sweetie-Cutie said. 'There will be lots of food to eat later.' She draped a brocaded silk saree around her body. She put on fake gold jewellery. Her hair was plaited with scented oil; her eyes were blackened with kohl and her cheeks were a bruised rouge-red. With a lurid lipstick she stencilled a pout on her lips. She wiped off traces of lipstick from her tooth with a swirl of her tongue.

'I am hungry,' I said again.

'We'll leave soon,' Sweetie-Cutie said and looped a string of jasmine into Arun's hair. She looked at Arun in the mirror. 'There, you look beautiful.' Sweetie-Cutie cracked her knuckles on either side of his head. Then with a delicate wave of her hand Sweetie-Cutie slapped Arun's rump. 'Soon you will be a woman.'

'Did it hurt?' Arun asked.

'Not at all,' Sweetie-Cutie said.

'Was it difficult being a woman?' Arun asked.

Sweetie-Cutie smiled; her eyes did not.

She explained that it wasn't easy being a woman: she kept stroking her crotch, searching for the missing lump of flesh as the tongue would seek a fallen tooth. And she couldn't pee properly squatting, at first. She tried to walk like a woman but it was difficult. When she was a man people teased her because she sauntered like a woman, so delicately, but as a woman her walk was ungainly. Her feet fell heavily on the ground. Her face was round and soft like a woman's before but when she had turned into one, her face was angular and hard; her eyes popped out of their sockets and her beard was coarse. Then she met a tailor. He made her a sexy red blouse. She never forgot her first night with him, having sex as a woman. She remembered the touch of his hands, warm between her legs, and knew she'd have been excited, if there had been something to excite...

She sat still, and then she patted her stomach. 'I am hungry.' She looked in her purse and held out a twenty-rupee note to me. 'Here, go buy some fruit and come back soon.'

I walked down the lane. The stalls on either side were festooned with tinsel. A profusion of glass bangles, cheap jewellery, cosmetics, brooches and hairpins, sarees, a variety of panties and bras with stiff pointed tips, and blouses and petticoats flowed from them. Film music blared through speakers perched on stands and brightly attired hijras with counterfeit breasts and hairy thighs danced to the throbbing music. And beyond were food, fruit and juice stalls. I returned to the hut with a large papaya. I had the remaining change in my pocket but I didn't give it to Sweetie-Cutie. She didn't ask for it.

Sweetie-Cutie cut the fruit into halves, discarded the globs of slippery white and black seeds, then cut one half into two. 'The youngest gets the biggest piece,' she said as she gave me the other half.

I walked to the window and sat on the ledge. I scooped the flesh with my fingers and stuffed it into my mouth, making sure the juice didn't drip on my skirt. I liked papaya more than any other fruit. I licked my fingers clean. Across the lane I saw an old man sitting on the ground holding a cord. The other end of the cord was tied to a monkey's neck. Dance, monkey, dance, the keeper shouted and as he sang, the monkey danced around him. Suddenly the animal stopped, threw its hands up in the air and looked at me. I remembered the evening on the beach when we were eating corncobs and a monkey had chased Rebecca. I had thrown the cob at the monkey and run after her. She had clung to me, crying, and I had held her close; so close that I could feel her heart throb against mine. I inhaled the scent of Cuticura Talcum Powder on her skin. I had remembered this. I remembered this. Would she call me to LA?

I took a moment to reflect on this. With eyes shut tight I was now inside my head, in every nook and corner of it. Numerous doubts ricocheted past, and sifting through them I tried to find the reason for who I was, and why I was here. Deep inside my inside world I had more perspective. At first I couldn't see anything other than the darkness of my thoughts. But then, deep deep down, where my feelings were stored, where Rebecca was stored, I recognised a pair of eyes – her eyes, looking back at me. Then I saw myself. Not Tara. Not us. But me. I saw Rebecca and me. I looked at the papaya in my hand, juice oozing out of the wound that I had made in it. I stabbed the papaya repeatedly with my thumb until it leaked out its orangeyellow blood.

'Tara! What are you doing?' Sweetie-Cutie screamed.

'I am not Tara,' I said.

'You are Tara, kanna,' she said blowing a kiss at me, 'and you are my beautiful princess. Now let's go.'

We walked out into the lane and joined the queue of hijras outside the guru's house. Inside, the air was thick with fumes of burning camphor, and the smells of jasmine and banana. Laxmi-amma was seated on the mattress. She wore a glittering gold saree, flowers in her hair, and fake jewellery. Two hijras beat the drums, and Sarojamma smashed a coconut open and offered it, like twin breasts, to Laxmi-amma. Then all the hijras walked to her one by one for her blessings.

Sweetie-Cutie pushed me forward. Laxmi-amma looked up at me and said, 'You are going to be a beautiful woman, Tara.'

25

I woke up startled, as if from a bad dream. I looked for Sweetie-Cutie. She wasn't there. I shook Arun awake; he didn't know where she was. In fact, nobody knew where she had gone, bag and all.

Later that afternoon Sarojamma locked Arun in the solitary hut. Several times through the day she fed Arun opium and milk to keep him intoxicated. Late in the evening, Sarojamma dragged Arun out of the hut and forced him down on a stone table under the huge banyan tree. Laxmi-amma and the other hijras were gathered around. I hid behind a bush and watched.

Laxmi-amma tied a cord tightly around Arun's balls. Two hijras held Arun down and he started to scream like a child: loud piercing shrieks, mingled with incoherent cries and sobs. Laxmi-amma raised the sharp knife in her hand and then in one swift movement she severed Arun's penis and balls. She bled the cut to drain every drop of Arun's manhood. She inserted a wooden plug into the wound, leaving an aperture. Then she poured hot oil over the gash and pressed a pad of herb paste on it to heal it. Violent drumbeats and shrieks of country flutes drowned out the cries of Arun until he passed out. I watched, my hands pressed to my crotch. My dry tongue stuck to the top of my mouth.

The torture was not over. Next morning all the hijras dressed up in their finery. Sarojamma combed my hair, fixed a string of jasmine in it and painted my face. We gathered once more under the banyan tree. Then, as the mob of hijras clapped and made ululating sounds, Laxmi-amma forced Arun down on the large pestle of the grinding stone until he bled from the anus.

The drops of blood were taken to signify the first periods. The initiation was complete and Arun was now fully a woman. He was renamed Aruna.

I was terrified. Aruna's tortured screams rang in my ears as I stumbled back to the hut. From under my mat I picked up the change I had left from what Sweetie-Cutie had given me and ran down the lane. I boarded the bus to Madras Railway Station. When it reached the stop I got off and strolled down the street. I looked at shop windows, at the mannequins dressed in fancy clothes. I stopped at a restaurant with a large glass window through which I could see people eating. I was hungry. I walked further and stopped by a roadside vendor. He was making dosas on a hot iron griddle. I sat down on the pavement under the tree. A crowd of people streamed out of the railway station and gathered around the vendor as he fried dosas for them. I watched them as they ate; hunger rumbled deep inside me. A truck drove up. The driver got out and stumbled towards the cart. He was short and bulky with small piercing eyes. He slapped the vendor on the back and then he saw me. 'Venkat, who's that young girl? A relative of yours?'

'Nah. I don't know who she is.'

The man walked up to me. 'What's your name girl?'

I looked at my skirt; I looked down at my toes. Sweetie-Cutie had painted them red. 'Tara.'

'How old are you, Tara?'

'Thirteen. No, fourteen.'

'You look much younger. Where do you live?'

'Machilipatnam.'

'What are you doing here alone?'

'I have no money to go home.'

The driver looked at his watch. 'I am going to Machilipatnam in ten minutes. You had better come with me.' Then with a smile he added, 'My name is Selvam.' He turned to Venkat and ordered two plates of dosas.

244

Selvam's was a badly bashedup Tata truck and its broken door was secured to the frame with a rope. I got into it through the driver's door and slid down to the other side. Selvam took off the red cloth tied around his head. He scratched his hair, inspected the grime in his fingernails, chewed at one, and spat it out. Then he got into the driver's seat. Soon we were speeding down the highway. Each time Selvam engaged the gears, the jolt rocked the entire framework of the truck. Now and again Selvam adjusted the plastic photoframe of Lord Krishna fixed above the dashboard. A string of cocktail lights were coiled around the frame. They blinked and winked at me. Then the truck screeched to a halt as a cow ran across the road and the plastic photoframe tumbled to the floor. Selvam picked it up, wiped it on his shirt then touched it to his forehead and eyes and put it back on its holder. With a loud rattling we drove on. I sat close to Selvam. When the truck lurched I fell against him. 'You must be tired,' he said, 'go to sleep, girl. We have a long way to go.' He bent down and kissed me on my head. I slept all through the long way.

Selvam shook me awake. A grey blanket of dusk had fallen over us. All around in the fields the crops grew tall. Sugarcane. The blades of the tall grass sissed in the breeze. Then he swerved the truck into a dirt road and stopped alongside rows of trucks not far from a shack with a newly painted signboard, red and yellow: Paradise India Hotel. The stink of raw rum hung in the hot air. Several drivers were sitting around a table outside. We got out of the truck and Selvam clasped my hand as we walked toward the shack. A rotund man with a ferocious moustache, red eyes and purpled cheeks stared at the blackboard in front of the door with the menu scribbled in chalk.

Mutton cury
meat pattis
seek kababs
brein masala
tava roti
rice plait

The man swayed and the stench of cheap rum hulahooped around his body. He drew all the saliva from deep inside his throat and spat at the board. The spittle ran down the menu, disfiguring it.

The drunk raised the bottle of brandy to his mouth and took a swig. Then he saw us, and let out a roaring laugh. 'You pluck them young, don't you Selva?' He raised his hand and stroked my cheek. 'With skin smooth as velvet.'

A woman passed by; she had hitched her saree up and her ankles were visible. She wore silver anklets that jingled as she walked. She carried a tray of food. The drunk put his fingers in his mouth and whistled.

Selvam held my arm and walked into the shack. We sat down at the counter. I looked at the blue-light fly killer fixed on the green wall in front of me. The flies were lured to it like a drunk to another drunk, and then with a spark and a ping they were incinerated. On the pink wall behind me were photographs of the chief Gods and their respective wives: Shiva-Parvathi, Vishnu-Laxmi, and Brahma-Saraswati. Each of the wives was equally buxom, their full breasts covered by see-through silks. Their faces were candy-pink and their lips blood red. Garlands hung around them: white and pink flowers, plastic. Next to them were pictures of the leaders of the nation, similarly garlanded: a young ebullient Pandit Nehru; a sweetly-smiling Mahatma Gandhi; and Indira Gandhi, who looked tired. Bleached lizards moved from the leaders to the Gods and back; they clicked their tongues and smacked their lips awaiting stray insects that had escaped the blue-light fly killer.

Several boys in vests and khaki shorts ran between the tables. One of them splashed water on a table, wiped it with a dirty rag, and then beckoned a man to sit down. The place was crowded with truck drivers gorging the last meal of the day before setting off into the night with full bellies. I wished that I had on my shorts and shirt. Amidst the burly men in the shack I felt an urgent need to be like them. The smells of boiled rice, fermented curd, spicy curries and chutney spun around my nose and mouth. Selvam ordered two rice plates, mutton curry, potato curry and onion pakoras, an orange drink for me and a quarter bottle of brandy for himself. The food and drinks came almost at once and I ate heartily, as did Selvam. Then he drank brandy, and now and then tossed a pakora into his mouth.

The drunk came in and sat down beside me. 'Mutton curry and rice plate,' he muttered to the man behind the counter. He scratched his face. 'No. Make it chikan curry and rice plate,' he said.

'No chikan. Only muttoncurry-meatpakora-meatroast-fishcurry-potatocurry-puri-roti-and-riceplate,' the man behind the counter replied. He was short and extremely lean. He seemed nervous and his hands began to shake.

'Chikan,' the drunk insisted, thumping the counter with a fist.

The woman returned. She stood behind the counter in front of the drunk. The palav of her saree had slipped off her shoulder; her blouse was cut low. 'Did you not hear what my brother said?' she screeched. 'No chikan, only mutton.'

'Chikan, I want chikan.' The drunk banged the counter again.

The woman said something to her brother. He ran off and minutes later returned with a bowl of chicken curry and a plate of rice. The curry was a bowlful of fatty broth, piled high with bones. The woman pushed the bowl towards the man. 'Eat.'

He didn't. He watched the woman's breasts through an empty glass, breathing hard and drooling. He mumbled: 'Left tit, right tit, in-between tits, tit-tits,' and laughed. Suddenly, the drunk leaned across the bar and pushed his hand into the woman's blouse. She pushed him violently and he lost his balance and fell against me. I fell to the floor.

Selvam pulled me up and led me out of the door. He walked me towards the crop of sugarcane in the field. He sat down on a boulder in a clearing and pulled me towards him, crushed me against his chest. I resisted, but his hand moved to my thighs. Selvam gasped. He pinned me against a tree, and pulled my skirt down and slipped down my underwear. 'You mother-fucking hijra!' Selvam slapped me across my face, hard. He boxed my eye and then my ear. I tumbled down. Selvam kicked my ribs, screaming obscenities. Then with the heel of his shoe he kicked me in the face. Pain rose in my nose like the aroma of an onion: tart, pungent. I passed out.

When I came to it was morning. I felt a smarting in my belly and, doubling up, I vomited. Slowly I got to my feet. Under a bush I found my clothes and put them on, my hands shaking. I stumbled towards the main road and collapsed in a heap. A truck driver who had stopped for a leak found me some hours later. He carried me to the truck and put me in the front. 'Where's your home, girl?'

***

The driver dropped me near the market. I stumbled up Gibbs Road; I could hardly walk. I had to stop several times to catch my breath, to contain the pain in my ribs, before I reached Victoria Villa. When Munniamma saw me standing outside the gate, badly bruised and dressed in a tattered skirt and blouse, she let out a long howl. Then she ran to me; her mouth was open wide and her breath escaped between her teeth: sis-sis.

The curtains sighed in the wind. I was in bed. Munniamma had cleaned the cuts and bruises, and rubbed ointment on them. She had helped me into fresh clothes and fed me dosas that Mani made. I could hardly eat. I felt the cold crawling up my skin and reaching up to my eyes, filling them with moisture. Tears streamed down my face. Then I heard footsteps up the stairs and Appa stood at the door. He looked at me for a long moment and then rushed to me, gathered me in his arms.

26

The rains come tentatively to Machilipatnam. By the middle of June the sky grows wishy-washy. Clouds dangle from it, almost bruised purple, the colour squeezed out of them. Then at night the rains come sputtering as if from a tap that has remained unopened for a long time. Through the next three months the monsoon winds rage over the coast. Leafy fingers of palm trees serrate these winds, which whine and blow over oilseed knolls, proceed over paddy fields, and part the wet green grass thisway-thatway before they swish away to the dry plains beyond. Then for days on end the rains lash down. Tree-branches flap, vines reel out their tendrils. The wet spindles of cobwebs snap. Flowers fluff out their scent and bees suck the wetness out of them. Rainmoths fly up into the air, fluttering their wings with such ecstasy that they come apart and fall to the ground like parachutes made of eiderdown.

It is only April, not June, and yet it has rained all month. It is a sign, this early rain, of things to come. I open the windows to admit a heavy-eyed dawn. I inhale the moist air deep into my lungs and feel the pulse pounding in my head. My hands are cold; my head sweats and I cannot swallow my spit: my throat is sore from all the crying. We are leaving for London tomorrow, Appa and me. We are leaving Machilipatnam for good.

A week ago, when I went to Vishnu-thatha's house I asked him about Amma: What if she returned? What If? We were out on the veranda. The stars had come out but the sky was inkdark; there was no moon that night. Vishnu-thatha looked up at the sky as though he was looking for the moon. He seemed broken. I saw the fear in his eyes – a silent fear, a disease that devoured cells and nerves, and then everything that was left of what was left. I knew this sort of fear – the fear of the unknown. I had felt it.

And a week before this I had met Sweetie-Cutie by the lake. The wind moved the water and slapped gently at its shores. We sat down under the chakka tree. Sweetie-Cutie hitched up her saree and crossed her hairy legs in front of her. She undid her hair and let it loose, then ran her fingers through it, plucked a fat louse and crushed it between two fingernails. 'I had a bad dream that night,' she said. Her face was tight. 'I dreamt my father was very ill. I had to see him. Sorry I went away.'

Her father was half his size, she said. Raw rum had cratered his cheeks and his eyes bulged out of their sockets. When he held her hand, his fingers felt cold and moist. She looked after him for a week and fed him mutton biryani every day. As he slept she sang songs to him and watched the tears roll down and collect in the well of his cheeks. Then she bought special mutton biryani with black kismis. She set the plate on her father's chest so that the smell would drift to his nostrils and remind him of those days they spent together. Then, pinching his nose, deliberately and slowly she fed him until his mouth was stuffed and he could eat no more. He died. He had wet his bed.

'I made a terrible mistake.' Sweetie-Cutie wiped her face with the end of her saree. 'I am a fake.' There was something definite and purposeful in the way she spoke: In her heart where her feelings were stored, she was a woman. In her head where her thoughts were shaped, she was a woman. But in her body she was a man. And deep in her conscience she was utterly indefinable. Because she never looked there, she betrayed herself: she held on to a fate not entirely her own. All the years, the effort she had made to be a woman meant she was being cruel to the man in her. But she had made a choice and she had to live the lie. 'It's good you ran away, Siva,' she said. 'You have to be who you are meant to be.' She stood up, ruffled my hair and went away.

I thought of what she said. The thought pained me, like a pebble in my shoe. It hurt as I walked home.

Appa's Ambassador drove out of the gates. Tommy-uncle stopped the car when he saw me. 'Confucius. So young man, are you looking forward to go to London?'

'I don't know, uncle,' I answered truthfully.

'It's better not to know. Because you shouldn't know what you know until you know what you don't know.' And with that he rattled down Gibbs Road.

Only last evening I was in the attic. I hadn't been there since I returned. The floor was littered with dried leaves blown in through the window, bits of paper, and dried morsels of food. Rats, squirrels, sparrows, cockroaches, mosquitoes and other insects had made the attic their home. I stood under the hole in the roof and watched the twilight sky. I saw a plane flying over. I saw its huge belly. I saw bird-bellies flying. The stars glittered above like an island in the sky. Our Para-dies, with tiny tiny stars.

And now here I am today, my last day in Georgie's villa. So many years... So many lives... My cockeyed fate with an ultimate plan has transcended all of them except Rebecca. We had met near the lake. Fireflies had dotted the night sky. I had kissed her and then run my tongue over my lips, testing, tasting, as though I was licking a new flavour of ice-cream. I had liked it.

I try to cry. I need to cry. But the tears don't come. The fan above turns slowly, then with a loud whirr it begins to rotate faster. I feel a whirlwind of emotions on the tip of my tongue; I taste each one: Sweet. Sour. Bitter. And then in a big gulp I swallow my spit. My mouth is dry, bereft of taste. I look around the room. The paint on the walls has yellowed in patches and looks like watermarks with burnt edges. I look at the old picture of Georgie on the wall. Depending on the light his expression changes. He looks terribly sad today. Did he find his son? I am curious to know how the end ends. I retrieve the ledger from the cupboard, and then sit down on my bed, flip through the pages, read the last entry, dated April 1862:

I had just finished reading the letter from my father, a fifth time. My mother had died suddenly of a heart attack. It had started with a mild cough; a week later she had succumbed. She had been utterly lost since the day Elizabeth left home.

Matthew came through the door. 'You must sleep now sar, you have a long journey to make tomorrow. You be back in your country and you will be happy.'

'And what the deuce will I do, back in my country?' I barked at Matthew. 'Leave me alone!' I was in a worse temper than ever.

After Matthew left the room I picked up my son's notebook from the table. I flipped through the pages: alphabets, words, a butterfly, then there were the sketches of the sea, so many pages of them, blue, endless, waiting... I took a deep breath and started to remember; it all came back, perfect as it used to be, my brief time with my son. I looked up at the picture of Elizabeth on the wall. She had been four months pregnant then. My head became cluttered with too many thoughts, too many memories: of John, Elizabeth, my dead mother, my old father, and my cold country. My thoughts shifted to my village in Somerset, to the trees and the river, the small animals, night smells of herbs and flowers, and the birds flying and the swans floating down the river, their huge white wings folded. I would have liked my son to see his country, his village, and his grandparents. But he has gone.

'The sea swallow me. It swallow daddy.' John's voice rang in my ears.

I knew what I had to do.

I ran up the stairs to my bedroom. I slipped out of my nightclothes and donned my uniform. I looked for my belt but I couldn't find it anywhere. Far away in the distance, I could hear the waves; they called out to me. My son called out to me.

'Daddy! Where are you?

It is only mid-April but it has rained nearly every day. This morning the clouds are empty of rain and the early sun has tinged the clouds with its colour, but blackness tears at my heart. Darkness fills me utterly. Soon I will cease to feel and before long, I know, I will cease to think...

As I read Georgie's words I am convinced the blueprint of my life exists; my Fibonacci sequence has followed through as intended. This new knowledge contains in it a strange stillness, absence, and deep silence.

I am afraid.

Why are you 'fraid?

Did it hurt?

Only for a blink of an eye.

Is it like Over? O-V-E-R.

It's not over. I was with you all the time.

I raise my left hand and stretch it out in front of me. Tara's hand touches mine, a cold glass in between our touching hands. I stretch out my right hand and feel Tara's hand warm against mine. I bend forward and touch my cheek to the glass, and I feel the softness of Tara's cheek. I touch my lips next and my breath leaves two dewy spots on the pane; they coincide with Tara's breathbubbles on the other side. I blow at them; they disappear, both the halves, quivering together, hand in hand, fingers locked. Tara's heart beats in my heart and through my lungs she inhales. Tara whispers and I hear her in my head.

I'm goin now.

Don't go. Please don't go.

I must.

I'll find you.

You won't. If you look for me, I am not here.

Then all at once I feel lightness in my mind – Tara is slipping out of it. I feel colourlessness behind my eyes – Tara has drained out. I feel emptiness in my heart – Tara's beat is missing. My lungs feel full and I exhale her breath. She hums in my ear but her voice is faint. Her fingers that she has locked into mine let go, one by one by one. She is gone. I am alone.

I know what I have to do.

I get dressed at once and into a bag I stuff Amma's saree that I had stored in the cupboard, the old ledger, the butterfly notebook, the photograph of Rebecca, Cyril and me taken in Sunrise Studios, and the wire rose with red cloth petals. I reach inside the drawer of the desk and retrieve the old goodluck coin.

Once when I couldn't decide which ice-cream flavour I wanted, Vishnu-thatha asked me, 'Siva, do you have your goodluck coin?'

I had groped in my pocket and held up the coin. Vishnu-thatha took it from me and tossed it in the air, caught it and closed his hand into a fist.

'Heads you choose the flavour. Tails, I choose, okay?' he'd said. 'But never forget, coins work only for choosing between small things and not big things.'

Heads.

I had chocolate ice-cream that evening.

I put the coin into my trouser pocket and run down the stairs and out of the house. I walk down Gibbs Road, my eyes on my feet, humming: Lala-la-la-la-lala. There are people on the street already. Some of them stare at me and whisper to each other as I pass them by. I walk past what used to be a bookshop. The sign is painted in the colours of an upside-down taxi, black-on-yellow: *Sweeties Saloon.* Hairpieces displayed in its window roll down in ringlets or are piled high on pink plastic heads. The beauty parlour undoubtedly belongs to two Chinese girls. Their names appear on the sign: Lin & Jin.

Farther along, MacOnly's board reads:

No Beef
No Pork
Muttan on Fridays
Waterless Chickans Always

MacOnly
Hambuggas
Be eating
Being Happy

In front of it is the signboard: *No English. Only the language of the soil. Only Telugu.* It is broken.

Closer to the Shiva Temple, people have collected under a new hoarding of Coca Cola. Momentarily distracted, I cross the road and push through the crowd to see the mob of the Hindu National Party dressed in saffron robes, ashlines intact on their foreheads. The pavement is wet with purpled water, slightly foaming at the edge, and Coca Cola bottles lie broken on the road next to the delivery vehicle. Swami is crouched on the road, scooping up the foaming purple liquid in the cup of his palms and slurping it up.

'No Coca Cola. No Colgate. No nylon,' the mob shouts. 'Indian products only. Buy Indian. Be Indian.'

The speaker of the party raises a hand in the air to quieten the mob and shouts: 'Beware, westernisation is corrupting us. Look around you, my brothers and sisters, look at the red soil, grab it in a fist, feel it, smell it, taste it: it will taste of our mothers' sweat and blood, our sweat and blood. Remember this is our mothers' land and we are the sons of this soil. We must fight for our rights; we must fight for our land, our mothers' land. Be Indian. Buy Indian.'

I press through the crowd and out of it. I hurry past the delivery van and almost slip on the wet road where Swami had been. He is not there. I walk on slowly, all the way to the beach. The morning sun has hardened, crisping the air. The muezzin taps the loudspeaker in the minaret, then wails into the moist atmosphere – la ilaha ila allah. From the Shiva temple the devotees chant: Shiva. Shiva. Shiva.

I see Swami with a tattered straw hat, possibly discarded by a tourist, perched on his head. Swami smiles and with a benevolent nod displays the knob of his leg, unevenly stitched. He crawls closer to me. 'You motherfucker! Bastard son of a mad woman.'

I turn away and dash to the sea. Baby crabs spring sideways. The waves reel, toss, and fold into themselves like sheets of mercury. I unzip my bag and pull out the old ledger. I fling it high into the air. It flutters open and plunges into the water: *Red –Yellow – Dark Blue – Brown-chocolate – Black – Purplebrown* – all soaks away.

Goodbye Georgie.

I take out the butterfly notebook. I pull apart the pages and toss them into the air. A paper wraps itself around my leg. I peel it off and look at it. It has pink and blue lines on it. At the top of the page is inscribed a capital A and somewhere at the bottom a capital Z. John had yet to fill in all the letters between A and Z. The paper slips from my hand and the breeze scoops it up; it dips and soars aloft. I watch it and for a moment forget the bitter ache in my heart. I take out the photograph and Rebecca's wire rose, and hurl them into the sea. The photograph floats, the waves tugging at it, slapping it this way and that; it washes ashore, only to be sucked back again.

I take out Amma's saree now, the brown one with peacocks and lotus flowers. I unfold it and wrap it around me. A familiar smell. A childhood smell. Ammasmell. Tarasmell. They will be together, Amma and Tara. Always. Forever. Connected by an umbilical cord of love. Perhaps for the first time I understand love: it grows eternally, undismayed by any eventuality or any end. A love so momentous it could last a lifetime.

But I don't have a lifetime.

I obliterate each thought until I am empty: empty in my heart, empty in my mind. I am in an empty place. Through the resounding emptiness all I can feel is the wind sweeping in from the sea, moistening my face, murmuring in my ears, innocent nothings. This moment has about it a certain intimate quality. It belongs to me. Not Amma. Not Tara. Only Me.

Shoving a hand into my pocket I clutch the goodluck English coin. This is a small thing, I think. I throw the coin into the air. The coin flies overhead, catches the light of the sun, winks, flips, and like a shooting star falls on the sand.

Heads.

My lips tremble and my knees buckle; my feet sink into the sand. I look far out to sea, like one in a trance. Tara, I call out, if you look for me, I am not here.

The sun shines on the water, a wave wets my feet, and...

Siva! Where are you...?

Acknowledgements

I want to thank, firstly and mostly, my son Ayush, who read the manuscript on his flight to London and texted me on arriving – 'Awesome Mom!'

For friendship and generosity I want to thank Jill Hughes who wrote to me out of the blue – 'Have you written anything lately?' and became a dear friend and agent who rigorously believed in my work and me despite my moments of doubt and desperation.

For kindness and grace, for the unrelenting enquiry of all things unfamiliar, and for the finest editing, I would like to thank Lin, Hetha and Kevin, the team at Bluemoose, who made the book what it is.

Most of all I am thankful for my granddaughter, Rosa Maia, who brings such delight to my days, and my daughter, Anshu who made this possible.